Papias and the Mysterious Menorah

Papias and the Mysterious Menorah

The Third Art West Adventure

Ben *and* Ann Witherington

PICKWICK *Publications* • Eugene, Oregon

PAPIAS AND THE MYSTERIOUS MENORAH
The Third Art West Adventure

Pickwick Publications
An Imprint of Wipf and Stock Publishers
199 W. 8th Ave., Suite 3
Eugene, OR 97401

Images are in the public domain or are the property of the authors or Mark R.
Fairchild, who has kindly granted permission for their use.

www. wipfandstock.com

ISBN 13: 978-1-60899-460-1

Cataloging-in-Publication data:

Witherington, Ben, 1951–

　　Papias and the mysterious Menorah : the third art west adventure / Ben
　　Witherington III and Ann Witherington.

　　vi + 262 p. ; 23 cm.

　　ISBN 13: 978-1-60899-460-1

　　1. Archaeology—Fiction. I. Witherington, Ann. II. Title.

PS3605 W55 2010

Manufactured in the U.S.A.

Flash Fore-word

IT HAD BEEN SITTING on a high shelf for over thirty years hidden under a red velvet sleeve. It was not an object of desire; it was not even an object of attention. Kahlil el Said had bought the golden menorah long ago. So filled was his shop with ancient objects that he had not given the menorah much thought—until now. The invitation to Grace Levine's wedding prompted him to ask, What could he give his dear friend and her husband-to-be Manny Cohen that would tell them how much he appreciated their friendship and how blessed he hoped their marriage would be? It was a gift fit even for royalty. But unbeknownst to Kahlil, this menorah had a notable, even notorious past, and it still held secrets yet to be revealed. Herein lies a tale of discovery involving ancient lore, mysterious objects and papyri, demons and the underworld, and the intertwined lives of three great friends, Kahlil el Said, Art West, and Grace Levine.

Part One

In Hot Water

PAMUKKALE IS AN INTRIGUING place. Set in the Lycus Valley in west central Turkey, which has Colossae and Laodicea as its two most famous biblical sites, Pamukkale (pronounced pa moo' caw lee) often is overlooked by Christian pilgrims. This is because the ancient city of Hierapolis, which is today called Pamukkale, is only mentioned in passing in the New Testament (Col 4:13). However, it is now and has been since before the time of Jesus, a local mecca because of its remarkable hot springs. But Christians on pilgrimage are not usually looking for places to get into hot water when they have already spent hot days in June or July seeing the biblical sites.

Art West was a different sort of fellow. A New Testament scholar and archaeologist of international reputation, Art enjoyed nothing better than searching for rare and historically important artifacts. West spent his summers crawling around biblical sites, not least because his Discovery Channel show required fresh material. On this particular beautiful evening, Art found himself soaking in the outdoor hot springs at his hotel, the Pamukkale Grand Palace, drinking a mango margarita, and mulling over his next move.

Art was on sabbatical this year, well earned after many years of teaching at Duke and Vanderbilt. Turkey was a veritable treasure trove of biblical, Greco-Roman and Ancient Near Eastern sites, many of them inadequately excavated or explored. When Art went to places like Hierapolis/Pamukkale, he could hardly contain himself. Having spent the day working systematically through the necropolis (graveyard) at Hierapolis, and then visiting the Hierapolis museum, he figured tomorrow morning would be the time for the hike up the hill to some of the early Christian sites.

As Art knew all too well, history only reluctantly gave up its secrets most of the time. But on a tip from his friend and fellow scholar,
Mark Fairchild, he had checked out a grave stele at the Hierapolis museum and he was beginning to think that sometimes secrets are hiding
in plain sight. Here for all to see was a second century AD grave stele
which read:

ΠΑΠΙΑΣ ΚΛΕΣΟΣ

ΠΟΙΜΕΝΕΡΟΣ

ΧΡΕΣΤΟΣ ΠΑΡΟ–

ΔΕΙΤΑΙΣ ΧΑΙΡΕΙΝ

Art had photographed the stone earlier and now was examining the
pictures on his little Sony Cybershot. The first line clearly enough desig-
nated the man's name—*Papias Klesos*. Could this be the famous Papias
who was Bishop in Hierapolis so long ago? But this stele, now in the
Hierapolis museum, was found in Laodicea, and tradition said Bishop
Papias died in Smyrna in the middle of the second century. On the
other hand, this could simply be an honorific stele erected in Papias's
memory. He was probably bishop of the entire region, which included
both Hierapolis and Laodicea in the Lycus Valley. But what should be
made of that second line which read *poimeneros*? It looked like an aug-
mented word for shepherd. And the next to the last word—*parodeitais*—
needed pondering as well. A voice from behind Art startled him out of
his cogitations.

"Another margarita, sir?" asked the tall waiter by the side of the
pool.

"Thank you, Hakan. As refreshing as it is, one is always my limit. I
still need to do some clear thinking."

"As you wish, but if you need anything, do not hesitate to ask," replied Hakan.

The sun was slowly slipping down over the hills on the far side of
the Lycus Valley, which Art could see plainly from his vantage point.
His hotel was near the top of the hill overlooking the limestone cliffs of
Pamukkale. The tourists were still walking over the slippery chalky de-
posits on top of the cliffs, but by 6 o'clock the site would close for the evening. Art was also reading the *Turkish Daily News*, the English language
paper, because it had an article on the new finds at nearby Laodicea.

"Just remarkable," said Art to no one in particular. "Who would have guessed that Laodicea was an enormous city by ancient standards, surely the largest city in the whole region, despite its formidable water problem? That water is so full of calcium carbonate that it's not even drinkable!" There was a picture in the paper of an ancient water sieve used to filter out the minerals—the original Britta filter!

Reflecting back on some of the Hierapolis inscriptions, Art mulled over what he knew about this particular city in the fertile Lycus region. Munching away on a pretzel in one hand with his guide in the other he mused, "Now what does the guide book say?" Next to the picture of the famous theater in Hierapolis he began reading:

Hierapolis means "holy city" or possibly the city of Hiera, the offspring of Herakles (Hercules). The hot springs of Pamukkale were used as a spa since the 2nd century BC. People came from near and far to soothe their ailments. Many retired and died here, which explains why the large necropolis is filled with sarcophagi. It is estimated that the Jewish population in the region was as high as 50,000 in 62 BC. Several sarcophagi in the necropolis attest to their presence.

One of the earliest structures still visible is the Plutonium, the shrine to Pluto the god of the underworld. Next to the ancient temple of Apollo, the Plutonium is actually the oldest local sanctuary. It is a small cave, just large enough for one person to enter, descend the inner stairs, and walk into a 10x10 foot square chamber. In this chamber, from a deep cleft in the rock, fast-flowing hot water releases various gases (probably sulfur and carbon dioxide). People died from inhaling these gases, giving rise to the idea that the gas was sent by Pluto, god of the underworld. In fact the entrance is now closed off to the public because several tourists who were exploring the shrine died from inhaling the noxious fumes.

An enclosed area of 2000 m² stood in front of the entrance. It too was saturated with poisonous gas, killing everyone who dared to enter. The priests sold birds and other animals to the visitors, so that they could test the deadly nature of the area. During the early years of the town, castrated priests of Cybele snuck in through safer, secret entrances, descended into the Plutonium, crawled over the floor or held their breath, and emerged safely to proclaim immunity to the killer gas. People believed a "miracle"

had occurred! Of course they believed the priests were infused with superior powers and divine protection! Visitors could ask, on payment of large sums, questions to the oracle of Pluto. This provided a considerable source of income for the temple.

Earthquakes in AD 17 and 60 left the city in ruins. But the city was always rebuilt with the financial support from the Roman emperor. It was during this period that the city attained its present Roman form. The theatre was built later in 129 when Emperor Hadrian visited, and was renovated further under Septimus Severus (193–211). The great baths, designed in the second century AD, were constructed with huge stone blocks without the use of cement. When Emperor Caracalla visited in 215 he bestowed on the city the much-coveted title of *Neokoros*, a provincial imperial city, according Hierapolis certain privileges and the right of sanctuary.

Through Paul's influence, a Christian church was founded in Hierapolis while he was still at Ephesus. Philip the Apostle spent the last years of his life here with his three daughters, all of whom remained active as prophetesses even after Philip's martyrdom (ca. AD 80). Sometime in the early 2nd century, Papias (ca. AD 80–155) became bishop of the Christian colony in Hierapolis. By the 4th century the Christians filled the Plutonium with stones, showing that Christianity had supplanted paganism. In 531 the Byzantine emperor Justinian raised the bishop of Hierapolis to the rank of metropolitan. The town was made a see of Phrygia Pacatiana.

Hierapolis was first excavated by the German archaeologist Carl Humann (1839–1896) in 1887. His notes were published in his book *Altertümer von Hierapolis* in 1889. Excavations began in earnest in 1957 by Italian scientists, led by Paolo Verzone. Restoration of the site has begun; for example, large columns toppled by the earthquakes now stand as they once did alongside the Domitian gate. A number of houses from the Byzantine period, including an eleventh century courtyard house, have been unearthed. After many statues and friezes were transported to museums in London, Berlin and Rome, the Hierapolis Museum was built in 1970 where the baths once stood. After the large white limestone formations became famous again, the area was renamed Pamukkale meaning *Cotton Castle*.[1]

"Hello, Professor West?" A sultry voice interrupted Art's mental trip through the travel guide. Art turned and, looking directly into a spectacular sunset, squinted at the black-haired woman towering over him. "Yes, and you are . . . ?" asked Art politely.

"I am Dr. Marissa Okur, but you may call me Marissa. I am wondering if I could have a word with you. I am one of the persons our government put in charge of the Hierapolis dig this summer."

"Right, I've heard your name. You're an archaeologist?"

1. The preceding information was taken from "Hierapolis" and "Pamukkale," wikiepdia.org, accessed Feb 10, 2009.

"That is true. Are you aware that you will require $50,000 and government approval to gain permission for a dig?" said Marissa in impeccable, albeit a bit stilted, English.

"Yes," said Art, "but I'm not really hoping to do a separate dig. I'd much rather join one in progress."

Marissa smiled, and Art sat up taller. "Ah, I was hoping you would say that as we will not charge you for being a consultant. In fact, we may be able to make it worth your while. We think we have just found something important and would like your opinion, as it is from the early Christian period."

Already intrigued, Art answered, "Why certainly, and what is it that you think you've found?"

"Well, it is all pure speculation at this point, but it appears we have found the house of Papias, the Christian bishop of the early second century."

Art literally jumped out of the hot pool, wrapped himself in a very large plush Turkish towel, and plunked himself into a deck chair, all the while excitedly asking, "What would make you think it might be Papias's house!?"

Marissa slowly sat in an adjacent chair. "Well, it appears to be the home of a well-educated man. Just this morning we found a scriptorium or library. We have begun to lift the rubble out, but our flashlight survey illumines a room with scrolls in it, and equally important, I have here a small portion of the lintel from the doorway into this room."

Art took off his dark glasses, and stared at the almost foot long but very thin piece of limestone Marissa held in her hands. Taking water from a pitcher that sat on his drink table, Art rubbed his hand over the carved stone. As if by magic, the following letters appeared: ΕΠΙΣΚΟΠ …ΙΑΣ. More rubbing produced the word ΙΧΘΥΣ. Art's eyes got bigger and bigger until he exclaimed, "Do you have any idea what this is!?"

"Well, we have a guess, but I am guessing you are about to tell me!" enthused Marissa.

"This may be the most important Christian find in Turkey in the last hundred years! Papias is the bridge figure between the apostolic age and the church of the second century. He lived in Hierapolis and was its bishop, but more importantly he wrote five commentaries on earlier Christian literature, including one on the sayings or oracles of Jesus. Up to now, we only have fragments of his work in Eusebius and other Church Fathers, but if you have found his house, that could all change. Just today I was examining an inscription from the Hierapolis Museum which may refer to Bishop Papias as the shepherd of the region. Wow, talk about converging lines of evidence!"

"Well, that is why I am inviting you to join us in the morning if you will?" inquired Marissa.

"Wild horses couldn't keep me away! Sleep will be hard to come by tonight! I'm pumped!"

Marissa smiled as she walked away, "I thought you would say something like that. We will collect you at 8 o'clock promptly. Please be ready."

"Yes, Ma'am" replied Art with his best Southern manners. "I was born ready for this adventure!" The visit to Hierapolis had already begun to pay dividends.

Nuptials in the Works

TO SAY TEL AVIV is hot in June would be a gross understatement. Between the relentless sunshine, the high coastal humidity, and the still air, only one word comes to mind—oppressive. Nevertheless, Grace Levine and Manny Cohen were bopping around in Grace's red sports car with the top down, trying to make yet more arrangements for their wedding.

Grace, long a single person and a successful academic who taught at Hebrew University, was considered one of the world's leading experts on first century Aramaic inscriptions. Manny Cohen, on the other hand, was one of the wealthiest of Israelis, owning not only a successful computer chip company but also the professional Tel Aviv basketball team, Maccabee Elite. Only last year his team had won their league championship, but this year they finished second behind their closest rival, the team from Eilat. Both Grace and Manny were hard-working, successful Jewish persons who took their religion seriously, although of late, in small doses.

The courtship of Grace by Manny had been rather like the courtship of two porcupines gradually summoning up the courage to get close to each other. There had been major obstacles along the way, not the least of which was the kidnapping of Grace last year by rogue agents from Hamas! It took a while for Grace to regain her bearings in life after that trauma. Manny abided his soul in patience for much longer than he was used to doing. But at last, some six months prior, Grace said yes to marrying Manny, which had so pleased Grace's mother, Camelia, that she basically underwent a personality transplant going from a glass-is-half-empty to a glass-is-half-full mother (and future mother-in-law). She had been bragging to anyone who would listen about how Grace had the good sense to wait in life until she could reel in the big fish when, in fact, it had been Manny who was doing all the casting. The long years of Camelia pestering Grace about getting married were finally over. Now she spent her time nagging about wedding details. On this particular day, Grace had made a final decision about her Dior gown, and Manny in turn had picked out an Armani tux. Grace, ever the iconoclast, had decided that white was too white for her age, and so had chosen a beautiful creamy yellow shade reminiscent of the roses Manny frequently sent. Manny, when Grace finally said yes, had felt like he had just won the lottery and the basketball championship all on one day. Instead of prompting him to be more boastful, it had actually humbled him. He had a profound sense that he was not worthy of the love of this remarkable woman, and so he was profoundly grateful to God and remarkably circumspect about how he described the matter. He was not like the chanticleer that struts around the barnyard crowing and preening. Instead, Manny felt like he was in some sort of dream world, and this all was too good to be true.

"So dear, what shall we do now that the costumes have been finalized? The day is ours," sighed Manny. Neither his business office nor his courtside office had seen much of Manny in recent days.

"Well, that's a good question," pondered Grace. Manny had already learned not to make any major decisions without talking with his new full-time consultant, the wife-to-be. "How about we head down to the beach and stop at that little fish restaurant we like for lunch—Steinmetz's?"

"Your wish is my command," said Manny. "But I already have the big fish I want right here by my side," grinned Manny.

"Boy, you do know how to flatter a girl, calling her a fish! Do I really smell that bad! Next thing you know you will be telling me we are going to stuff ourselves to the gills at Steinmetz's . . ." At this both of them laughed until they cried. They were at a place of settled contentment, now that the dating game was over. What they could not foresee was how many challenges they would face as mature persons set in their ways, getting married for the first time in mid-life.

3

Back on the Home Front

CHARLOTTE, NORTH CAROLINA WAS a city on the rise, and had been since the early seventies. The population had climbed to 1.2 million in greater Charlotte over a 35-year span. Art West's roots were in this town, and his mother Joyce still lived on the south side. She readily complained about the increasing glut of buildings and traffic. Joyce saw far too little of Art between his teaching, speaking engagements, and summers in the Lands of the Bible. Fortunately she liked to stay at home, do things at church, attend her book club, watch her favorite soap operas (something Art could never fathom), and generally enjoy the company of her senior friends.

But recently she had acquired a very unique lodger with a funny accent—Jake "the Cat" Arafat, as he now dubbed himself. The former Ishmael Arafat, the star of the Maccabee Elite basketball team, had indeed made the roster of the Charlotte Bobcats after an extended tryout closely observed by Michael Jordan himself, part owner of the club. It was Jordan who had seen the man's promise and had come all the way to Tel Aviv to watch "the Cat" play. Ishmael's 44-inch vertical leap made Jordan smile, and reminded him of his own feats at that age when he had just joined the Bulls.

The story of how Jake had come to live with Joyce was intriguing. Ishmael had a very protective Palestinian Christian mother, all the more so, since her other son Issah had been brutally murdered in Bethlehem the previous year. She had given her blessing to her remaining son to try out for the NBA team on condition that if he made it, he would find a good Christian home to live in, and get himself grounded in a solid church community. Having caused his mother so many years of grief when he was involved with Hamas, Jake was all too ready to agree to this proviso, if it would set his mother's heart at rest about her remaining son. So it had come to pass that when Mrs. Arafat had asked Art West where her son could find a good Christian home in Charlotte, Art had replied, "I know just the person you are looking for—my mother! She is actually looking for a lodger to keep her company and help with a few things around the house." Little had Joyce West realized that her so-called lodger was famous, and indeed a millionaire, for by the time his second year in the league had begun, the team had renegotiated his contract to keep him for years to come.

Jake the Cat's first basketball season in Charlotte had been an up and down affair. There would be moments of sheer brilliance, followed by long stretches of inconsistent play. There would be a game where he would score 20 points, and then one where he seemed to disappear into the hardwood floor. Such was the life of most NBA rookies. But what grounded Jake, and gave him the stability to do his best and grow into his new career, was living with "Aunt Joyce," which is what this 6'4" Palestinian had come to call Art's mother.

Joyce, after some initial awkwardness because of the cultural differences, had warmed to this young man with a bright basketball future, and had even been coaxed into going to a game or two sitting in a box seat Jake reserved for her. This explained why Joyce was wearing a Bobcat sweatshirt this morning while watering her plants in the kitchen. She had become something of a fan of the local team on the rise.

"Says here in the *Observer* that 'Jake the Cat Arafat' shows great promise of becoming a star in this league, if he keeps progressing," said Jake while munching his raisin bran muffin and quaffing orange juice, all the while devouring the sports page.

"Well just remember, that in your profession a meteoric rise can just as easily lead to a meteoric fall. You have to go out and prove yourself every time—no slacking off. In fact, last I checked, meteors always come crashing to the ground. On the other hand," smiled Joyce, "I did notice you were doing a better job in defending your man last night."

Jake slumped a little, as he was fishing for bigger compliments, but in his heart he knew she was right. One thing about "Aunt Joyce"—when she gave you a compliment, you could be sure she really meant it, and she rationed those things in small doses.

Joyce didn't much like the culture of stardom. It didn't fit well with the culture of thriftiness that was part of her Great Depression upbringing. So she figured it was not her main job to stroke the ego of Jake Arafat. He got plenty of that at the new basketball stadium in downtown Charlotte. On the other hand, she was ever so pleased that Jake, without prompting, had joined the young adult singles class at Myers Park Methodist. Jake often went to events with his classmates, some of whom were awe-struck to see him there. In all, Mrs. Arafat was pleased with the regular progress reports Joyce sent through e-mail.

"I'm off to practice in a minute. Anything you need from the Fresh Market? I could pick it up on the way home this evening."

"Well, now that you mention it, we do need a few things. Could you get a box of Quaker Instant Grits, a package of fresh okra, a pound of green beans, and a small piece of fatback? Also stop by Spoon's barbecue, just down the road from the grocery store on South Boulevard, and bring home a pound of barbecue, plus slaw and hushpuppies."

"You know, Aunt Joyce, I never realized going grocery shopping was such a cross-cultural event! I haven't ever even heard of half the things you just mentioned, but I am sure someone in the store can help me when I get there," said Jake as he took down a few reminder notes. "You spell okra how?"

"Just ask anyone," grinned Aunt Joyce, "and okra is O-K-R-A. You need to get to know that vegetable."

"Vegetable? I thought that was the name of a TV star—Okra Winfrey—right?" and Jake grinned big.

"No son, that would be Oprah Winfrey, but you were close. Remember to save the receipt so I can pay you back."

"Well, I don't think I'll be accepting reimbursement since you have been giving me Charlotte's lowest discount rate on rent. Your money is no good with me." And so the playful banter went on back and forth for a while, like an ancient honor exchange. Joyce West would not accept "charity" but if it sounded like a fair deal, she would relent.

"Alright," said Joyce, "but I'm buying the next time we go out to McCormick and Schmick's for dinner after Church."

"Fair enough," said the budding basketball star. He had learned that even in America haggling was an art, and you needed to know "when to hold 'em, and when to fold 'em, and when to walk away, and how to lose graciously," as Kenny Rogers would put it. Reciprocity exchanges with

Aunt Joyce were just way too much fun. Jake was enjoying his new home and his extra mother.

As the Highlander hybrid pulled out of the newly paved driveway, Jake waved goodbye to Aunt Joyce, and she turned to those corn muffins she had been cooking in the oven, saying quietly to herself, "That boy can eat me out of groceries in about five minutes flat. He's still a growin' boy, and I like what he's becoming."

4

The Mediterranean Market

CHARLOTTE WAS AN INCREASINGLY multi-cultural town, and one aspect of that was the growing number of people of Middle Eastern descent moving to the Queen City. Most of them sought to blend in with the larger culture and make their contribution to society. But some had other ideas in mind, ideas about striking daggers into the heart of the American system, which was assumed to focus on wealth and materialism and entertainment—all in excess. These particular Charlotte residents retained their contacts with their Middle Eastern friends and relatives, and looked for a day when they could make a difference on behalf of a more radical sort of living out of the Muslim credo.

One person in particular, Ahmed Arafat, was in fact a distant cousin of Jake Arafat, and he knew all about Jake and despised him. He despised him for abandoning his role in Hamas, for playing a frivolous game like basketball, for becoming part of the immoral entertainment industry in America, and most of all for converting to Christianity. This man had even changed his name from Ishmael, a good Muslim name, to Yakov or Jake, which surely was a Jewish name! This was insufferable, and Ahmed was biding his time working at the Mediterranean Market while looking for an avenue to do something about this act of apostasy. For a radical Muslim like Ahmed, conversion to Christianity, a polytheistic religion as far as Ahmed knew, was the ultimate insult to the one God Allah, an insult so grave it required a response. But what to do about this situation? Security was tight at ball games these days.

Ahmed was mulling these things over as the late afternoon sun shone through the shop window, when the little bell attached to the door tinkled and in walked a tall, dark-skinned man sporting a bright orange

Bobcats t-shirt. Ahmed's eyes got big when he realized it was none other than the famous Jake Arafat himself. "Speak of the devil," Ahmed muttered to himself. "Good morning. How can I help you?"

"*Salam aleichum*," said Jake. "The folks at the Fresh Market told me there was a Middle Eastern store, but I had a difficult time finding you all the way over here on West Boulevard. I would love some fresh hummus and pita bread, and I gather you have some wonderful shwarma as well?"

"You have come to the right place for that. How much would you want?"

"Oh, three or four man-sized portions should do for now," smiled Jake at the man in the black and white kefia who handed the order slip to a young woman. "Are you from Palestine?"

"Yes, but I left many years ago, before the Intifadah."

"A wise move," nodded Jake. In due course, a woman with a head covering came out from the back with the food items in a large plastic bag. Ahmed handed the food over, and Jake paid with cash, saying, "*Shokrun*. It sure is good to find some real food in this town."

"*Afwan*. Come by anytime," said Ahmed without a smile. His patience had been stretched to the limit already. As Jake walked out the door, Ahmed had come around the counter and followed him to the door so he could get a good look at his vehicle. As the green Highlander sped away, the man in the shop jotted down the moniker on the NC license plate, which read, THE CAT. "It always pays to plan ahead," Ahmed said to himself.

5

Much Ado at the Antiquities Shop

KAHLIL EL SAID WAS still a formidable man, even though he had entered the golden years of his life. He was indeed tall, dark, and handsome, reminding some of Omar Sharif, something his daughter Hannah often teased him about. Kahlil ran perhaps the most famous antiquities shop on the Cardo Maximus just inside the Damascus Gate in the Muslim quarter in the old city of Jerusalem. Kahlil had begun to gradually turn over the shop to Hannah now that he had reached the seventh decade of his life, the biblical three score years and ten. Yet he loved to keep his hand in the trade, and on this morning as he drank his cup of Turkish coffee he was inspecting a new cache of small pieces of papyri he had purchased from a scholar who was currently staying at École Biblique, the French Catholic school in Jerusalem.

Kahlil's biblical and early Christian Greek was only passable, but with the help of his Greek lexicon he was working through the translation of the largest of the papyri, which had a substantial portion of Eusebius's *Ecclesiastical History*, the first full-fledged church history written in the fourth century, after Christianity had ceased to be considered a *superstitio* (superstition) by the Roman government. Kahlil was puzzling over what Eusebius was saying about Papias, the Bishop of Hierapolis. Art West had asked Kahlil before he left for Turkey that if anything in his new cache of documents contained information about Papias or Hierapolis he would be pleased to hear about it. What was odd was that this version of the *Ecclesiastical History* seemed to be a value added version, that is, it seemed to have more in it than the Loeb edition of the Greek text that Kahlil had open before him.

"Hmmm," said Kahlil, "this is very odd, but at the same time very interesting."

"Why father?" said Hannah with a quizzical look on her face. "What is special about this piece of papyrus?"

"Well, if I am interpreting the Greek correctly, this papyrus says that Bishop Papias met John of Patmos who *is* the author of the Book of Revelation, but *is not* the author of the Fourth Gospel or the three letters. What it says is that Papias developed his millennial views, which Eusebius clearly disagreed with, from a certain conversation Papias had with John of Patmos, and presumably from reading his Revelation."

"Well, what is so special about that?" said Hannah, who was not as well versed in biblical scholarship as her father.

"Many things," replied Kahlil. "It would mean that the elderly man that Papias met was John of Patmos, and *not* John the son of Zebedee who was the Apostle John and would have been long-since dead anyway. Secondly, if Art West is right that the Beloved Disciple is Lazarus, and not John the son of Zebedee, this in turn would mean that the Apostle John had nothing to do with any of the Johannine literature. He is neither the Beloved Disciple nor is he the John of Patmos. The Catholics and Orthodox won't much like this news. Further, despite Eusebius not much liking Papias's views of the end times, he clearly confirms that Papias had been in contact with one or more of the original figures from the apostolic generation. Come look at this passage for a minute and see if you agree."

Hannah was relatively small of stature and her father towered over her, so he had to back away from the old wooden worktable so she could come close and look at the photocopy of the Greek scroll, which Kahlil had interspersed with an English translation as follows:

> Ουκ οκνησω δε σοι και οσα ποτε παρα των πρεσβυτερων καλως εμαθον και καλως εμνημονευσα συγκαταταξαι ταις ερμηνειας, διαβεβαιουμενος υπερ αυτων αληθειαν. ου γαρ τοις τα πολλα λεγουσιν εχαιρον ωσπερ οι πολλοι, αλλα τοις ταληθη διδασκουσιν, ουδε τοις τας αλλοτριας εντολας μνηνευουσιν, αλλα τοις τας παρα του κυριου τη πιστει δεδομενας και απ αυτης παραγιγνομενας της αληθειας.

> [Papias himself writes:] "But I shall not hesitate to arrange alongside my interpretations as many things as I ever learned well and remembered well from the elders, confirming the truth on their

behalf. For I did not rejoice, like many, over those who spoke many things, but [rather] over those who taught the truth, nor over those who related strange commands, but over those who related those given by the Lord by faith and coming from the truth itself."

Ει δε που και παρηκολουθηκως τις τοις πρεσβυτεροις ελθοι, τους των πρεσβυτερων ανεκρινον λογους, τι Ανδρεας η τι Πετρος ειπεν η τι Φιλιππος η τι Θωμας η Ιακωβος η τι Ιωαννης η Ματθαιος η τις ετερος των του κυριου μαθητων α τε Αριστιων και ο πρεσβυτερος Ιωαννης, του κυριου μαθηται, λεγουσιν. ου γαρ τα εκ των βιβλιων τοσουτον με ωφελειν υπελαμβανον οσον τα παρα ζωσης φωνης και μενουσης.

[Papias continues:] "And if anyone chanced to come along who had followed the elders, I inquired as to the words of the elders, what Andrew or what Peter had said, or what Philip or what Thomas or James or what John or Matthew or any other of the disciples of the Lord [had said], the things which both Aristion and the elder John, disciples of the Lord, *are saying*. For I did not suppose that things from books would profit me as much as things from a living and remaining voice."

Ενθα και επιστησαι αξιον δις καταριθμιουντι αυτω το Ιωαννου ονομα, ων τον μεν προτερον Πετρω και Ιακωβω και Ματθαιω και τοις λοιποις αποστολοις συγκαταλεγει, σαφως δηλων τον ευαγγελιστην, τον δ ετερον Ιωαννην, διαστειλας τον λογον, ετεροις παρα τον των αποστολων αριθμον κατατασσει, προταξας αυτου τον Αριστιωνα, σαφως τε αυτον πρεσβυτερον ονομαζει.

[Eusebius then explains:] "It is worthwhile also to pay attention here to his twice counting the name of John, the first of which he groups with Peter and James and Matthew and the rest of the apostles, clearly indicating the evangelist, but the other John, with a change of wording, he arranges with others away from the number of the apostles, and clearly names him an elder."

Ως και δια τουτων αποδεικνυσθαι την ιστοριαν αληθη των δυο κατα την Ασιαν ομωνυμια κεχρησθαι ειρηκοτων δυο τε εν Εφεσω γενεσθαι μνηματα και εκατερον ετι νυν λεγεσθαι· οις και αναγκαιον προσεχειν τον νουν, εικος γαρ τον δευτερον, ει μη τις εθελοι τον πρωτον, την επ ονοματος φερομενην Ιωαννου αποκαλυψιν εορακεναι.

[Eusebius then adds] "As also through these words he shows the story to be true of the two men in Asia called by the same name and that there are two tombs in Ephesus, and both are still now said [to be his], to which it is necessary to direct the mind, for it is likely the second, unless someone should be willing [to say] the first, that saw the apocalypse which bears the name of John."

Και ο νυν δε δηλουμενος Παπιας τους μεν των αποστολων λογους παρα των αυτοις παρηκολουθηκοτων ομολογει παρειληφεναι, Αριστιωνος δε και του πρεσβυτερου Ιωαννου αυτηκοον εαυτον φησι γενεσθαι· ονομαστι γουν πολλακις αυτων μνημονευσας εν τοις αυτου συγγραμμασιν τιθησιν αυτων παραδοσεις. και ταυτα δ ημιν ουκ εις το αχρηστον ειρησθω.

[Eusebius adds] "And the aforementioned Papias now confesses that he received the words of the apostles from those who followed them, and says that he was an earwitness of Aristion and of the elder John. At least he mentions them by their name often and gives their traditions in his writings. Let not these things have been said uselessly by us."

Kahlil had cut and pasted the above, which is found in the Loeb edition of Eusebius with the additional material found in the manuscript he had which read in translation as follows:

"For Papias, I have no doubt, got his strange views about the future from the chiliasts and from a certain reading of the Revelation of the elder John, who after all was not John son of Zebedee, and indeed not one of the Twelve, which is why his visions are disputed by our church to this very day."

"Now Hannah," said Kahlil, "what is so intriguing to me about all this, is that Eusebius seems to think that the Apostle John, son of Zebedee, is buried in Ephesus along with John of Patmos, but in fact there is only *one* shrine or Johannine church known to this day in Ephesus. I have seen it sitting up on a hill overlooking the old temple of Artemis, and it commemorates only one John. I am betting it is John of Patmos, not the one who was originally a member of the Twelve. Eusebius, who apparently never visited Ephesus, seems to have made a mistake about the shrine, but not about there being two Johns, or about Papias meeting only one of them. My overall impression is that John of Patmos assembled the memoirs of the Beloved Disciple as well, which may explain how it came to be called a Gospel *from* John. In any case Eusebius adds the following pejorative remarks about Papias:

Εν οις και χιλιαδα τινα φησιν ετων εσεσθαι μετα την εκ νεκρων αναστασιν, σωματικως της Χριστου βασιλειας επι ταυτησι της γης υποστησομενης. α και ηγουμαι τας αποστολικας παρεκδεξαμενον διηγησεις υπολαβειν, τα εν υποδειγμασι προς αυτων μυστικως ειρημενα μη συνεωρακοτα.

[Eusebius adds:] "Among which also he says that there will be a certain millennium of years after the resurrection of the dead, the kingdom of Christ being established bodily upon this very earth. Which things, I suppose, he got by having welcomed the apostolic accounts, not having seen that the things spoken through them were spoken mystically, in patterns."

Σφοδρα γαρ τοι σμικρος ων τον νουν, ως αν εκ των αυτου λογων τεκμηραμενον ειπειν, φαινεται· πλην και τοις μετ αυτον πλειστοις οσοις των εκκλησιαστικων της ομοιας αυτω δοξης παραιτιος γεγονεν, την αρχαιοτητα τανδρος προβεβλημενοις, ωσπερ ουν Ειρηναιω, και ει τις αλλος τα ομοια φρονων αναπεφηνεν.

[Eusebius adds]: "For indeed, that his [Papias'] mental capacity was very small, as is proven from his words, is apparent. But he also was responsible for so very many of the churchmen after him being of his same opinion, putting forward the antiquity of the man, like Irenaeus then, and any other if he has proclaimed that he thinks the same things."

Kahlil added, "This is how Eusebius distances himself from Papias and his millennial theology, all the while admitting that Papias had been enormously influential in getting other theologians to embrace the theology of John of Patmos in Revelation. Papias, you see, was not only a chiliast, a believer in a future messianic millennium, but also one who believed miracles and visions were still happening in his own day. There are traditions as well that Philip and his prophesying daughters retired to Hierapolis and had contact with Papias also. You will find especially interesting this next addendum in my scroll's version of the Eusebius text which adds:

"[Eusebius said]: But perhaps the clearest sign of the limited mental capacity of Papias is that he not only accepted the prophesies of John and Philip's prophesying daughters, he believed it perfectly appropriate for women to pray, prophesy, and *even preach within the congregational meetings*, but as we know, this cannot be what our Savior and the original apostles wanted."

"Here again," stressed Kahlil, "Eusebius is attempting to do damage control and re-orient how his audience would read Papias and his pneumatic teaching and views, urging them to disagree with some of his views."

Hannah sighed and said, "It is ever thus father, for men feel threatened in the presence of a gifted or inspired woman, and sadly have used religion to silence them. But this Papias gives me hope that not all the Church Fathers were like that."

Kahlil smiled. "Some were more enlightened by God. I cannot wait to share these two little additions with Arthur and see what he says."

"You are a true friend," said Hannah. "I am sorry he is not here in Jerusalem this summer to share the excitement of this find."

"Ah, but you are forgetting Grace's wedding which he will surely be attending."

"My, I nearly forgot! What shall we give them for a present?"

"I thought you would never ask, my dear. I have just the thing." And unveiling a metal object, which had been under a velvet covering, Kahlil said, "How about a genuine menorah, worth no little amount of money."

Hannah gasped! "Father, how can we afford to give that away!? I know you recently put it on display with a 'not for sale' sign. So I thought you would never part with it!"

Kahlil smiled. "True, I could never sell it. For me it is too precious an object. I have enjoyed looking at it lately. But what could be better than to give it to two dear friends who will really value this treasure?"

"How you model the virtues of our Islamic faith," said Hannah, beaming at her father, and with that she gave him a big hug. "Grace and Manny will realize just how much you value their friendship. If only all relationships between Jews and Muslims could be like that."

"Indeed, ensh'Allah [as God wills]," replied Kahlil. But just then the phone rang.

"Hello, Kahlil, guess who this is?" said the male voice.

"I am thinking it is my favorite Christian scholar," laughed Kahlil.

"You're never going to believe what happened here at Hierapolis," gushed Art. We may have found the home of Papias, plus a scriptorium and a grave stele was found in Laodicea that also point to Papias."

"Well, your timing is impeccable as I was just pouring over a new manuscript attributed to Eusebius. And it has value added. It may be an early copy of Eusebius originally lodged in the famous library of Celsus in Ephesus."

"No!" said Art breathlessly. "I just came from giving a lecture at the Ephesus meeting that Levent Oral sponsors each year, and we met in the beautiful setting of the Celsus library. Unfortunately, a thunderstorm came up complete with lightning over the library and we had to run for cover. Trust me, it was very dramatic. The grave stele that I just mentioned may have been erected to our Papias. It reads: '*Papias Klesos*, shepherd, anointed, to those passing by, greetings.' It seems odd that there would be a formal stele with decoration set up to a mere shepherd, but if 'shepherd' here is used in its metaphorical New Testament sense, then we are on to something. It is more likely this refers to an honored higher status person."

"I think you are right," said Kahlil with excitement. "This whole conversation is a harmonic convergence that reflects the hands of the Almighty."

But just then the shop bell rang, feet stomped loudly, and Kahlil jumped from his stool. It was the Israeli Antiquities Police, and they did not look happy. "I must go, Dr. West. We will talk of this later. The IAA police have just shown up." Kahlil rang off abruptly.

The mausoleum of a famous businessman
named Flavius in Hierapolis.

6

Marissa's Memoranda

MARISSA OKUR WAS AN unusual Turkish woman on many counts. She earned two honors degrees from the University in Ankara; spoke four languages (Turkish, German, English, and French); and understood the gist of various ancient languages (Sumerian cunei-

form, Latin, Greek, and some Northwest Semitic languages). Earlier, she successfully led the archaeological work at the ancient Hittite city of Hattusa, uncovering its lion gate. Now, all before the age of forty, she was beginning to produce results in Hierapolis. Marissa, like so many of her educated peers, came from a family of self-described "secular Muslims" who embraced the secular values of the founder of modern Turkiye (as it is properly spelled), Ataturk. She had no patience with fundamentalists, especially those that sought to repress women or prevent them from getting an education, good jobs, and the like. She refused to wear a head covering on principle, and could be brusque with those who objected. She could also be quite charming and vivacious, not to mention she had a nice figure and a dark Mediterranean complexion with raven-colored hair. She intimidated most men after only a few minutes, and few had been brave enough to date, much less court her. "My life is in ruins," she liked to say when asked about either

her profession or her social life. She was married to her profession and she loved it passionately.

On this morning Marissa had gotten up quite early to watch the sun come up over the Lycus valley. She had taken a walk from her hotel all the way to the old city of Hierapolis to look once more at the famous tomb near the Domitian gate, the tomb of Flavius Zeuxis, the man who bragged in his epitaph that he had made some 72 journeys to Rome and back on business. The ancients, as it turned out, were more mobile than we might think.

Chewing on an apple as she passed a Jewish part of the necropolis, Marissa was reading a passage from Strabo, the ancient traveler and geographer, about the Plutonium near the temple of Apollo. Strabo writes:

> The Plutonium is a fissure wide enough for a person to enter. It is very deep. An area of some 30 ft in width surrounded by a fence is covered by a thick mist which makes it impossible to see the actual place. The air outside the fence is quite clear, and when no wind is blowing there is no danger in approaching it, but any living creature that enters dies on the spot. Large animals that enter the fissure immediately collapse and are brought out as corpses. We sent birds in as an experiment and saw them drop dead immediately on entering. Only the eunuchs of the temple of Kybele are able to spend a short time within the cavern without being affected.

Whipping her notepad out of her back pocket she scribbled a memo to herself: "Bring in scientist to test the air in the Plutonium cave. Needs to be explored and photographed extensively." Turkey's constant problem was that it had too many interesting archaeological sites and too little money with which to excavate them. The government controlled everything, and they doled out money sparingly if one was talking about a largely Jewish or Christian site, or even the Jewish or Christian part of a site. There was more money for ancient Anatolian excavations, or for some Greco-Roman ones, but Marissa was more interested in the Christian period in ancient Hierapolis. She had been cagey enough to put in her grant application indicating that she would explore further the Greco-Roman ruins in Hierapolis, all the while knowing that it was the more specifically Christian Greco-Roman ruins in which she was interested.

By now the hill on which Hierapolis set was in full sunshine, and Marissa realized she was about to be late to collect Art West. After taking a few more pictures, she raced down the hill to her hotel, and, breathing heavily, hopped into her jeep. It was going to be an interesting day.

FYI, the IAA

THE ISRAELI ANTIQUITIES AUTHORITY is a diverse agency of the Israeli government responsible for policing the 1978 Law of Antiquities by regulating excavations, encouraging site conservation, and promoting research. It even had its own antiquities police, who among other things spy on archaeological sites to make sure no illegal activities are going on. Periodically they made surprise search and seizure visits to the antiquities shops in the Holy Land, especially those in Jerusalem. On a normal day, they could do a routine inspection of at least one antiquities shop, to make sure 'everything was Kosher'. By this was meant that an antiquities dealer had no permission to sell any truly precious artifact uncovered in Israel after 1977. If the object had come into the dealer's hands before 1977, then the dealer could do what he or she liked with it. Today, Kahlil el Said's shop was the object of scrutiny.

"To what do I owe the pleasure of your personal visit today Dr. Cohen?" asked Kahlil in his deep booming voice. Dr. Sammy Cohen, director of the IAA since its reorganization in 1999, had come in person because of an anonymous tip that there was a suspicious menorah in Kahlil's shop. The report suggested it had come from a recent dig site. Kahlil to date had a completely clean record and reputation, so Cohen could hardly believe this report, which in his mind sounded like malicious gossip. He had decided to come in person.

"I am sorry to bother you, but the boys and I are here on a report that you have an ancient menorah for sale. I found this report hard to fathom, so I decided to come check in person, as I am well aware of your reputation."

"I have absolutely nothing to hide, and indeed I do have a menorah, but it has been in my shop, in my family really, for more than thirty years, and as for the suggestion I was going to sell it, in fact I was about to give this precious menorah away," said Kahlil with a devilish smile and a wink.

"Give it away!" exclaimed Sammy incredulously.

"Why yes, I was going to give it to Grace Levine and her beau as a wedding gift, and a nice one at that do you not think? Here it is, for your inspection."

Lifting the velvet cover from the menorah, Sammy suddenly feasted his eyes on a truly beautiful artifact, and let out a gasp when he saw the gleaming bronze menorah with its delicately carved seven branches with detailed filigree work, the sign of real artisanship.

"You would give this amazing menorah to a Jew, and you a Muslim?" said Sammy slowly and softly.

"Yes," said Kahlil. "For there are many things in life more precious than a gold or bronze object, however valuable, and one of those is true friendship. If you do not mind, let me recite a few lines from the book of my namesake, Kahlil Gibran. He says,

'And let there be no purpose in friendship save the deepening of the spirit. For love that seeks aught but the disclosure of its own mystery is not love but a net cast forth: and only the unprofitable is caught. And let your best be for your friend. If he must know the ebb of your tide, let him know its flood also. For what is your friend that you should seek him with hours to kill? Seek him always with hours to live. For it is his to fill your need, but not your emptiness. And in the sweetness of friendship let there be laughter, and sharing of pleasures. For in the dew of little things the heart finds its morning and is refreshed.'

"This is from the nineteenth chapter of his famous work entitled, *The Prophet*. Perhaps you will have heard of it?"

"Yes, of course," murmured Sammy. "I believe he is Lebanese."

"Indeed, and my personal favorite," affirmed Kahlil. Kahlil was a Sufi Muslim, given to mystical reflections and meditation on such poetry. He actually lived out his life guided more by such poetry than just by this or that verse of the Koran.

"For the sake of formality, do you have the authentication papers for this menorah?" asked Sammy.

Kahlil nodded, walked to the back of the shop, parted the sheer mesh curtain hanging in the doorway, and entered the private quarters where Hannah was cooking. He asked her, "Can you find the file of authentications for 1976 please. The IAA needs to see the papers for the menorah. Dr. Cohen and two associates have come to visit us."

"Certainly, Father!" said Hannah excitedly. "Please, ask the gentlemen if they would like some Turkish coffee. I have a pot ready!"

Returning to the shop, Kalil relayed Hannah's offer, which was accepted. But as Sammy sat and waited, the menorah sitting on the counter became a strong reminder that he had failed in his attempts to court Grace Levine, whilst that other more famous Cohen had succeeded. It was a painful reminder, but Sammy was mature enough not to act out his personal pain in ways that would sully his professional behavior. Finally, Hannah emerged from the back room with a slightly dusty folder of documents. A minute later she handed a file to her father who, in turn, handed it quickly to Sammy.

"Well, you must forgive us, but our filing system is, not surprisingly, antique! This file is very old and I have not looked at it in a long time. Nevertheless, here you will see that the menorah was bought before the law changed in 1978, and from none other than Yigael Yadin, our most famous archaeologist. I knew him well before his death in 1984. Where he got it, the paper work does not say, but he sold it not long after the famous Moshe Dayan scandal. You will remember that Yadin had to deal with Dayan's 'theft' of important artifacts from certain archaeological sites. In one instance, where the thefts were commonly attributed to that famous one-eyed general, I remember that Yadin remarked: 'I know who did it, and I am not going to say who it is, but if I catch him, I'll poke out his other eye too.' My point is just this: Yadin was a person of absolute integrity, unlike Dayan, in these sorts of matters. I do know enough to know that if this object was found by Yadin himself, we would expect it to have come from some synagogue in the vicinity of Hazor, Masada, Megiddo, or even here in Jerusalem. But this is just conjecture."

Sammy had stood up and had gone over to the counter to examine the menorah more closely. Picking the heavy object up, he noticed on the bottom a sort of bung or plug. Gently shaking the object, he heard a small rattle.

"Had you noticed that the menorah seems to be hollow?" inquired Sammy.

Kahlil, with a quizzical look on his face said, "I have not closely examined the object in many years. This is news to me."

"There is a recessed area in the bottom, so it might be easy to miss. Do you mind if we try to extract the plug?"

"No, I do not mind at all. The menorah is the gift. The contents are another matter. But it may take some time to extract whatever is inside, so could I suggest you come back this evening, say at sundown. I will work on this today in between clients."

"Yes, we did not really think you of all people were up to anything nefarious, so we will return at 5:30, if that is convenient," said Sammy.

"That is just fine, *shalom* until then," boomed Kahlil with a smile.

Kahlil could not wait to start opening the menorah's secret chamber. He loved mysteries. With gloved hands and a stiletto-like knife, Kahlil very gently pried away on one side and then the other of the little metal plug in the bottom of the religious artifact. Eventually, the plug loosened and with a small set of forceps Kahlil coaxed the plug out of the hole it was filling. What happened next was completely unexpected.

8

The Cat and the Bobcats

THE CHARLOTTE BOBCATS WERE not exactly the toast of the town. Their predecessors, the Charlotte Hornets, had left town under sad circumstances, moving on to New Orleans, and had become far more successful than the fledgling Bobcats. Since the beginning in 2004, the Bobcats had posted a losing record. Yes, they had some promising athletes over the years, both experienced and inexperienced, but injuries had kept the best young players from reaching their potential. Finally, however, a player of such skill and style had arrived in the person of Jake the Cat Arafat who, like LeBron James and other such phenoms, could not be kept out of the starting lineup for long. Indeed, the Bobcat coach had decided that next fall Arafat would be in the starting line up.

Summer practice sessions were often intense, with a "no blood, no foul" kind of rule designed to toughen up the young recruits. Everyone knew they were practicing now for playing time in real games. But like his idol Michael Jordan, Jake had a grace and quickness that allowed him to slide and slither around huge blocks and crowding defenders to get to the hoop for layups or thunderous dunks. Even some of his veteran teammates had to admire his athleticism and infectious spirit. It was so clear how much he loved the game and the competition that honed his skills.

"So Jake," said Raymond Felton the point guard, "where did you learn to jump like that?"

"Well, when you are growing up in Palestine and the bullets keep coming your way, you have to be cat-quick and able to jump at a moment's notice."

"Dude, for real?" asked Felton with widening eyes.

"For real. My brother was killed by Hamas in Bethlehem."

This sudden revelation stopped the conversation altogether. Felton had grown up in Latta, South Carolina and knew what the face of prejudice looked like, but he had never met anyone who had lived where it was daily taken a step further. This gave Jake some instant "street credibility" with his teammates.

"Let's run the post play drills one more time before we break for the day." Coach Larry Brown, himself a former Tar Heel like Ray Felton, had been making some progress towards team chemistry through these summer sessions, and he had begun to see Jake as the catalyst and game changer he had been looking for. He blew his whistle as the drill was winding down and called Jake over to the bench.

"Now listen, son," he said. "You've been doing well trying to blend in with the team, but I don't want that to squelch your creativity. I've noticed that you have the ability to come up big in crunch time. You don't let that scare you. So I have a question. You're a rookie. Why aren't you scared of those situations?"

"Well, coach, I have told you something of my story. To be honest, basketball is my passion, but it is not life and death like living in Palestine. I have been shot at, and I have seen my brother brutally murdered. After that, basketball is no pressure at all. It creates excitement, not anxiety. I am not afraid of failing in basketball. The bigger challenge is not failing in life."

Coach Brown adjusted his glasses, cupped his chin in his hand, and then smiled. "Jake, maybe you can inject some of that perspective into your teammates, but in any case I look forward to putting you in the starting line-up in the fall and seeing what happens."

Jake straightened up taller than ever, and responded, "Really!?"

"Yes, really; you are ready for the big leap forward, so let's make it a good one."

"Yes sir! I can't wait to tell Aunt Joyce and my Mom!"

As Jake left the practice floor there was a look of contentment on his face and relief in his gut. He had finally become an integral part of the Bobcats.

9

The Scripts in the Scriptorium

WHEN 8 O'CLOCK ROLLED around, Art had long since been up and ready for Hierapolis. Art looked the part—khaki shirt and shorts, backpack, water bottle, and Red Sox hat. He was pumped up about the new discovery at Hierapolis. That stone with the Christian symbols, which Marissa had shown him, had really gotten the adrenaline flowing. Could this really be the house of Papias, the famous Bishop of Hierapolis? What was hidden in the back room of the newly excavated house? The long-awaited knock at the door finally came.

"Good morning, Professor West," said Marissa all business-like. "You appear to be quite ready."

"You bet! But please call me Art. I've had some weird experiences on digs, but this could prove to be a great day! Did I ever tell you about the time I got trapped in a tomb. . . ." Art just rambled on with his story as they climbed into Marissa's old green jeep. The sun had already crept across the Necropolis and up the hill to the old city, illuminating the Christian ruins. They would ride past the Domitian gate, up to the general parking lot, and then walk up the hill past the Roman baths that had been turned into a Christian basilica. Coming into the archaeological site they paused to watch the sun play off the limestone or travertine cliffs. Even Art smiled at the unusual beauty of the so-called "cotton castle." The view was spectacular.

Art broke the silence. "I've seen the white cliffs of Dover, but the formations here make this chalk so much more interesting. Watch how the sun's rays literally change the color depending on the angle of the light."

"Yes," replied Marissa. "Every morning there is something new and quite beautiful to see. Let us hope the same will be true up the hill at the site itself."

Walking up the steep incline, the two archaeologists passed the ruins of the Temple of Apollo on their left and kept heading upward. Arriving finally at the current dig site, they found a beehive of activity.

"Professor West, I would like you to meet Professor Mehmet Ertegun from Istanbul University." Art looked up at an imposing man built like a barrel with a traditional Turkish moustache. His cap barely covered his lengthy black hair. He looked like a warrior ready to brandish a *kilij*, a deadly Turkish saber. Art swallowed hard and felt intimidated for a moment before he acknowledged the introduction.

"We are pleased to welcome you to our own Big Dig in Hierapolis— with some apologies to my colleagues in Boston," laughed Mehmet. "I was recently at a symposium at Harvard. Your name did come up in conversation! We know of your work in Israel, and are so very glad to have someone who is familiar with the Christian history of our country."

"Well, to be honest," replied Art, "my expertise is in the New Testament period, not the second century, but I am honored to help. I can tell you I'm a big admirer of Turkey and its archaeological sites. More tourists should come here!"

"Please do your best to get that good word out!" pleaded Mehmet. "But for now, let Marissa show you our wonderful site."

Grabbing his arm, Marissa led Art into the fenced off region where the current digging was progressing in typical but painfully slow fashion. When something significant is found, then the archaeological work has to go into slow motion to make sure nothing is missed, nothing is damaged, and nothing is lost. "Here is the fallen stone door that leads into the central living area. In this room we found a few potsherds, a couple of broken vessels and plates, and two small oil lamps. The lintel I showed you was not from the front door, but rather from this fallen entrance into what looks like a scriptorium."

Getting down on his hands and knees, Art shone his light into the chamber and sure enough, there seemed to be some papyri on the floor of the chamber. There was also a small crease in the stone wall at the back of the room that looked like an opening into yet another chamber. "Have you noticed that space at the back? Any thoughts?"

"Yes. We believe there might be another room beyond the chamber. Getting to it, however, will be a long, slow process and funds are already limited," sighed Marissa.

"Or perhaps a tunnel or passage way?" mused Art lost in thoughts about treasure not finance.

"I had not considered that possibility," replied Marissa. "But a passage to where?"

"Don't know. Do you have someone here who might be able to safely wriggle down into the room and retrieve some of the papyri?" asked Art.

"We have considered many options. But today let us try something new," said Marissa with a mischievous smile. She produced what looked like a golf-ball retriever. It was gold in color and easily extended some eight feet, but at the end it had a little scoop-like device to pick up a small object. Art was left-handed, and so he positioned himself so that his left arm could extend into the chamber. He slowly extended the retriever into the chamber while laying down flat on his belly.

"Can you please shine your big flashlight into the hole?"

Marissa obliged by lying down next to Art to produce a steady beam into the chamber. She was so close Art could hear her breathing, and her perfume was so intoxicating that for a second Art lost his train of thought. It had been a long time since he had been this close to an attractive woman who was "eligible," as his mother would say.

"Thanks," whispered Art, returning to the task at hand. Extending the calipers of the scooping mechanism, Art carefully maneuvered to reach the first piece of papyrus he could see. The trick was to lift the papyrus *very* gently. It was after all an ancient and rare artifact. For what seemed like an eternity Art manipulated the device like an astronaut trying to capture the Hubble telescope. Finally, finally he was rewarded. "I have the papyrus," he whispered.

"Now take your time and pull it out very, very slowly. No sudden motion. Keep the scoop level," urged Marissa also whispering.

Art slowly crawled back up until he was on his knees and then could take both hands and bring the extender out of the hole more easily. As the calipers emerged, Marissa put both her gloved hands gently around the prize and extracted it from the scoop. "We have special equipment back in the main tent to look at this piece of papyrus. Even then I am reluctant to open it here, rather than at the museum." But it was obvious by the look in her eyes, that even she couldn't wait that long. Art knew the first examination would be minutes away. They walked back in awed silence, collecting Mehmet on the way. At the tent, the precious papyrus was placed upon a glass slab for its first read in probably 1900 years.

"What have we got?" asked Art breathlessly, as Marissa professionally unrolled a bit of the papyrus.

"We have early Christian Greek in *scriptum continuum*. All the letters are run together; all the letters are in caps; and there is no punctuation. You can see here and there the symbol for a contraction of the *nomen sacra*, in this case Jesus Christ, and the first three words that jump out at you at the top left hand corner of the papyrus are *Logiōn Kuriakōn Exēgēseis.*

"Yikes!" shouted Art. "Do you have any idea the significance of that title?"

"No, but we are waiting for you to tell us right now!" laughed Marissa.

"If I'm right, then it's one of the lost works of Bishop Papias! If so, it could confirm that the excavation is indeed his very house! The title literally means "Oracles or Discourses of the Lord Exegeted/ Interpreted." Papias produced a five-volume work that is all but lost except for the fragments we have in Eusebius and some other Church Fathers. Papias's writings include some of the earliest reflections on the origins of the Gospels, the collection of Jesus's sayings, comments on early Christian eschatology, and things Papias learned from one of the last of the early Christian leaders who had been in touch with the eyewitnesses, John of Patmos. It could unlock many mysteries about the origins of various New Testament documents. I'm sure that Papias's work would provide a list of *agrapha*, or otherwise unrecorded traditions of Jesus's sayings."

"That is most impressive, but let us not get too carried away at this point," cautioned Marissa. "Remember, we have only about one page of this manuscript, and possibly its beginning. That bodes well for finding more pages, do you not think?"

"Well, yes, there appears to be much more in the chamber. Besides this is such a good beginning that I'm sure it warrants all the excavation money the government can spare! For now, can we take a non-flash series of photos of the full text so that I can begin a real translation? I presume you have a very safe place to store the artifacts found at this site."

At this point, Mehmet intervened, "I assure you that we are well equipped to safely store the document. Of course, our main concern is deterioration from the heat and humidity. You seem to be a useful addition to our team for now, Dr. West."

"Please, call me Art. And please post a special night guard at the entrance of the house until we can extract all the documents and other artifacts," requested Art.

"Of course, I was just mentally making the arrangements. I believe the antiquities authorities are currently camped at the Laodicea dig. I will contact them as soon as possible," promised Mehmet.

The rest of the day was far less exciting as Art was asked to do a survey of the whole site and see if anything required more detailed analysis. It's always helpful to have an extra pair of eyes at a dig site. Nothing of real significance came to light, and when 5:00 p.m. rolled around, Marissa asked, "Would you like to join me for dinner tonight at the Pamukkale Grand Palace?"

"Why, thank you," expressed Art, a bit nervously. "I'll be happy to pay for my meal."

"What! And not let us show you our famous Turkish hospitality after you have worked all day for no pay! Not a chance!" she chided.

Mehmet watched as the two archaeologists rode back down the hill in the jeep. What were they thinking, he wondered? What Art was pondering was why Marissa's perfumed presence distracted his train of thought so easily. One way or another, he was going to need to figure that one out.

10

The Demons Only Come Out at Night

RIGHT ON TIME THE IAA came trooping into Kahlil's musty shop at 5:30. "Well Kahlil, what revelations do you have for us?" asked the chief, Sammy Cohen, while Agents Simon Levi and Josef Dershowitz waited eagerly.

"You are not going to believe what I found!" responded Kahlil with pride, as he looked at the three men, and winked at his daughter.

There was a collective gasp when Kahlil, with gloves on, painstakingly rolled out the papyrus, and placed a piece of glass gently over it. No one in the room had ever seen a papyrus like this before, especially with its drawings. There, plain to see, were two demons, various nondescript letter sequences, and a Greek text, which Kahlil, even with all his training, could only partially decipher. As Kahlil poured over the manuscript using his magnifying glass, with the IAA peering over his shoulder, his wonder only grew.

"Gentlemen, here is what I think. Since we have clear ancient evidence of people placing rolled up curse formulae on small pieces of metal and papyri and hiding them in a holy place in order for the curse to be enacted by the deity in question, my suspicion is that this scroll was inserted into our menorah as a means of protecting it from theft or vandalism. We know very well that in early Judaism demonology had developed on a grand scale long before this menorah was ever made in the second or third centuries. In other words, this papyrus was meant to place a curse on anyone who mishandled this object, with threat of them being plagued by demons!"

"That would certainly cause the thief to take notice," chuckled Sammy. "If only we were so lucky to have curses on all our sacred artifacts! There would be a real spiritual deterrent to their being stolen! But of course all that is just ancient mythology. Modern people do not believe in that sort of spooky stuff."

Kahlil looked up and replied emphatically, "Not so fast. In the first place many very modern people do believe in curses and demons, even many well-educated persons, so I would not be so quick to dismiss the notion. If you talk to orthodox Jews, Christians, and Muslims they all believe in the reality of demons and even curses. I, in any case, am more than a little thankful we discovered and extracted the scroll before we gave the menorah to Grace and Manny, and I would suggest we not mention this whole matter to them. I cannot imagine having to tell the couple, 'There was a curse scroll in your wedding gift, but do not worry; there are no such things as curses!'"

"I see your point," smiled Sammy. "But may I suggest that you sell this papyrus to the IAA, and get it off your own premises, especially if *you* believe in curses. We would be delighted to take this very interesting document off your hands and give it further study. If we find it is genuine, we will pay you a good sum for it."[1]

Kahlil nodded his head. "That sounds fair enough. I would appraise this very rare papyrus at 350,000 shekels or 100,000 U.S. dollars. Does that seem fair to you?"

1. Thanks to Don Barker for a better picture of this genuine papyrus now housed at Macquarrie University.

"I dare say it would bring three times that amount on the open market. Let me write out an IOU and sign it now. We will take the papyrus with us and have it professionally examined in short order," promised Sammy.

Kahlil turned to Hannah. "My dear, would you please get one of those promissory note forms out of the filing cabinet?" She knew they could certainly use the money, as business had not been all that good, what with the tourist trade being way down due to the huge increase in plane fares in the past six months.

Expeditiously the paper work was completed. Kahlil rerolled the papyrus and placed it in a secure dark container. Sammy could see the concern on Kahlil's face.

"Do not be so worried, my friend," said Sammy softly. "You know we will be careful not to expose this precious papyrus to the elements."

Sammy shook hands with Kahlil and quickly exited the shop with his two burly companions. Turning left and heading toward the Damascus Gate, Sammy had not gone ten feet before he tripped and fell flat on the massive stone pavement. The long, round container slipped from his hand and began to roll wildly into the street. The cap popped off, and the precious manuscript began slipping from the container. Agent Dershowitz scrambled and grabbed the container before a vegetable wagon being pushed by a stooped elderly lady nearly flattened the drum. He gently poked the manuscript back down into the container, and safely capped it once again. Meanwhile, Agent Levi helped his director back to his feet. Sammy had stubbed his toe badly and his hands were scuffed up, but it was mainly his pride that had taken a beating.

"Are you alright, chief!?" exclaimed Agent Levi.

Sammy groaned as he brushed himself off. "I will be fine as long as we did not lose our prized possession."

"Oh, I have it," reassured Josef. "But it was nearly squashed by that rickety wagon. Well, you know what they say about demons."

"Uh, no, but do tell me," encouraged Sammy with raised brows.

"They only come out at night," pronounced Josef. But Sammy Cohen had no idea what sort of trouble he had just brought upon himself by agreeing to purchase this curse scroll.

Late that evening, Sammy was rubbing his hands while sitting at his desk in his new IAA office located within the Rockefeller Museum in East Jerusalem. They still smarted from the fall on the Cardo outside el Said's shop. The demon papyrus, as it had now been officially dubbed, was safely ensconced in a climate-controlled storage room. Sammy did not believe in curses coming from ancient manuscripts, but he had to admit it was weird that he had stumbled the way he did on the Cardo. Normally, he was very sure-footed. And strange that Simon started sneezing on the way back—some sort of allergic reaction to mid-June pollen they imagined.

Sammy continued nursing his coffee while thumbing through numerous reports, including the latest one on the latest hot artifact, the so-called Gabriel Stone. Ada Yardeni had authenticated its script, and it seemed to provide evidence that before the time of Jesus some Jewish person had thought of the notion of a dying and rising messiah figure, though there was no mention of crucifixion as the means of death. It had to be admitted though that the crucial line in question in the text had gaps and was blurry in places—yet another artifact which provided the source of endless debate and speculation. Why exactly had the stone's inscriber written with ink on stone rather than engraving it? This seemed very odd to Sammy. Suddenly the phone startled him back into the moment. "Yes, this is Sam Cohen. What? Surely not! I'll be there quickly."

The person at the other end of the line was Dershowitz's hysterical wife. Her husband had been rushed to the hospital. Cohen was racing to his car to head up the hill to Mt. Sinai Hospital, and one part of his brain was asking, "Could this scroll be the kiss of death?"

11

It Takes Two to Tango

He couldn't concentrate. He just couldn't. He wanted to be thinking about what questions to raise about the new Papias manuscript find, but he was distracted by other thoughts that kept crowding into his brain. For some reason, Art West was as jumpy as a frog on a hot rock. He kept asking himself, "Why am I so nervous about a simple dinner with an archaeological colleague whom I barely know?" For years Art had simply channeled all his passions into his work as a confirmed bachelor. These newly awakened feelings were awkward, unexpected, unbidden, and there was a part of him that was in denial that this sort of thing could be happening to him.

Truth be told, Art had not been entirely comfortable with his feelings even when he was around someone who was just a dear friend of the opposite sex, like Grace Levine. Their religious differences had served as a sort of psychological fence, which kept the relationship within platonic bounds, and now that Grace was about to be married, Art was somewhat relieved. What little personal or sexual tension there had been between Art and Grace had been removed from the equation. But now, here came a new feeling of tension in a relationship Art had not sought. Nevertheless, he went through his usual hygiene routine—face shaving, teeth brushing, hair combing—but he drew the line at cologne sprinkling! He was determined not to see this as a date. After all, he had not had a date in decades, so *this couldn't be a date!*

Going down to the hotel lobby, he found Marissa already waiting, and she no longer looked like a field archaeologist. No pith helmet on now. Instead she was wearing a long, silky floral-patterned dress. Her jet-black hair flowed down her back, and makeup accented her natural features. To Art, she looked amazing, and perhaps for the first time in a long time he actually wanted to study a woman. In his teenage and college years he had dated off and on. But then the vision of ministry and work convinced him that he had *much more important things to do for the Kingdom.* So he tended to see dating as pointless or superfluous. What woman would put up with a husband who ran around the world lecturing and digging and exploring? These were some of the convoluted thoughts racing through Art's head as his pulse began to quicken in the lovely presence of a woman who was indeed *la femme très formidable.*

"Well, you clean up nice," said Marissa rising from her seat and smiling.

"I was about to say something similar about you," replied Art somewhat awkwardly. Art himself was wearing a colorful sport shirt, dress chinos, and his matching brown Turkish leather belt and loafers. "Shall we go into dinner, and talk about everything and anything?"

He was startled when Marissa actually took his left arm and escorted him into the hotel restaurant, aptly dubbed the Cotton Castle Club. More like a lounge than a restaurant, the club was dark and intimate with candles on the tables and a small jazz trio playing quietly in a corner.

"So, being native, what do you recommend?" asked Art, after he had helped Marissa get seated.

"The chef here is from Istanbul, and he knows all the traditional dishes. I am especially partial to the stuffed pepper dolma, the mujver, and the fantastic doner kebab."

"Your culinary preferences are right up my alley," said Art. "But shall we start with a meze platter? I could really devour some baba ghanoush. The eggplant here seems to be prepared with a very unique smoky flavor that I like."

"You are right. In Turkish it is called *patlican ezme,* but I admit most Westerners refer to our aubergine or brinjal or eggplant appetizer as baba ghanoush. How long have you been coming to our fair land?"

"Well, the first time was about twenty years ago, on one of those Journeys of Paul and Churches of the Revelation sorts of American tours. I was the talking head lecturing at various sites. At that time I met a tour guide that I have continued to work with ever since—Meltem Çiftçi. Maybe you know her? "

"Know her!" exclaimed Marissa. "I went to school with Meltem in Izmir. She is one of the very best guides in all of Turkiye. Her scope of historical knowledge is just about unmatched among all guides in this country. And she tries very hard to understand the Christian religious significance of the sites, a trait that is so appreciated by the Christian tourists."

"Tell me about it. She is constantly surprising me with new information, and she keeps me up to date on the latest digs, which is why I am here."

"Where is she now?" asked Marissa. "I've lost track of her in recent years."

"Right now she is doing one of those interesting archaeology cruise tours of the southwest coast, starting in Bodrum. I hardly see her any more except when we occasionally do a tour together, but we keep in touch by e-mail."

Suddenly the waiter appeared dressed all in white, except for his hat, looking sort of like a Turkish fez. "Will you both be having an aperitif?" he asked politely.

Marissa answered, "I will have a dry martini."

Art followed with, "I've become attached to the frozen margaritas, especially with mango. You have such wonderful fresh fruit here in Turkey."

"Shall we have a bottle of wine with our meal?" When Art nodded, she picked a simple white table wine from the region of Cappadocia. "Good vintages have become very expensive—a point of contention— but grapes have been grown here for millennia."

This encounter was going far too smoothly. Art was beginning to feel like he was on a preordained escalator boldly going up where his feelings had not gone in living memory. Could he really have found a woman with whom he felt comfortable—one who would allow him to be himself? The voice inside Art's head told him it was too soon to ask that question—he needed to focus.

Grabbing her large satchel, Marissa produced a photocopy of the papyrus fragment which they had extracted from the inner room now being called "the Papias House." Handing it over to Art, she asked, "I have had a quick look, and it seems to be the opening passage from one of the books of 'the Oracles of the Lord,' but I am unsure which one. What do you think? Is any of this new information not found in Eusebius or elsewhere?"

Art scanned the manuscript looking for clues, and frowned. "This photocopy is a bit fuzzy. All in all, however, this appears to be the very beginning of the document itself, indeed the part that Irenaeus tells us was in the preface. Look at these lines here, while I give a rough translation. I think Papias is being honest and setting out his credentials for being able to do an exegesis of the Lord's oracles and sayings."

Ουκ οκνησω δε σοι και οσα ποτε παρα των πρεσβυτερων καλως εμαθον και καλως εμνημονευσα συγκαταταξαι ταις ερμηνειας, διαβεβαιουμενος υπερ αυτων αληθειαν. ου γαρ τοις τα πολλα λεγουσιν εχαιρον ωσπερ οι πολλοι, αλλα τοις ταληθη διδασκουσιν, ουδε τοις τας αλλοτριας εντολας μνηνευουσιν, αλλα τοις τας παρα του κυριου τη πιστει δεδομενας και απ αυτης παραγιγνομενας της αληθειας.

"But I shall not hesitate to arrange alongside my interpretations as many things as I ever learned well and remembered well from the elders, confirming the truth on their behalf. For I did not rejoice, like many, over those who spoke many things, but instead over those who taught the truth, nor over those who related strange commands, but over those who related those given by the Lord by faith and coming from the truth itself."

"Most of the first book of the Oracles is missing, is it not?" asked Marissa anxiously.

"Yes, but these lines I do recognize as also being in the works of Irenaeus. This particular papyrus, though tantalizing, mostly confirms what we already know from the excerpts in Irenaeus and Eusebius. Maybe some of the other papyri in that room will provide new evidence. Our new papyrus confirms that we can rely on the snippets from Papias found in Irenaeus who apparently quoted him accurately. Papias, you see, was engaging in archaeology as it was originally meant. Remember that *arche* really refers to something original or the origins. So Papias was actually an early archaeologist; he went back to the original source of things to get at the truth of the matter. He wanted to know what Christ and the original apostles actually said and meant. He was, like us, of an historical mindset."

So engrossed were these two scholars that they were surprised when the waiter showed up with their drinks and the meze platter all at once. "Fantastic," enthused Art, "I am thirsty and hungry."

Marissa grinned, "So let us toast to an evening of fun—not work. If the music is to your liking, perhaps we can join some of the couples over there on the dance floor if you like."

"Well, I am not a very good dancer," said Art honestly and nervously. "But if they play something smooth, slow, and familiar, I guess I can get by." Just then the band began to play one of John Coltrane's classic ballads, "Stardust," a tune Art knew by heart especially since Coltrane, born in his own hometown of High Point, NC, was his favorite saxophone player. Art was astonished, and asked, "You didn't bribe them into playing that number just to get me out on the dance floor, did you?"

Marissa laughed quite long at that suggestion. "Why I have no idea what you are talking about, Professor West. What sort of woman do you take me for?"

Art began to really wonder about that question. The dinner had gone extremely well, and Art had found himself more and more interested in Marissa Okur, and thus far the interest seemed mutual. As they were finishing their last coffees she suddenly said, "Shall we have a little dance on the floor?" Art had learned over dinner that Marissa had spent her early years growing up in Boston. This explained her proper English, and some knowledge of idioms, albeit somewhat dated. Summoning up his courage, Art tried to reply nonchalantly. "Sure, why not, just so long as you understand this is not 'Dancing with the Stars.'"

The band was playing the Miles Davis/Bill Evans/John Coltrane classic "Blue in Green" and the piano was working its way through a nice solo in the middle, with the saxophone blending effortlessly. Art found Marissa's hand remarkably soft, considering they were often digging in the dirt, and she smelled for all the world like the flowers printed on her dress. Art could not really believe that he was enjoying dancing, but enjoy it he did. As the song came to an end, Marissa turned to face him. Not inches away she sighed, "This has been a wonderful evening, but we have much work to do tomorrow, so we had best call it a day."

"Whatever you think best, Marissa," Art heard himself saying as softly as he had ever spoken. Walking Marissa to the door of the restaurant, he almost gave her a little hug, but they parted to their own rooms. He felt like a kid again, but he knew he needed to temper the rising tide of hopes and expectations with a dose of reality. As he opened his hotel door he murmured to himself, "Don't make too much of it, at least not yet." But already he knew he was fighting a losing battle with his heart. "What will my Momma say about me going out with a non-Christian, Turkish girl?" moaned Art as he turned in to bed for the evening.

12

RSVP ASAP

THE WEDDING INVITATIONS WERE being hand addressed by Grace, with Camelia stuffing the envelopes, licking the stamps, and putting a large rubber band around each batch of the embossed, cream-colored announcements.

Camelia sighed. "Do you realize you invited 100 people to your wedding? And Manny another 100? How will we care for them all in some synagogue ruins in Capernaum? Is that even kosher? What if it rains? What about the heat? Why can't we have the wedding here in Jerusalem? I will faint away in Capernaum!"

"Mother, we have been over all this," sighed Grace loud enough to silence her mother. Just think how beautiful it will be late in the evening as the sun is sinking below the horizon. And you know it never rains in July! And remember we will all adjourn to the Scots Hotel in Tiberias. And I showed you the pictures of the lawn area overlooking the Sea of Galilee where we can eat and toast and cut the cake and dance and ..."

"Well I see you have got it all figured out without me," interrupted Camelia. "I hope those ruins will be accessible to old folks like me. I will break my hip for sure!"

"Mother, you know that Capernaum is a top tourist attraction—and very safe. After all, the synagogue is one of the oldest in the world. And did you know that beneath the fourth century synagogue, there are remains of yet another, older synagogue, maybe even from the first century! Imagine that!"

"I will feel better when I am back in my own bed," moaned Camellia.

"We are renting the Scots Hotel and the Ron Beach Hotel for three nights to accommodate all our guests. We cannot expect our friends to come to Galilee from near and far and not be hospitable to them. And yes, we've made sure the catering will be kosher to the max, with a non-kosher table for some of our non-Jewish friends. After all, Manny can easily afford all this extravagance once in his life. Any man who buys a diamond ring so large that I am too afraid to wear it in public most of the time can afford all this quite readily."

Secretly, Camelia was proud and relieved that Grace had taken charge of all the arrangements. She sighed again, but mainly because she was so enjoying this time with her daughter on this fine morning. But Grace had more to say.

"Mother, I have one other somewhat delicate subject to broach with you just now. As you know, I will be moving to Tel Aviv and commuting to Jerusalem two to three days a week for work. I have a request, and hope you will not say no. Manny has purchased a nice little beach bungalow right on the Mediterranean that is only a mile down the road from the seaside house where we will live. Can I please persuade you to move there, so we could continue to be close? Manny and I would both like that very much, for as you know both of Manny's parents are deceased."

Camelia began to weep, as she had assumed she would be losing the almost daily contact with her one daughter. She would lie awake at night wondering how she would cope living alone in Jerusalem. "*Todah rabah*," replied Camelia, as she wiped her eyes and blew her nose. "Thank you, child. I promise not to be any trouble!"

"Whoever said you were trouble?" Grace winked at her mother, who had indeed been a bit of a task to manage in recent years. "This is your chance to enjoy the sea air, and get away from the problems in Jerusalem. We will have some good times there; I know you love the Mediterranean."

And for once in her life, Camelia was so happy, and so overwhelmed that she was totally and absolutely at a loss for words. She and her daughter embraced and looked forward to the time after the wedding. But for now, there were urgent tasks at hand. The wedding was only weeks away, and they hadn't even mailed the invitations yet. So they wrote at the bottom of each reply card—RSVP ASAP! That ought to get everyone's attention.

13

From Hummus to Hamas

AHMED HAD BEEN ON hold now for what seemed like ten minutes, waiting for the operator to connect him to his cousin in Gaza. The phone system there was primitive because the cell tower had been disabled by one of the periodic Israeli airstrikes meant to disrupt things in Hamas headquarters. Meanwhile Ahmed's wife was busy making the hummus for tomorrow morning so it would be ready before the Mediterranean Market opened for the day's business. Things had not been good for Hamas ever since El Tigre, the great mastermind of international terror, had been captured in Jerusalem. Worse, El Tigre had disappeared from the face of the earth as far as Hamas could determine, and not coincidentally this happened right about the time Ishmael (Jake) Arafat had stopped being their conduit for money and influence in the Middle East. It was hard not to connect the two events, though in fact there was no clear proof they were connected. Indeed, Ishmael Arafat had seemed to be the victim of his brother's own malice as he was used as a hostage to obtain the release of Art West from his Gaza captors last year. Or was he? Could he have been part of the plot to release West, even after he had been part of the plot to capture Grace Levine in the first place, as a way of catching the bigger fish, West?[1]

All this was hard to decipher, but what was certain was that Hamas had taken a major hit when Ishmael Arafat had suddenly left the country and ceased to be the conduit for the very life blood of the revolution, money. For this alone he deserved some punishment. As Ahmed fumed over the defection of his distant cousin, *in order to play professional basketball no less,* he had devised a strategy in his mind to get some revenge.

1. This story is told in *Roman Numerals: The Second Art West Adventure.*

Ahmed, truth be told, had no stomach for murder and he was not sure Ishmael deserved to die, but theft was another matter. Ahmed knew very well the usual Muslim punishment for a serious theft, and so he had formulated a plan that did not require him to invade Ishmael's space, or the basketball arena where so much openly lascivious and drunken behavior went on, but rather to abide his soul in patience and be ready to dole out the punishment when the time and place were right. Now if he could just clear this sort of plan with headquarters in Gaza.

Finally the connection went through: "*Salam aleichum*, it is very late here, what do you need?" Ahmed had made the mistake of thinking there was only seven hours of difference between Charlotte and Gaza, but in fact at this time of year there were eight.

"Forgive me, Muktar, this is Ahmed, but I needed to consult with you about an important matter. I have devised a plan to punish Ishmael Arafat, who has betrayed our holy cause, and I wanted to see if you could help me."

"Yes, go ahead, but this had better be good. We have lost several key operatives and are strapped for money now, since both el Tigre and Ishmael are no longer working for us. Do not even think about asking me for money, as I have none to spare. Even our investments for Hamas have gone down due to the economic crisis spreading around the globe."

"Yes," said Ahmed meekly, "but what I am devising is a plan to punish Ishmael and prevent him from enjoying his ill gotten gains from pro basketball. Did you know there is even a rumor he has been going to a church here in Charlotte?"

"You are saying he has become an infidel? Is that what you are saying?"

"I believe so, though I am not absolutely certain. I suppose he could be playing a role in order to get money, and maybe he was planning on sending us some in due course. I am not absolutely certain. He could be an infiltrator, like some of us in the US."

"But if that were true, surely he would have advised us of his plan, instead of just falling off the face of the earth, and going completely silent for all these months."

"Well, yes, but didn't el Tigre used to do that as well?"

There was a pause on the other end of the line, and finally a response: "I suppose you are right, so you had better test him about Issah, hadn't you, before doing anything drastic."

"Right, test him first; punish him second, if he fails the test. But what do I do after I punish him? Where do I go? My wife and I barely get by here in Charlotte, and I do not know where the safe houses and other operatives are."

"There is time enough to talk about that later," growled Muktar. "For now do nothing drastic. You have a good cover there and no one suspects anything yet, but once you take action against Ishmael then you will have to disappear quickly. So think on how you will test Ishmael—perhaps ask him about his name change when he comes in again, and ask him how he views Issah, not his deceased brother, but the more famous prophet for whom he was named. Ask him if he believes Issah is greater than Mohammed, and if he died on a cross. If he says yes to those two things, you will know."

"I had not thought about testing him first, but you are right of course. But will he not get suspicious if I ask such questions?"

"Not if you ask them in an unassuming and simple and pleasant way. So you must practice by being friendly to the man when next he enters the shop. Ask him about his basketball games, or something like that. Show some interest in the man and beguile him a bit."

"Yes, Muktar, I will do as you say, *aleichum salam* to you, I will ring off now."

And as the phone went silent, Ahmed was lost in his thoughts. He must approach this carefully, so as to not scare away his prey. Jake Arafat must not suspect he was being silently and subtly stalked.

14

Demons on the Loose

A GENT DERSHOWITZ WAS INDEED in the hospital suffering with pro-gressive paralysis. He was on oxygen, which seemed to have relieved some of his symptoms, but the doctors were baffled. Sammy Cohen sat patiently with Dershowitz's wife, trying to console her a bit. Naomi was non-responsive. She just sat quietly weeping.

After about another thirty minutes, which seemed like an eternity to Naomi, Dr. bar Ilan came into the waiting room to speak to Naomi. Sitting down and looking her right in the eye, the doctor said, "Mrs. Dershowitz, we are still not sure what is wrong with your husband. He seems to have been affected by an unknown substance to which his body is reacting violently. We examined him from top to bottom closely and we didn't find any wounds or infected places, but something poisonous has gotten into his system. We are still doing blood work and will prob-ably send a sample to a high-tech lab for analysis. Do you have any clue as to how he could have come into contact with something toxic, and if so what? We need an antidote!"

"I honestly have no idea, but perhaps Dr. Cohen might," Naomi said coldly.

Sammy, looking surprised, hesitated, thought for a moment, and then replied, "No doctor, I can't think of anything that could explain this, but let me ask you a question. Could contact with an ancient manuscript convey some ancient contagion? Would a disease last that long enclosed in an object for two thousand years? Agent Dershowitz did briefly touch an ancient document with his finger tips yesterday."

"I shouldn't think so. Other than some endospores, most microbes would surely have died a long time ago. But a contaminant, like a quick-acting poison, that would be another matter. Could someone have coated the document in question with poison?"

"I guess I should find out," said Sammy looking guilty. "Our labs will begin an analysis immediately."

"I guess you'd better, and you'd better do it quickly," said Naomi, her anger rising.

At this juncture Sammy realized he needed to beat a fast retreat. "Doctor, I promise to have the manuscript chemically tested. It will be top priority. I will get back to you ASAP."

"See that you do," said Dr. bar Ilan, frowning even more than Naomi. "The situation may be grave, since we do not know yet what we are dealing with."

As he was leaving Mt. Sinai, Sammy flipped open his cell phone and called the office. Susan, his secretary answered. "Susan, would you please get one of our top scientists to do a residue scan and analysis of the demon papyrus immediately. I don't care what other projects he needs to set aside to get this accomplished. And tell him to take extra precautions! Don't touch that papyrus! Agent Dershowitz may have been harmed through contact with that ancient scroll."

"At once boss. I'll get right on it," and she rang off.

As he raced to his car, Sammy muttered to himself, "What have I gotten myself into by purchasing that papyrus?"

～

Josef Dershowitz had been better, but he had also been worse. Right now he was weak as a kitten. He had indeed been poisoned by some of the residue on the demon papyrus. The chemical analysis revealed a powdered form of hemlock, specifically the chemical conium! Hemlock, the very thing that killed Socrates. Josef was not feeling very philosophical about what had happened to him, and his wife Naomi was mad as a wet hen about it. She wanted her husband out of this line of work. Skullduggery should be left to those who were numbskulls! He was now being nursed along on chicken soup. The goal was to get him out of the hospital in about a week's time.

Meanwhile, the demon papyrus had been stirring up trouble in another quarter in another way. Sammy Cohen was having the devil of a time deciphering the script. Some of it seemed to be just gibberish, nonsensical syllables piled one on top of another; some of it seemed to be cursing, and some of it seemed to be a string of deity names. What in the world was this conglomeration of things supposed to convey? Sammy was out of his element and out of his league with this papyrus. Among other things, he needed an expert in ancient scripts and early Jewish demonology, but alas Grace Levine was not available at all these days.

"What in the world is going on with this manuscript?" said Sammy to no one but the ghosts in his IAA office. On the one hand, it looked like a child's doodling while being bored at school, but this surely must be more significant than that. And why was it stuffed inside a menorah? So many questions, so little time. But Sammy was determined to get to the bottom of things. He was not about to allow those demons on the papyrus staring him in the face to get the better of him.

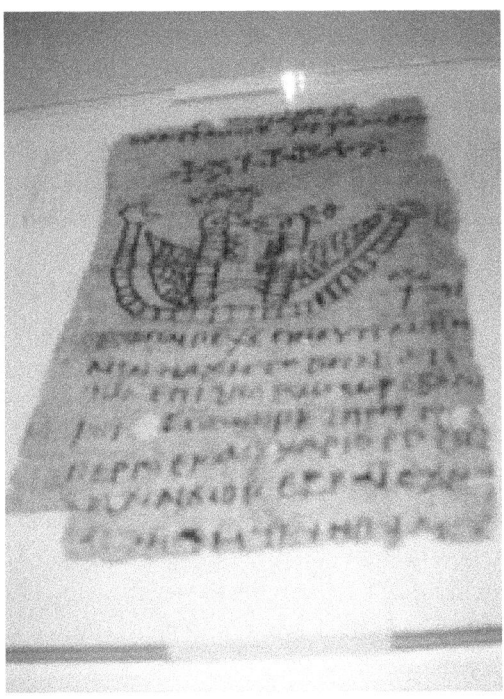

15

Pondering the Papyrus

UNABLE TO SLEEP, ART had stayed well past midnight with his magnifying glass, carefully reading and translating the photocopy of the first Papias papyrus fragment. There could be no doubt this was a fragment of the introduction to Papias's famous five-volume work, which begged the question whether there was more of it in that dark chamber. Thus far, Art had learned nothing new about Papias, except that he was a truth seeker wanting to get back to what Jesus himself actually taught and did.

Sleep had finally overcome him, but it seemed like minutes later when he was startled out of a sound sleep by the jangling of the phone. "Hullo," moaned Art as he picked up the phone in his hotel room.

"Good morning. Aren't you cheerful this morning?" said Marissa in her melodious voice.

"Well, you see, I think any hour before eight in the morning is the result of the Fall," replied Art, gradually becoming more alert.

"What in the world do you mean by that?" queried Marissa.

"Oh, it's an old joke based on the theory that when Adam sinned it affected everything, even the way day and night affected human beings. I'll explain it to you sometime."

"Regardless, it is time to rise and shine. I plan to continue exploring the Papias chamber. One little piece of papyrus already known from other sources does not a larger government grant produce. So shall I meet you downstairs for breakfast in thirty minutes?"

"Fine," agreed Art. "I'll just freshen up and head downstairs with all my usual paraphernalia. A good breakfast and Turkish coffee could wake the dead."

"TTFN!" said Marissa in place of "Good Bye."

Art scratched his head and muttered, "Ta, Ta For Now! Where did she learn that British abbreviation? This woman is full of surprises." Just how many surprises, Art had only begun to discover.

Art had sent an email to Grace asking for info on the timing of the wedding and the duties of an usher. He applauded Grace's choice of the Capernaum synagogue ruins for the festivities, though he found it rather ironic, since this was also the probable locale where Jesus himself had preached on more than one occasion. It would be good to have Jesus's blessing on this marriage, just as he blessed the wedding at Cana.

Checking his smart phone as he ran a comb through his hair, he discovered that Grace had indeed sent back all the particulars, and even booked him a room at the Scots Hotel.

"That woman is on the ball," said Art, "even when she has every right to be frazzled with all the wedding plans." Art wondered what it would be like to get married, and have a family. It seemed a little late for the latter in his case, but still he wondered about it. In this day and age, certainly Grace could have children. What a thought!

Having put on his exploring clothes, including his most service-able pair of working jeans, Art was prepared for doing some crouch-ing, crawling, squeezing, reaching, pushing, shoving, digging, dusting, or whatever was required to get into that chamber. Those other scrolls needed to be rescued, and quickly before someone unscrupulous got their first. Despite security precautions, no dig was truly safe.

As the elevator door opened, Art saw Marissa waiting for him to go to the hotel café to wolf down some food and get started on an exciting day.

Marissa smiled. "You need to eat hearty at breakfast because we may have to work right through the day to get into the chamber and extract those scrolls. Mehmet generally has lunch brought in, but I can't promise gourmet cooking."

"You sound like my mother," laughed Art.

"Well, an archaeologist can't live by artifacts alone," quipped Marissa.

"So true," replied Art. "Let's eat. Turkish breakfast buffets are a true feast around here. Some days, however, I miss grits and cheese and sau-sage." But as the couple walked into the café, they were being observed closely by an increasingly jealous man—Mehmet Ertegun.

16

A Gift from God

JAKE ARAFAT CUT QUITE a figure with Aunt Joyce on his arm, walking into Myers Park Methodist Church in Charlotte. Even the ever-so-Southern and polite members of that church couldn't help but stare. Picture a six foot four, well-built athlete with dark, olive skin and jet-black hair, wearing a gray three piece suit and shiny black loafers. On his arm is a five foot four, slightly plump, elderly woman with gray hair recently curled at the beauty parlor, wearing shiny red lipstick and a colorful floral dress. Staring was not only natural, it was almost mandatory when it came to this couple heading down the middle aisle. The usher, Lou Bledsoe, an old friend of the West family, led them into their usual pew near the front on the right. "Here you go," said Lou with a smile. "So good to have you with us this morning." From here Joyce could recognize the choir members and see the flower arrangements. Yesterday, there had been a wedding. Arrangements of white magnolias were laced with delicate vines of sweet-smelling jasmine. The aroma was heavenly.

Joyce went to church, as they say, religiously. She almost never missed a week, except when she was feeling poorly, and lately her diverticulitis had been plaguing her some. But she enjoyed the preaching of Rev. James Howell, even if he did have some novel rhetorical hand gestures from time to time.

She was old school in her religion, and not likely to join the "happy clappy" praise crowd in the other wing of the church, singing what she considered endlessly repetitive praise choruses. Joyce had been a classical piano teacher; thus she liked things that in her mind had class, especially when it came to worship. Give her a choir and an organist, not a guitar and drums, any day. She preferred traditional worship; for example, she did not like taking communion informally without the proper peniten-tial prayers and liturgy. No Kool-Aid and crackers communion for her. As for Jake, the only kind of Christian religious service he had ever at-tended was very traditional, liturgical, high church. He had never even witnessed a contemporary "praise" service in his life. As he looked up into the vaulted ceiling, stared at the beautiful stained glass windows and listened to the organ play, this seemed like "home" to him.

As they settled into their pew, and the organ played a subdued pre-lude, Joyce noticed the various people staring at Jake. Myers Park was no different than any other Charlotte church in this respect—it was loaded with sports fans. They were mostly college basketball fans pulling for Duke or Carolina, but there were a few avid NBA fans as well, and so there was some recognition of who Jake Arafat was, especially among the young adult males.

In the pew behind Joyce and Jake, two of these aforementioned males were whispering to each other. "I'm telling you man, that is Jake the Cat Arafat. The Cat is in the house this morning." At this point Jake turned around, and putting a finger over his lips while smiling his mil-lion-dollar smile, "Shush, what matters is God is in the house!" Properly chastened, the two young men obediently shut up.

This morning there was a procession down the central aisle. As the crucifer and the acolytes went by, and everyone was singing, "All glory, laud, and honor, to thee Redeemer King . . ." Jake flashed back to that horrible day in Bethlehem when they had to bury his brother, Issah. So many hundreds of Issah's friends had shown up. He thought about the big difference between sports fans, and those who admired Issah for his noble Christian character. Jake resolved once more to strive to be more like Issah (the Arabic word for Jesus), both the original one from Nazareth and his brother. He would deflect the praise of fans, and try and point people to the one true God. Before everyone took their seats, Dr. Howell led them in the Apostle's Creed.

"Let us all unite in affirming this historic and most ancient sum-mary of our Christian faith: 'I believe in God the Father almighty, maker of heaven and earth . . .'"

Joyce, as she said the words, was actually thinking, "It's just like God to put two such different persons as Jake and myself together in church. It's hard to put aside prejudices, but if I can do it, there's hope for every-one!" It was a good morning to be in church.

~

Grace had hit a snag in her wedding preparations. She wanted a ring of baby's breath for the bride's maids' hair to give them a sort of natural look, but it was not going to be available from the florist. What to do, what to do? Her second choice was to go with some sort of aromatic flower pinned to their hair—a magnolia blossom perhaps? Grace had never considered these details. She was a no nonsense academic who had reached middle age without getting married, and so she was swimming in uncharted waters. She decided to ring up her girlfriend Sarah who ran Solomon's Porch coffee shop on Ben Yehuda Street in Jerusalem. Flipping open her new razor thin cell phone, a gift from Manny, she said, "*Boker tov*, girlfriend, this is Grace. Have you a minute to help me out of a wedding planning jam?"

"Sure, but I told you this was going to happen when you refused to hire a proper wedding planner. What were you thinking?" chided Sarah.

"Thinking didn't really enter into it," said Grace. "I just imagined that since I was only getting married once, total immersion was the way to go, rather than sloughing these decisions off on someone else."

"I hear that, but now you are paying the price. There are a million little last minute decisions, and some of them have to be changed on the fly."

Wrinkling up her nose, Grace replied, "Don't I know it? As the old Swedish proverb goes 'We are too soon old, and too late smart.' Anyway, I am trying to decide what to do about flowers for the bridesmaid's hair, and since you are one of them, I am taking a one-person poll on this. Here's the problem. You can't get baby's breath here in Tel Aviv at this time of the summer."

Sarah just laughed. "What's so funny?" asked Grace a bit testily.

"Well, hearing you stressing out about wedding minutia rather than ancient manuscripts is hysterical. I never thought we'd see this day come."

"Please remember that 'this day' is bearing down on me like a freight train, so help me out. What do you think of a magnolia blossom with greenery for you girls?"

"Well, that depends on the size of the magnolia blossom; some of them are as large as hats!" quipped Sarah. "The wedding is in the evening right? I have the perfect flower for you—jasmine! The flowers open in the evening; they smell so sweet; and they are always available. And would you believe, jasmine comes from the Persian word meaning 'Gift from God.' Now isn't that just perfect!"

"Sarah, I'm so impressed! How do you know all this?"

"Simple, I have a jasmine plant in my apartment." At that Sarah began to ponder the possibility of giving Grace and Manny a beautiful sweet-smelling jasmine vine for their new home. Her thoughts, however, were interrupted by Grace's obviously frazzled voice. "Thanks! I promise I will hire a wedding planner for the rest of the arrangements. She will probably find all the things I've totally lost track of."

"Well, better late than never," said Sarah. "Wait a tick; before you go I have a joke for you. Seems there was a nervous bride who was paralyzed at the back of the synagogue and couldn't make her feet go forward. The rabbi told her, 'Just concentrate on one thing at a time. First look at the aisle, then look at the altar, then look at your groom. You got that?' 'Yes,' said the bride, 'I think so.' And as she started walking down the aisle she was overheard muttering to herself, 'Aisle, altar, him. Aisle, altar, him.' And one lady who heard this said, 'Good luck, dear!'"

Grace broke out into raucous laughter. This joke had helped break the tension in her mind. Sarah signed off thinking, "Grace is going to need a vacation *after* her wedding, and *before* she gets back to real life." Just how much Grace would need a break from her work thereafter, she would not discover until the honeymoon itself.

17

The Journey to Pluto

ART WEST ALWAYS GOT a tingling feeling when he thought he was on to something big, and today his nerves were charged as he rode with Marissa to the tel. Marissa was quiet, lost in her thoughts and not sure what to expect. She was reflecting on last night's wonderful evening, dining and dancing with Dr. Art West. Did she really want to pursue a serious relationship? She realized that she instantly liked Art; in fact, she was actually flirting with him! Now in a more rational and business mode, she was thinking, "I hardly know him! This will never work!" But that was not what her heart was telling her. Art West had the prerequisites she wanted in a man right now. He was intelligent, respected in his field, youthful enough to get excited about his work, not hard on the eyes. And most importantly, actually because of their cultural differences, he actually respected the rights of women to pursue a career.

As they passed the temple of Apollo, Art was asking himself the same sort of questions, and ringing in his brain over and over was the biblical phrase "it is not good for man to be alone." But then there is also the phrase about not being unequally yoked—religious differences *do* matter. But the very minute he sat down next to Marissa this morning, his body stirred up certain feelings that seemed to override his worries about cultural differences. For now, he decided to put dilemmas aside and concentrate on the tingle of excitement related to archaeological digs only.

Arriving at the site, Mehmet was already present with the day laborers who had just begun clearing more debris from the entrance to the Papias chamber. The sun was already threatening to beat down on the ar-

The sealed up entrance to the
Plutonium at the Temple of Apollo

chaeological site, hence the need to get as much done as possible before taking a break in the afternoon.

They had placed a guard on the site overnight to make sure absolutely nothing was pilfered, since they now believed they were on to a major discovery. The guard, a small Turkish man carrying a rifle, walked up to Marissa as she hopped out of the jeep and said in Turkish, "All is well. There were no prowlers last night." It was important to him to exercise some measure of authority before this woman.

"Excellent work, Heido," said Marissa politely, "Thank you for your helpful service. We will be working this morning under my supervision, and then this evening Professor Ertegun will be in charge from four until sundown, as I must go down to Laodicea for a meeting with our supervisors. Let's start by getting that small crane over here, and hoisting that huge block of stone that is blocking our way. Could you go ask Ali to drive the little crane over here, please, Dr. West?"

"Certainly," said Art smiling rather fondly at Marissa.

It was all Mehmet could do to watch this cordial but sappy interchange. How is it that the American had jumped in front of him in the pursuit of Marissa's attentions? He could not understand this, not least because he secretly despised most Americans. His father had been an imam totally opposed to Turkey having alliances with the West and with NATO. He had vigorously opposed the U.S. Air Force base at Adana, especially when those planes flew missions over fellow Muslim countries. Gritting his teeth he said to Marissa, "And what shall I begin with this morning?"

"Thank you for asking, Mehmet. Could I get you to supervise the sorting of the potsherds over there in tent, since pottery is your specialty?"

"Indeed, and I will check back later in the morning. We should all lunch together, do you not think?" But Mehmet was thinking, "How convenient to shut me out of the dark chamber room. Apparently, she would rather spend her morning with Dr. West. How has it come to this?"

The three-hundred pound stone was ever so gently lifted from the doorway of the house of Papias. Art did not want to appear over eager, but he could not resist saying to Marissa, who was wiping her brow with a red kerchief, "Shall I reprise my normal role as one who slithers into holes and recovers artifacts?"

"If you still have energy after all we've been doing in this beastly heat, go right ahead," replied Marissa, giving Art the nod. There was now a triangular opening wide enough for even a large man to slip through. It was no longer like the rich man trying to squeeze through the eye of the needle, but the thought crossed Art's mind. Art also remembered the day when he had tried to impress various girls in the neighborhood by climbing a sweet gum tree, only to get stuck in a fork between two huge limbs. The girls giggled and fetched the burly neighbor, Mr. Cornelius, who brought his ladder and extracted Art. The humiliation of that occasion he had no desire to repeat.

Art stretched his legs into the hole and finally dropped into the chamber, which was a good five feet below ground level. The room was cool and pleasant, and Art, holding the penlight with the laser-like brightness in his mouth, had gauged his landing spot to be sure not to fall on anything delicate, like a piece of papyrus. Quickly surveying the room, he immediately remembered the strange crevice at the back. Yelling up to Marissa, he asked for his camera and a larger lantern, both of which were gently lowered down.

Snapping away at a rapid rate, Art discovered that this was not a crevice but some sort of doorframe. Could there really be an easily accessible chamber behind this one? But first things first, there were three rolled up scrolls on the floor next to an upturned table. It looked like the room had been turned upside down, not by some man-made occurrence but by an earthquake, which had certainly happened in this area before and after the time of Papias.

His survey located three pieces of papyri. Ever so carefully he picked up a papyrus with his gloved hand, and placed it in the basket attached to the retriever. "Okay," he shouted, "Pull it up, please!" And gradually the retriever disappeared back through the hole. "Send it back down! There are two more scrolls to load up!" hollered Art.

While he was waiting, his eye constantly went to the crevice. If there was a room behind this, would it be subterranean? Could this have been a secret underground Christian meeting place? Could it be a tunnel leading somewhere? Inquiring minds wanted to know. Shining his light up and down the recessed stone area, Art found a series of letters faintly carved into the stone. They appeared to say ΠΛΟΥΤΩΝ.

The spelling was not perfect, but it sure looked like *Plouton* to Art. There were probably letters missing. The Plutonium was down the hill and next to the Temple of Apollo. Surely this word was meant to read Plutonium.

But from this spot well up on the hill it would be a considerably long underground tunnel, and for what purpose? The pagan priests had gone down into the Plutonium to demonstrate their sanctity and purity, and perhaps to get inspired so they could speak prophecies. They did this from the entrance near the temple of Apollo. But what had that to do with Papias? Yes, Hierapolis had been the center of Christian prophecy in the late first and early second centuries, but was there some connection here? And hadn't the Christians filled in with stones the other entrance to the Plutonium in the 4th century? Why would they have a passageway open to the Plutonium from another locale?

As he was pondering these things, Art began crawling back up into the blinding daylight, and he saw Marissa and two workers standing above waiting to give him a hand as he came forth. "Are the scrolls okay?" asked Art immediately.

"Yes," said Marissa, "and I am taking them to the safe immediately. We are not leaving these precious things lying around on this site."

"There does seem to be a further chamber or passageway behind that little room, the scriptorium I am going to call it. And the funny thing is that I found these letters inscribed on the recessed stone back there." Taking a pen he wrote out on his palm, ΠΛΟΥΤΩΝ.

"Well, I doubt this means 'here lies Pluto," joked Marissa.

Art grinned but shook his head "No, but there was a small directional arrow beside the letters, and I would guess it means 'to the Plutonium,' though there are some letters missing. I suppose it could also mean 'to the underworld.' There are cave entrances all over the Mediterranean crescent which the ancients believed led down to the river Styx."

Marissa headed toward the jeep. "How odd to find all this in the back of a Christian bishop's house. Could this house have belonged to a pagan priest before it belonged to Papias?"

"I hadn't thought of that," replied Art. "But that might make some sense of things. Anyway, I intend to explore some more during the evening dig session."

"I will be away this evening at a meeting, but I should be back by eight. I'll stop here first. There won't be many workers around. Mehmet is in charge and will probably work on his potsherds. Do be careful getting in and out of there."

"Me, careless?" replied Art with a sly grin, "perish the thought." And as the two got into the jeep and drove down the hill to the hotel to clean up and have a late lunch (without Mehmet), both were lost in their thoughts, each in different ways. Marissa was thinking about Art, but Art was pondering the connection between Papias and the Plutonium. After lunch was wolfed down, Marissa left for Laodicea, and Art decided to read for a while which he knew would inevitably lead to a nap.

When the alarm went off at 4:30, Art had been sleeping for a couple of hours, and as he splashed cold water on his face, his excitement level began to rise. Staring into the mirror, he had a conversation with himself. "What do you suppose is behind that closed door? Can I get it open? Should I?" Realizing his reflection wouldn't be any help at all, Art quickly dressed in cool, comfortable clothes and walked up the hill the mile or so to the dig site. He was already sweating profusely when he arrived and saw Mehmet barking orders at a couple of interns. He did not know what to think of Mehmet. His credentials were good, but even his first encounter left him with mixed feelings. Art didn't much like him, but he didn't know why.

"I need to get myself back into the chamber and explore its back wall some more. Can you lend me a hand to get down into the chamber again? I think I can easily climb out later."

"But of course," said Mehmet, with a sort of sly smile.

This time Art packed his penlight, camera, water bottle, power bar, notebook and pencil into various pockets. The rest of his gear he left in his backpack in the leader's tent.

The second time into the triangular hole proved to be easier, and once he dropped into the chamber, Mehmet said, "I must return to the pottery tent for a while. I promise to check back with you periodically. I can't spare a man to stay with you right now, so don't get lost in that small space," and he laughed out loud.

Scratching his head, Art couldn't quite figure out the intent of that remark, but he quickly forgot all about it when he started investigating the back wall. Slowly his hands worked over the stones, searching for the crevice and possibly other carved letters. It was slow work. Occasionally he poured some water on the stones, thinking he may have found a letter or symbol. Nothing.

Suddenly, to his enormous surprise, when he pressed on the engraved word ΠΛΟΥΤΩΝ he heard creaking. A huge panel in the stone wall began to pivot, opening inwards into darkness! He looked back at the sunlight flowing into the main chamber. Art knew he should call for help. But the demon of self-justification whispered in his ear: "Maybe there's nothing behind the door. Why get everyone excited for nothing?" Besides, Mehmet said he would be back soon to check on him. So Art made an executive decision to slip by the partially opened stone panel.

Shining the lantern straight ahead he saw a series of stone steps heading downward. To the left, a small chamber carved out of stone with a

table and benches came into view. Perhaps it was a dining or meeting room. Could this have been one of the first underground churches in Turkey? It had a remarkable little door-like entrance to it complete with ornate columns.

Art decided to explore this magnificent find later. He was always itching to get to the bottom of things; thus, he wanted to see where the stairs actually led. "One careful step at a time," he told himself. Soon, however, he began to smell something funny, something remarkably like rotten eggs. He had climbed down some

20 steps when he suddenly realized he was beginning to breathe rapidly. He felt dizzy and flushed. The passageway was damp and clammy, but the temperature was perhaps 65 degrees at the most.

Then, quite suddenly, Art was hit with a wave of nausea, and he had the most extraordinary phantasmagoric image pass before his eyes. It looked like a dragon for a second. He realized that breathing was getting difficult, and so he decided he must turn around and head back out. Pausing to rest a moment his light caught a little inscription in Greek on the right side wall, which read, "Not to every man's liking is the journey to the underworld, but every man must one day go...."

But as he began back up the steps, the dizziness got worse. He retched to the left of the stairs. Suddenly, feeling quite weak he sat down for a minute, while more strange images passed through his brain. He looked up to the top of the stairs and heard the sound of creaking. Utter darkness enveloped him. As he rose to begin climbing again, he stood up too fast and dropped his penlight, which rolled quickly down the steps. Groping his way up the stairs one at a time, and panting as he went, he had enough sense to realize he was in trouble. Instead of calling out, he decided to hold his breath and just climb, climb, climb. He had conquered fifteen steps when again he took a breath and fell on the steps. Suddenly, an old southern folk tune came into his head from out of nowhere—

"The water is wide, I cannot cross o'er
But neither have I, the wings to fly.
Build me a boat, that will carry two,
And both shall row, my love and I."

The last thing he remembered was pain. Then he went blank.

PART TWO

18

Jerusalem—Shared or Splintered?

KAHLIL, AFTER MUCH PRODDING by his daughter Hannah, agreed to begin a walking program for his health. One too many rich meals of Middle Eastern delicacies had added one too many pounds to his girth since he had gotten out of the hospital last year. His memories of being shot by Patrick Stone still left him with some sleepless nights.[1] Regular

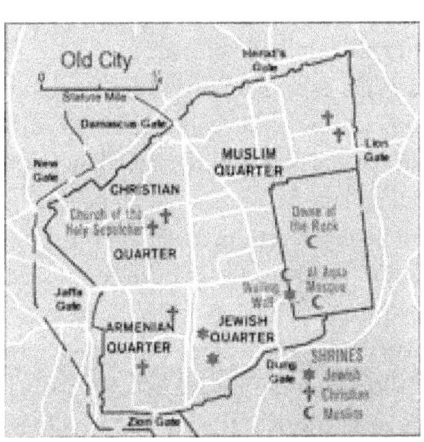

walks around the old city walls would do them both a world of good.

With over 20,000 people packed into the Muslim quarter alone, privacy is a rare commodity. The Muslim quarter is the largest parcel of the old city, followed by the Jewish, Christian, and Armenian enclaves. They walked north along the northern extension of the renovated Cardo which at this point separates the western Muslim and eastern Christian quarters. They well-remembered all the efforts made to reconstruct the Cardo or market road that stretched north-south through the old city of Jerusalem. Most of the work was done in the Jewish Quarter. At ground level, the work revealed ruins of Byzantine Jerusalem dating to the 6th century. Today, a lovely covered arcade blending old columns and new shops is now finished. The true Roman ruins exist twenty feet below street level,

1. A tale told in the first Art West adventure, *The Lazarus Effect* (2008).

and one area is accessible to tourists who want to explore the markets there. Kahlil was very fortunate to have his antiques shop located along the Muslim section of the busy Byzantine Cardo.

In silence they continued until they passed through the Damascus Gate and out of the old city. As they turned right, the massive walls built by Suleiman the Magnificent in the 1500s rose to the sky. In quiet they walked until they reached Herod's Gate. Up until 2004, the IAA was still sponsoring digs in this area. They continued around the northeastern point of the wall and headed south down the edge of the east wall to the Lions Gate. Many times Kahlil had watched pious Christians begin the Via Dolorosa at this very gate, following in the footsteps of Jesus from judgment to death. Kahlil and Hannah turned into the Lion's Gate and slowly wound their way through the alleys of the Muslim Quarter toward their own little home at the back of the shop on the Cardo.

Finally, Kahlil broke the silence. "It is still true, you know. Whenever I want to see a big man, I simply look at myself in the mirror!"

Hannah sighed, "Yes father, you are now too big a man. Too much of your fame and fortune are now to be found around your middle. But I suppose I am partially to blame. After all, I do love to cook!"

Kahlil laughed and patted his belly. "And I do love your cooking. With the economy down and tourists scarce, however, we can now save some money by eating smaller portions. This reminds me that I am pleased that Grace's wedding will take place before Ramadan begins in August. She must have taken that into consideration, don't you think?"

"I know she did," replied Hannah. "She has always been impressed by the true meaning of Ramadan—a time of fasting, prayer, and good deeds to teach patience and humility. She says that all of those practices are compatible with the Jewish and Christian faiths. Grace believes that our Ramadan practices are very similar to those of the ancient Israelites. And she is quite sure that Jesus himself would approve of all people taking time out to quiet their lives and focus on their God. I will have to ask Art how this works out in his Christian faith."

Kahlil heartily agreed with his head pumping up and down. "Yes, and with the economy so slow, this will be a special year for us to help the poor and provide presents for our family and friends. At least something good will come of all this. If only every Muslim would practice the tenets of Ramadan as Mohammed would have wanted it. Yes, this year I will truly purify myself. Allah must forgive me for over-indulgence. Food for the poor will be more important than food for my body," vowed Kahlil. "Hannah, explain to me what will happen at Grace's wedding. How is it different from a Muslim wedding, for example?"

"For one thing, the religious service will be longer, and it will involve a brief speech by the rabbi, as well as some vows and blessings. On the other hand, like a Muslim wedding, the celebration takes place somewhere other than in the synagogue proper, usually in a hotel," explained Hannah.

Kahlil suddenly perked up. "Yes! I saw on the invitation that we would be staying at The Scots Hotel in Tiberias. Most tourists must think that is a very strange name for a hotel on the Sea of Galilee! Did you know that a Scottish missionary, Dr. David Torrance, started the guesthouse and hospital in 1884? Imagine coming from Scotland to start a medical mission here when the Turks were still in power! He was very brave; many of his family members died there. I'm impressed that the Church of Scotland agreed to make the hospital grounds a first-class hotel. The brochure claims the hotel should be a place of reconciliation for all people including Jews, Christians and Muslims. So we are going to a tranquil Christian place for a multi-cultural celebration. Now that sounds like a very good day!"

"This wedding will be so much fun! Maybe we can go up a few days early and tour around the Galilee. I've always wanted to take a boat ride and see the sun set on the sea!" said Hannah poetically.

Kahlil was amused but then realized his daughter rarely traveled outside the city. So he promised himself to make her wish come true. "And speaking of gifts, do you have any ideas for wrapping our famous menorah?"

"No, I was hoping you would help me with that. Should we leave the menorah in its velvet sleeve? What about a box—maybe it should be wooden! Do we need to guard this precious gift? Where do we buy paper for a Jewish wedding? I can't make frilly bows, you know!"

"Relax!" said Hannah laughing. "Yes, we will leave the menorah in the velvet sleeve, put it in a strong box, and wrap it with big yellow ribbons. You can help! It will look grand when we finish!"

19

Art Imitating Life

WHEN MARISSA RETURNED FROM her meeting about 8:00, she went straight to the site and found Mehmet still sorting potsherds by a dim light. "So what did we get accomplished in the evening session today?" she asked quietly.

"Ah, Marissa! You look very nice in the evening light. Sit here and I will show you some fascinating Greco-Roman pottery." Mehmet carefully held up a Roman clay lamp in the shape of a foot. The big toe had a hole in it with a wick protruding through. Mehmet lighted the wick. Both of them watched as the foot/lantern glowed in the night. "Now that is what I call a hot foot!" exclaimed Mehmet delighted at his own sense of humor.

Marissa laughed diffidently at the old joke, and then asked, "Where is Professor West? Have you seen him in the last little while?"

Deflated, Mehmet replied testily but truthfully, "No, I have not seen him for awhile. I myself have been swamped here in the pottery tent. I am not worried about American archaeologists who lack our desert stamina."

"Right," said Marissa hastily getting up and heading for the tent door just as Mehmet was making his way toward her. "I will catch up with you in the morning. I need to speak with Professor West! The Laodicean team needs him to evaluate something they found."

As she drove to the hotel, a premonition came over her that something was not right here, but she could not put her finger on it. If Art had gotten back to the site around six or so to avoid the heat, it was not like him to quit after only two hours, unless there was some good reason for doing so. And wasn't he going to check the chamber wall in the Papias house? What had come of that exploration?

Walking into the lobby of the Pammukale Grand Palace, Marissa strode purposefully across the gleaming marble floor to the front desk and asked the attendant to ring Art West's room. Looking out the window she could see the sun starting to go down over the far ridge of the Lycus valley. It would soon be dark. After many a ring, he said curtly, "I am sorry, but there is no answer."

Looking into the restaurant where they had dined previously, there was still no sign of Art. Going back to the front desk she asked if anyone had seen him come in the hotel in the last couple of hours.

The man frowned and said a bit nervously, "I would have done so, since I have been here for five hours now. His room key is still in that pigeon hole right behind me." He pointed emphatically to a key with a green fob.

At this announcement Marissa's internal alarm went off. She ran out the door, jumped into her jeep and raced up the little lane that led to the top of the hill and the archaeological site. When she arrived, she shouted at Mehmet who was just leaving by a path down towards the Apollo temple, "Wait! Something is terribly wrong! Art never returned to his hotel, which means he may be here still. Get the large search light and bring it down to the Papias house at once!"

Mehmet did not argue but instead turned, trotted up the hill, and grabbed the larger of the two conical lights in the pottery tent. By the time he arrived at the Papias house, all he could see was Marissa crawling into the chamber. Looking up through the hole and seeing Mehmet she urged in a loud voice, "Throw the light down to me, I'll catch it!"

Doing as he was told, he gingerly dropped the light through the hole into her hands. She switched it on at once. Sweeping the chamber revealed nothing. Art was not there. But she could see that the dirt floor had been recently disturbed at the back of the chamber. Marissa frantically ran her hands over the wall, prying away at the crevice where the doorframe seemed to be. Then she saw it—the inscription that Art had described earlier. Wiping here hand over it she revealed all the letters—

ΠΛΟΥΤΩΝΕΙΟΝ, "Plutonium." Instinctively she put her hand on the inscription again. And just as Art had found earlier, the door began to pivot, creaking very slowly.

Pushing with all her might, she got the door open just enough to slip through. Frantically shining the light to her left, she saw the little room Art had seen, and quickly realized he was not there. Turning the full capacity of the light downward, down the declining stairs, she yelled out "Art, where are you!?" But there was no response. She had climbed down about three big stairs when again she shone the light straight downward, only this time she saw something on the stairs another five or so steps down. At this point she let out a blood-curdling scream! There below her was the slumped form of Art West, covered with several large brown wolf spiders, which seemed to have been exploring him for a while.

Mehmet now stood at the top of the stairs watching this melodrama play out. Marissa implored, "Use the cell phone and call the Pamukkale rescue squad. West may be in deep trouble."

"At once, but I must climb back out of the chamber to get reception. It will take a moment. Then I will return to help you," said Mehmet rather too calmly.

Taking his own sweet time, Mehmet slowly climbed out of the chamber, called the squad, gave the necessary report, and went back to assist Marissa. No doubt she would want his full support in this crisis, and he meant to get further into her good graces. By this point Marissa was hunched over the body of Art West, having turned him over. He was bleeding from his arm, which seemed to have been pinned beneath him, breaking his fall. Marissa at this point noticed a smell in the tunnel, an odd smell, an evil and noxious smell. Hesitantly, she started CPR. By now she heard a siren in the distance wailing louder and louder coming in her direction. Fortunately they were only a couple of miles away from the local hospital.

"Mehmet, we must drag him up these stairs. Come help me!" Carefully walking down one step at a time, Mehmet finally arrived. Each taking an arm, they began the arduous task of pulling Art's inert body up the last eight stairs to the light. When they arrived back in the chamber, Mehmet could hear the EMT people shouting, "Where are you? Where are you?"

"Down here. Reach down and grab the body," he replied.

"The body? You make it sound like he's dead!" said Marissa indignantly. "He might simply be unconscious."

"Of course, Marissa, of course," said Mehmet. "But is he breathing? You started CPR. Right? How long has he been like that? Do we know these things?"

Rather than have an argument, the two of them pushed the limp body up and out of the chamber, and the three men above gently pulled Art through and carried him to the stretcher. An oxygen mask awaited. The EMTs, led by a slight, wiry man with a curly Turkish moustache, checked all his vitals as quickly as possible. In another couple of minutes both Marissa and Mehmet had extracted themselves from the chamber. Art's vitals were very poor: shallow breathing and low blood pressure, temperature, and pulse rate. One of the other EMT men was overheard to say, "We need to work fast to stabilize him en route. ETA in about 10 minutes."

Marissa was exhausted from dragging Art up the stairs, and now she was at the point of a complete loss of control, so unexpected was this to her. She began to weep profusely, and Mehmet offered her a handkerchief, which she gladly used. He remained as silent as one could be. As the stretcher was taken over to the EMT van, Marissa said, "I am coming with you. He has no family here. You will need me."

Mehmet started to protest, and then realizing this was pointless, said, "I will close up things here." As the van quickly pulled away with siren wailing away, and the sun disappearing over the horizon, a little smile came across the face of Mehmet, who wondered whether the sun had not merely set in the west, but on the West.

20

The Finicky Felines of Ferris Phillip

FERRIS PHILLIP WAS AN odd bird. He made most eccentrics look normal, so bizarre were some of his habits. For example, he left the doors to his house, both front and back, wide open at night. Why? He claimed he just liked the breeze, but perhaps it was because his house smelled so bad. Ferris was a cat lover, and he had seven felines, all Siamese if you please, who ruled the roost. They had free reign over the whole house, and came and went through the cat door. Since he fed them generously with Fancy Feast, they rarely strayed far. He was convinced that if they did lose their way, they could look up and spot his weathervane, which he had specially made to include the silhouette of a cat, not a rooster. Add to that a stained glass window with a cat motif, a birdbath complete with a cement cat ever watching, hundreds of kitty knick-knacks, and a doorbell that sounded out "meow"—there would be no mistaking the home of Ferris Phillip. Basically his "kittens" as he called them dictated both their own and Ferris's lifestyle.

His enthusiasm for cats was not shared by his back door neighbor of twenty-six years, Joyce West. Whenever they wandered onto her property, she got out her broom. Ferris couldn't much understand this behavior, but he tolerated it, because at heart, while he loved cats, he was timid as a church mouse.

Many years ago he had been a respected professor of ornithology at Central Piedmont Community College, which in itself was odd since birds and cats don't exactly get along. He regularly went on birding expeditions, wearing the most outlandish outfits—bright yellow shorts with a black shirt, black knee socks, and a Sherlock Holmes hat. Cutting quite a figure, he had cultivated long mutton chop sideburns that nicely framed his thin, narrow face complete with granny glasses perched on the end of his nose. Being six feet tall but hardly weighing 150 pounds, he reminded Joyce West of her mental image of Ichabod Crane. In fact she had once pointed out to him the resemblance, but Ferris's only response was, "Why, thank you ma'am. I'll take that as a compliment. You may call me any bird you like, except the vulture." It took Joyce a while to make the connection.

On this particular morning Ferris was herding his cats around the back yard—his way of giving them some exercise. He had a picket fence around his back yard near the top of which he installed a foot-wide wooden ledge. Every sunny morning, he would place the cats on the board, one by one, and then lead the feline around the full three quarters of the square before giving each kitty a favorite treat. Being smart Siamese they learned the route quickly. A committed bachelor (Joyce commented frequently that he ought to be "committed"), Phillip had no one on whom to shower his affections except his cats. Joyce suspected that his will would leave everything to the feline friends.

Joyce knew the usual morning ritual was in progress, because Ferris had an old record player that blared the Disney film tune, "We are Siamese if you please. We are Siamese if you don't please." Sighing, she said to Jake who was sitting at the breakfast table, "You know the only cat in this neighborhood I truly like is you Jake."

"Purrrr-fect," quipped Jake. His toothy grin prompted a giggle on her part. Though she had not told Jake this, she thoroughly enjoyed his company. It had relieved the ache of many years of being alone.

"So what's on your radar screen for today?" asked Joyce. "Will you be in for supper? I thought I might fix some meatloaf—Art's favorite. Imagine baked ground beef, minced onions, Worcestershire sauce, and bread crumbs all mixed together with catsup on top."

"Sounds edible to me. I will be up for that later. My plan is to go to practice, then shower at the stadium, and run over to Green's hot dogs for lunch. Maybe I'll take in a movie at the classic theater over on Sharon Road. Would you be up for a movie?"

"That depends, what's playing this time?" inquired Joyce.

"Um, it's a double feature lasting all afternoon: *Lawrence of Arabia* with Peter O'Toole and then *The Bird Man of Alcatraz*."

Joyce looked up and said, "Well, I don't have to go to the movies to see that last one. I can just look out my kitchen window. But I wouldn't mind seeing Lawrence again. It's been decades since I saw that movie. Can you carry me to the theater, after your hot dog feast?"

"I could carry you, but I'd rather take the car," said Jake quizzically as he searched around for his Nike bag. "We can skip the second film, which by the way does not star Ferris Phillip. Indeed I doubt he has ever been near a movie, though someone should make one about him, don't you think?"

"Amen to that," said Joyce. "It could be a feature film by Looney Tunes."

"Now, now, Aunt Joyce, that's a tad uncharitable. You know he's quite harmless."

"You're right, Yacov," said Joyce properly chided. "It takes all sorts of people to make up the world. I think God must have a great sense of humor!"

And she could just hear Jake say "Amen" as he walked out the door and got into his Highlander.

21

Always the Bridesmaid

Hannah el Said, being Muslim, had never been to a Jewish wedding, but when Grace had asked her to be a bridesmaid, she immediately said yes. At the rehearsal, however, she was having second thoughts, especially since she discovered she was the only Muslim there. It wouldn't be good for her former husband's family to find out about this. Many years ago Hannah had been married to a man who was incensed with the Israeli treatment of Palestinians. As a result, he joined Hamas, and died in the first Intifada in 1989.

For years, Hannah had been bitter, not knowing whether she was angrier with her deceased husband for getting embroiled in that whole scenario, or with those who took his life. And yet, as time had gone on, the wounds healed, but that episode in her life left uneasiness about being around Jews. She did not feel this way about her good friend Grace, but when she was around strange Jews, especially in a setting where casual talk would rule the day, she was more than a little uncomfortable. And there was something else she was feeling as well. Grace was getting married, and Hannah in recent months had missed being married. Had life passed her by? All these things were running through her head when suddenly the newly hired wedding planner barked at the 'girls' and she snapped out of her reverie.

"Ladies! This is an outdoor affair, an early evening affair. You will need to be dressed and ready at the synagogue for pictures by 4 o'clock," commanded Naomi Meir. "We can't deal with a wardrobe malfunction or make-up disaster in the hour before the wedding. I am setting the alarm for eight at your hotel. That gives you time for breakfast, shower, dressing, makeup, and manicure all before the luncheon. Are you listening?" There was a collective groan from the bridesmaids. They imagined a party, not boot camp. Naomi Meir had come highly recommended. She had done the weddings for prime ministers and rich families in Haifa and Tel Aviv. She knew first hand that Murphy's Law operates at most weddings: What can go wrong, will go wrong—flowers wilt; bridesmaids faint; zippers break; rings disappear; rain falls; flower girls cry. Naomi believed in order—all girls with the same gown, the same shoes, the same hairdo, and the same nail polish (not black!).

Hannah, being an independent, Muslim woman, did not much like being ordered around by any woman, however accomplished in her profession. It was all she could do simply to keep her mouth shut. She would do her part for Grace's sake, however much it prompted feelings of loneliness and longing in her own heart. Hannah loved her work with her father in the antiquities shop, but when your work becomes your life, it's time to broaden your life.

"Hannah, we need you to be third in line here going down this side of the aisle starting from this spot," said Naomi pointing to a spot in the stone synagogue floor in Capernaum where she had placed a little X using colored tape. Hannah was feeling relieved that she knew only one of the other bridesmaids, Sarah, who owned Solomon's Porch coffee shop on Ben Yehuda Street. Only Sarah knew that Hannah was Muslim, and she preferred that information stay secret.

"Sarah, a quick question. Grace asked that we set up a little kiosk outside the synagogue here with cold drinks so that people can refresh themselves. Has that been taken care of?"

"Yes, Naomi," said Sarah, "my catering crew plans to be here early in the afternoon to set everything up, and we have brought our own portable generator to keep the drinks cold." One of the real problems with having the wedding at the ancient synagogue in Capernaum was that there was no shade to be found anywhere. The site was fully exposed to the sun. Naomi had arranged not only for Sarah to have a little refreshment tent outside the synagogue, but also for several more tents with fans where people could hide from the sun until entering the synagogue. It was something of a logistical nightmare, but Naomi had faced bigger challenges. Now she was fretting about getting the portable chairs into the synagogue in the heat of the afternoon. So many things could go wrong at the last minute.

As the rehearsal was winding down, Sarah came over to Hannah, and in a low voice whispered, "I know you are probably uncomfortable here, but don't worry, your secret's safe with me. We will just have a good time and celebrate Grace's big day, right?"

Hannah looked at Sarah, and a smile of relief came across her face. "Right," she replied. "Grace deserves to have her big day without incident. She will not believe what my father and I are giving her as a wedding gift!"

"Oh? Do tell girlfriend; my lips are sealed with superglue," said Sarah.

"Would you believe a gorgeous ancient menorah from right here in Galilee from the 2nd or 3rd century?"

Sarah gasped. "Holy smokes! You really know how to light up Grace's life. That may eclipse the wedding cake as the center of attention at the reception."

"Well, I just hope Grace likes it. My father had saved it for something special, and this is it. We have it all wrapped in Grace's favorite red wrapping paper and we are going to bring it with us when we come to the wedding." When the wedding planner wagged her finger again, and shuttled the two women into position for one more stately practice walk down the aisle, Sarah and Hannah jumped to attention, for all must be perfect for Grace's one and only wedding day, which was only a week from Saturday.

"I can't wait to see Art West's reaction to all this, can you?" whispered Sarah to Hannah.

"Yes, it will be good to see him again. He's been in Turkey for so long. I hope he doesn't have any trouble making the trip." Actually, Art had been making a very different sort of journey—into the Underworld.

22

Art in the Underworld

THE PAMUKKALE HOSPITAL WAS small, and ill equipped for dealing with major problems. Normally its emergency room dealt with tourists with sunburn or locals who fell on Pamukkale's slippery slopes. Now, however, the situation was far more serious. Art West seemed unresponsive in the ambulance. As he was wheeled into the emergency room, there was a sense of foreboding on the part of the staff. Marissa raced through the lobby of the hospital and ran right into emergency before anyone could protest.

"You can't let him die!" she screamed. The doctor who had just walked into the ER turned and shouted, "Get this hysterical woman out of here!" The technicians were speedily hooking Art up to every available monitor. The doctor barked orders for blood work. "His heart is still beating faintly; switch to a rebreathing mask. I want the oxygen flow up to 70%. Keep his airway clear. Get that lady back here! I need to know what she knows! And get me the blood gas work stat!" What the doctor did not know is that Art had inhaled a good deal of carbon dioxide.

Meanwhile Art's brain had wandered into visualizing Dante's *Inferno* as he relived his trip down into the Hierapolis Plutonium. Art imagined himself standing in the upper echelons of Hades with the dead. In his mind he saw three shadows drifting ever closer to him—the Stoic philosopher Seneca, the Greek physician Galen, and Socrates himself.

Socrates was saying to Galen, "You know it really wasn't so bad, the taking of the hemlock. There was a sharp pain at first, and then I was sailing down the rivers of Lethe to this place. But how came you to be in this place? Could you not heal yourself, physician?"

"No sadly, I was helpless to do so," sighed Galen. "I was felled by some sort of fever and disease for which there was no known remedy. But what about you, Seneca? How came you to be in this place?"

"Nero," said Seneca abruptly. "He finally drove me mad, when I realized I could never reform him. As a Stoic I realized I needed to accept the things I could not change, but then I also realized that there was a way out of the madness. It was only logical at that point to take my own life."

"Yes," said Socrates. "It is logical, but what is strange is that so many people think it is shameful to do so, as if one is offending the gods by taking one's own life."

Galen interrupted and said, "But that is precisely the problem isn't it? You did not create your own life; it was a gift from the gods through your parents. You do not have an inherent right to do what you will with it. Why, if you did not create your life, would you assume you had the right to take it, in the end? That is a philosophy I cannot follow or understand."

Art was fascinated by this conversation, which was all in Greek. Seneca's spoken Greek seemed a little odd or affected, but Art was able to follow along. What surprised him was that the conversation was so real, so vivid, and yet these three Shades seemed not even to sense Art's presence, as if he were an invisible bystander. Art wandered down the corridor of Hades and looked in another room.

There Art saw Alexander the Great, one of his childhood heroes. He was lying on a divan with his head propped up by his right hand, his famous golden locks unshorn and flowing over his shoulders. He was drinking a cup of wine, and conversing with his sister, Thessaloniki. In life, her interaction with her older brother Alexander would have been minimal, as he was already under the tutelage of Aristotle in "the Gardens of Midas" when she was born. She was only six or seven when Alexander had left on his Persian expedition. She was only nineteen when Alexander, king of the known world, died. They seemed now to be catching up with each other, making up for lost time.

"I deeply regret, dear sister, that we did not have more time together on earth, but now, we have all the time in the underworld," and Alexander laughed and raised his cup to Thessaloniki.

"I have always wished to know what prompted you to jump into that frigidarium which led to your premature death. Such a foolish act!"

Thessaloniki was sitting upright on a couch across from Alexander and slowly sipping from a cup.

"You will no doubt think this odd," said Alexander, "but it was not so much to cool off from a high fever I had for several straight days. I actually thought I heard the pool beckoning to me, luring me into its cold embrace, as if it was my destiny to die young, and I realized I had already accomplished almost everything I had set out to do. What does one do when there are no more worlds to conquer?" Alexander suddenly looked up and spoke to Art.

"Ah, you must be the poet I summoned. I gather you have a poem about me. I hear it is quite moving, but also tragic."

Art was startled. When he was in college and took Greek History at Carolina, he had indeed written a poem about Alexander's rise and fall. Normally Art was never nervous, but on this occasion he began to sweat.

"I will have to recite it from memory," said Art, in a shaky voice, his throat burning.

"Of course, we all prefer the living voice to something that is merely recited from a papyrus. Carry on!" cried Alexander in his usual imperial manner.

Clearing his throat, Art timidly began. "The poem is entitled 'Fire on Ice.'"

"Already I like it," said Alexander, "a pure paradox, a conundrum. That was me."

Art took a deep breath and continued.

> Fire on ice, ice on fire,
> Unbridled ambition, Unending desire,
> Golden hair, Midas touch,
> "I am Alexander."
>
> Ice on fire, fire on ice,
> Gory glory, beyond advice,
> One world vision, flickering flame,
> "I am Alexander."
>
> Macedonian monarch, Aristotle's ward,
> The great commander, without reward,
> Without peers, without an heir,
> "I am Alexander."

All the world's glory, all the acclaim,
The Greek colossus, the mythical name,
Builder of empire, finder of fame,
"I am Alexander."

Child of the gods, destined from birth,
Harvest of Hellas, spread through the earth,
Conqueror conquered, food for the worms,
"I was Alexander."

There was silence after the poem, and then Alexander stood up and began to applaud.

"Bravo," shouted Alexander, "you have captured the tragedy and irony of my life. The one who conquered the world, was conquered by the lowly worms. What do you think Thessaloniki?"

"Life seems all in vain when it ends in that fashion after so much triumph and success. It seems hollow, pointless."

Art was about to reply and tell them about Christ, but suddenly he had the sensation of being pulled backwards up a tunnel as if he were being sucked back into the world above ground and the next thing he knew he opened his eyes and saw bright lights, and he began to cough into the oxygen mask that was on his face. His heart was now racing and he was breathing fast through the pain. The doctor removed the mask.

"What am I doing here? And who are you?" wheezed Art. Before the doctor could reply, Art had scanned the room looking for a familiar face. Through the glass door, he saw a woman standing outside with long dark hair, weeping. Art thought that he should know her, but he couldn't recall her name. Turning to the doctor he asked quite timidly, "Who's that woman outside the door. Do I know her?"

The doctor replied, "Well Professor West, she certainly seems to know you. That is Marissa Okur, the archaeologist who is responsible for rescuing you earlier today. You are suffering from hypercapnia—excessive carbon dioxide in your blood."

"Rescuing me?" said Art, "Rescuing me from what? I really don't remember." And then the tears came flooding down his cheeks, for it seemed to Art he was all alone, and he could remember nothing of what had happened to him in the last 24 hours. His famous photographic memory seemed to have failed him altogether on this day.

23

Dabbling with the Diabolical

Sammy had finally managed to get through to Grace and had been able to ask her a series of questions about the demon papyrus. Her best guess, without actually examining the document closely, was that it was an incantation scroll, a scroll including what would appear to the modern person as nonsensical syllables and deity names and words for curses meant to incite the demons to act in particular ways. Grace, like Sammy, did not believe in demons, but nevertheless she did find peculiar what had happened to both Sammy and Agent Dershowitz, who, after being released from the hospital and recovering from the poison that had so drastically affected him, had tendered his resignation. Sammy was glum about this as Dershowitz was an excellent investigator, but Mrs. Dershowitz was at the end of her wits. Maybe sanity would prevail in a week or two.

What Sammy wanted to know more about was the ancient practice of cursing and its effects. Why exactly would a scroll like this be placed in a menorah—to protect it from theft? But then wouldn't it be God instead of demons that would do the protecting? Why not ask God for the help? Or could this menorah have fallen into the hands of non-Jews, or at least syncretists, those who tried to blend Judaism with one or more pagan religions? Sammy was leaning in the latter direction on this morning as he stared again at the papyrus now safely enclosed entirely in a glass sleeve of sorts. Were there really such things as curses and blessings that actually had evil effects once someone pronounced them? And then Sammy had another thought—could this scroll have contaminated the menorah, making it a deadly wedding gift? He'd better call Kahlil and make sure the internal part of the menorah was thoroughly cleaned before it was gift-wrapped. A demon-infested or poisonous menorah would never do as a wedding gift! In fact, he decided to ring Kahlil right now on this Friday morning.

The phone rang two times, and then Hannah picked up. "El Said Antiquities, how can I help?"

"Hannah, this is Dr. Cohen over at the IAA. Good morning to you."

"And *salam aleichum* to you sir. What may I do for you?"

"I have been worried a bit about that menorah. You realize that the scroll is contaminated with some poisonous powder. I was just wondering if you folks had managed to thoroughly clean the menorah, inside and out, before wrapping it. We wouldn't want it to be a deadly present."

"No indeed, we wouldn't, but we had not realized that there had been a poisoning. Whenever we handled the menorah, we wore gloves so as not to tarnish the metal."

"I'm sorry. We must have failed to tell you about the plight of Agent Dershowitz. He actually touched the scroll and became violently ill, ending up in Mt. Sinai hospital."

"That is terrible! Well I am glad you told us now! I will un-wrap the menorah and we will clean it thoroughly and carefully before rewrapping it. Thanks for the warning!"

"It was the least I could do," replied Sammy, and he hung up. Why was he still uneasy though, even after telling Hannah about this? Was this a premonition of more trouble or just irrational fear?

The Mediterranean Market was doing a big business on this day, and in the middle of the mayhem in walked Jake Arafat with Aunt Joyce in tow. He had wanted to show her where the market was so she would know where he had been getting all the delicious Middle Eastern food he kept bringing home and cramming into the refrigerator. But when the other Mr. Arafat behind the counter got a glimpse of Yacov and the accompanying older woman it just made his blood boil. He was going to have to do something about this situation. He could not stand idly by much longer, as he was sure now that Jake had become one of the infidels. How could he live with the shame of turning a blind eye to such a thing among his own extended family, for he was Jake's second cousin? Jake was a thief and an infidel he had concluded. Something had to be done soon, before the basketball season when he would become even more famous. Not being a brave man and knowing that a direct assault on Jake could ruin his own family's life and their larger mission in America, the other Mr. Arafat had devised a new plan to frighten Jake so badly he would never go to church or Bobcat practice again. Smiling a devilish smile as Jake finally became first in line at the counter, he said, "*Salam aleichum*, Mr. Arafat, will we soon be seeing you on television?"

"*Aleichum salam.* I suspect so, once the season starts in the fall. Do you have any fresh hummus today?"

"Of course we do, and some excellent shwarma and doner kebab as well."

"Good. Please prepare us a sampler platter. I want Aunt Joyce to try one of everything! Add a good supply of pita bread, hummus, brown rice, and some cucumber dolma, please."

"What's dolma, Jake?' asked Joyce.

"You're going to love this. It means stuffed, like stuffed bell-pepper or stuffed zucchini."

"Sounds interesting," said Joyce cautiously.

Then the shop owner said to Jake, as he handed him the food, "We will really have to hand it to you if you become a star this year."

"Time will tell," said Jake as he dropped all the packages in his own embroidered shopping bag—a gift from his mother.

"*Ensh'Allah*, as God wills," said the other Mr. Arafat, but already he knew what he would do to help his vision of Allah's will along the right track.

24

The Scent of a Woman

THE DOCTOR'S ANALYSIS OF why exactly Art West had gone into a coma was succinct and to the point—he had inhaled far too much carbon dioxide and sulfur gas while descending into the Plutonium. These were the very gases that had led to the delirium of the pagan prophets of old who were connected with the temple of Apollo in Hierapolis. Fortunately he had not ventured that far into the cave and after he knocked himself out on the steps, his breathing had become quite shallow. His blood gas tests indicated high, but not lethal, levels. Art would not suffer permanent brain damage. While lying in bed the following morning, still trying to clear his head, he tried to read a hospital handout on the effects of inhaling carbon dioxide. The report, typed out in English for his benefit, read in part:

> 1) Asphyxiation. Caused by the release of carbon dioxide in a confined or unventilated area. This can lower the concentration of oxygen to a level that is immediately dangerous for human health.
>
> 2) Kidney damage or coma. This is caused by a disturbance in chemical equilibrium of the carbonate buffer. When carbon dioxide concentrations increase or decrease, causing the equilibrium to be disturbed, a life-threatening situation may occur.

Well, both of these things had happened to him in some measure. He still had a slight headache. Though he had been conscious now for some hours, he had not yet felt the need to go to the bathroom, even though they had been pumping all sorts of liquids into his system. What most disturbed Art was his loss of memory. He had no memory at all of the last several weeks. No memory of coming to this hospital or

Hierapolis in Turkey; no memory of participating in an archaeological dig; and worst of all, no memory of this woman who continued to sit in the waiting room, hoping for a doctor to permit her to talk with Art. Who was she, and why was she not familiar to him? Her face seemed vaguely familiar, but that was all. Had his brain been damaged by the gas, or the fall or just the sheer stress of it all?

This whole situation was especially anxiety producing because, at least for some things, Art had a photographic memory. For example, he had never kept a date or appointment book; rather he had kept all those things in his head. And almost never had he forgotten an appointment except in a time of extreme stress—like now. When a person with such a clear and extensive memory capacity suddenly starts forgetting things entirely, it produces enormous stress. He had the disorienting feeling that he had lost control of himself, his circumstances, his life in general. He felt his abilities slipping away, maybe even his grasp on reality slipping a bit. While he was mulling all this over, and his pulse was rising with the anxiety, in walked a nurse who asked Art in broken English, "The lady outside, you want her come in?"

Art pondered this for a moment, thought about saying no, but then realized that she might help him remember the recent past. So he replied in his slow Southern drawl, "Sure, let her come in. What can it hurt?"

The nurse looked alarmed and said, "She no hurt! She help!"

The woman who came through the door was lovely: long dark hair, Mediterranean skin, great figure, and a nice smile at the nurse as she passed her. The room Art had been shuttled into was very small, which meant that Art and his visitor would be very close, whether they wanted to be or not. There was a single chair jammed up next to the bed where Art was resting.

Marissa immediately blurted out, "Oh Art, I am so sorry all this has happened to you, but glad to see you awake and alert again. I feared for your life when I found you unconscious in the cave!"

"Unconscious in a cave?" said Art incredulously. "I assure you, ma'am, I am not a spelunker. Forgive me for asking, but who are you?"

At this Marissa dissolved into tears. "Who am I? You don't know who I am?"

"No, I am afraid not," said Art. "Should I know you?"

"Yes!" Marissa responded with some volume. "We have become friends and are working together up the valley at the Hierapolis archaeological dig. Are you honestly saying you don't remember this?"

"No ma'am, I have no recollection of such a thing. The last thing I remember was getting on the plane from the U.S. to come to Turkey for something. Otherwise, in terms of recent memories, I draw a blank. But perhaps this information sheet will explain a bit of this. This is what they handed me about the effects of overly long exposure to carbon dioxide. I had assumed they were trying to tell me indirectly that I had tried to kill myself somehow."

Looking startled, Marissa took the sheet and read over the bits about asphyxiation, coma, and the general health effects of over-exposure to carbon dioxide. "No Art, you may have acted a little foolishly, but you didn't try to kill yourself. You were exploring behind the Papias house in an underground passageway, which probably leads to the Plutonium. You were overcome by the latent gas in the chamber. Do you by some chance have your camera still with you?"

Pointing to the tiny closet next to the bed, Art replied, "I think my clothes are in there."

Rummaging through his various pockets, finally Marissa found Art's Sony Cybershot, turned it on, and saw the last picture Art had taken.

Letting out a squeal of delight, Marissa turned the camera around and showed Art the picture. "Do you not remember seeing this? This must be in the entrance way to the corridor, part of some kind of underground meeting place or church structure perhaps."

Art studied the picture for a while, and then said, "No, it does not look familiar, but I can tell you something I do remember. I remember, though it surely must have been a dream or a fantasy, being in the Underworld and meeting various famous people—Greek philosophers and Alexander the Great."

"I've heard of dreams of grandeur, but that takes the cake," said Marissa smiling. "You actually remember this?"

"Indeed, it is the most recent and vivid memory I have. It was very exciting to meet and converse with Alexander and to hear a conversation between the likes of Socrates and Seneca and Galen."

"Well you certainly landed in the more interesting part of Hades, that's for sure," said Marissa, but inside she was deeply worried. Art was not himself at all, and he was being rather stiff and formal with her, calling her ma'am. She figured she had best start over.

"Art, my name is Marissa Okur. I am in charge of the dig at Hierapolis, and a week or so ago you agreed to consult and help us. We needed your expertise in things Christian when we found the house of Bishop Papias."

At this Art looked startled and said, "You found what? The house of Bishop Papias? Was there anything in it?"

"I'll say there was! You helped us extract at least four parts of scrolls there, including a piece with the introduction to his famous 'Commentary on the Oracles of Jesus' and the like."

"No way!" said Art.

"Yes, way!" insisted Marissa.

"And yet I have no memory of this at all. Horrible, as this would be something I would care deeply about and be deeply interested in. This is not like forgetting where you put your wallet. This is a big forgetting, at least for me. It scares me. Can I trust my mind any more? Miss Okur, please forgive me for being so out of sorts, but you say we are friends? Are we, ah, close friends?" Art began blushing slightly.

It was Marissa's turn to cry again, and so the response was slow in coming, "Yes Art, we were becoming close." And at this, she leaned over and gave him a little chaste kiss on his forehead. As she did so, Art smelled something, something he did have a vague memory off—perfume!

"I vaguely remember dancing with someone who wore that perfume. When I close my eyes I see the couple dancing. Was that us?"

"Oh, yes, it was us Art, it was us!" Marissa, encouraged by this sudden jarring of a little memory, added, "But you are tired, and this sudden exercise in lost and found must be a strain on you. I should go, as my ten minutes are up, but fear not. I will be back and we will find what was lost, gradually."

"Good, then," said Art who was suddenly about to fall asleep. "Thank you for your patience with me."

"No actually," said Marissa, "you are a patient who is with me, and I will be back soon." And as she rose to go, she smiled that million-dollar smile once again, and Art felt a bit reassured that things would get better. As she headed out the door, Art said in a weak voice, "Pray for me please. I am not myself."

"I will," replied Marissa and with that Art turned over on his right side and fell fast asleep.

25

Wedding Jitters

MANNY COHEN WAS KNOWN to be a passionate guy, but he was usually cool under pressure. As the wedding date loomed nearer and nearer on the horizon, however, he was having trouble sleeping, which led to his drinking too much coffee, which only increased his jitters and irritability. Naturally, he didn't want to take his frustrations out on Grace, or his employees, so he resorted to shouting at the walls in his office. This morning he had been throwing his little stress Nerf ball up against the wall about one hundred times before his budget meeting. There were important decisions to make about both his computer business and his professional basketball team, but he had been too swamped with wedding things to get much done. Manny was beginning to crack under the pressure.

"I said sell those blasted stocks!" shouted Manny over the phone to his broker. On top of everything else, the American economy was tanking and Manny thought his broker knew when to sell certain stocks, but when he turned on his computer this particular morning and saw he still had them in his portfolio, this only added fuel to his fire, and he blew up! He hadn't gotten to the top of the business world by sitting around and watching his assets depreciate. This was one stressor too many, and now he was pacing around his office like a wild cat. Through the glass wall his secretary watched this melodrama while doing her best to lay low. "Keep your head down and keep typing," she murmured to herself. It was right then that the phone jangled and jarred the secretary's nerves. It was Grace for Manny. For a half second the secretary considered taking a message since Manny wanted his calls held this morning, and then decided she had better not.

"Good morning, Grace," she said, "I'll put you right through."

When the phone rang in Manny's office, it was about the last straw. He seized the phone like a man grabbing a baseball he was about to hurl, "What!" he bellowed into the phone.

"Don't take that tone with me mister or you won't get your best fiancé award today," said Grace. Knowing he was stressed out, she had given him extra space in the past several days. "I just wanted to remind you that we do have our little chat with the rabbi this evening. Will that be a problem, dear?"

"Oh, Grace, I completely forgot. I have a meeting late this afternoon, but I can cancel. I assume the meeting with the rabbi is here in Tel Aviv?"

"No, dear, I told you last Tuesday, while you were busy doodling on the sports page over brunch that it is here in Jerusalem."

At this Manny was about ready to blow a gasket, but he paused, took a deep breath and said, "Okay, what time do I need to be there, and where are we meeting?"

"I hoped that you would pick me up at four. We meet with him at four thirty at his office next to Beth Israel synagogue near the Knesset. We really need to be very nice to this man since he will be schlepping to Tiberias for the ceremony."

"Right. I will try and take a chill pill before then and become Mr. Congeniality."

"Very good. I will see you at four, and I will treat you to a wonderful dinner," said Grace calmly, hoping her mood would rub off on Manny. But as soon as she hung up, another call came in. It was Kahlil. What could he want this morning?

"Grace, I have some unhappy news," said Kahlil in somber tones. "Our dear friend Art is in a hospital in Pamukkale. He was nearly asphyxiated by poisonous gas in some cave, though he seems to be beginning to get things back together."

"Oh, my goodness! How do you know all this? Why didn't he call me!" gushed Grace. "That man cannot stay out of harm's way. Do you know the prognosis? I sure hope this doesn't mean he can't come to the wedding!"

"First of all, I tried to contact him concerning, let's just say, a special artifact that I have. He did not answer the phone. Instead, I talked to another archaeologist named Marissa Okur who filled me in on all the details from Turkey. I can assure you that if the wedding were today, he would not be there. I do not know whether he even remembers your name, let alone your wedding, as Dr. Okur referred to some short-term memory loss. So, this is just to let you know that she is expecting me to call again today. I will keep you informed."

"Yes, please call me back as soon as you learn more. I really want to talk to him," stressed Grace. "Let's both pray for him, shall we?"

"Of course. Hannah and I have been doing that this morning. *Shalom* to you," said Kahlil and he rang off. But Grace just sat there holding the phone, thinking about Art, and beginning to worry. Had he finally gone too far with his risky explorations? What was he doing in a cave? Inquiring minds wanted to know.

26

Cat Food

THE SMALL, SQUARE, BROWN box sat on the back steps of Joyce West's house in Charlotte where UPS had the habit of leaving things. It was ten in the morning and she was expecting Jake back from an early workout any minute. They had planned to go to lunch over at McCormick and Schmick's, a favorite for both of them. But the box had been sitting out there for about an hour. Joyce was in the shower when the UPS man rang the bell then left the package. But it had not by any means gone unnoticed.

Ferris Phillip's felines had all smelled it at once and all seven of them pussy-footed their way over to Joyce's house to check out the smelly box. Within seconds the cats were clawing and growling and hissing at each other. When Jake's Highlander pulled into the carport it startled the cats, but so intent were they in catching the prey that they were not deterred even by the arrival of the SUV.

Hopping out of the car quickly, Jake ran toward the cats like a wild man—screaming and waving his arms. Joyce rushed out with curlers still in her hair. "Whatever is going on out here!?"

Jake paused and said, "I don't really know, but the cats sure liked it. I guess it must be some sort of food, but it sure does stink!"

"What does the label on the package say?" inquired Joyce.

"Not a lot. The return address is just a post-all place here in Charlotte and the line at the top says 'A Fan(atic)' and it's addressed to me, 'Jake the Cat Arafat.'"

"Interesting! Last week somebody mailed you shish kebab skewers because they heard you like cooking on the grill. I don't know where people get these ideas—we don't have a grill! Anyway, it's probably just another present from an admirer. Let's sit on the porch—I'll get my letter opener."

Jake slowly slit the top of the foot square box, and folded back the flaps. At first all he could see was some sort of crystals, like large salt crystals, but then as he began to rummage into the box, he felt something soft and malleable. Brushing away the crystals quickly, he saw what looked like fingers emerging, and then a whole hand, severed at the wrist, with a note attached, in Arabic.

When Joyce saw that it really was a decomposing human hand she screamed, backed up, and fell into the rocking chair. Jake dropped the hand like a hot potato and turned to see if Joyce was all right, but he had this sick feeling in the pit of his stomach. "Are you okay?" asked Jake.

"Get that horrid thing out of my house. Go throw it in the trash behind the garage and make sure the lid is on tight. It's too early for Halloween pranks. Some fan!" said Joyce breathing rapidly and trying not to gag.

"Just sit over there for now. There's a note attached to the middle finger. It's in Arabic. Do you want me to read now?" Joyce nodded. Turning the little card, he read these words that were written from right to left: "'This is the punishment for traitors who have betrayed Hamas. You know the even more severe penalty for becoming an infidel. We look for a sign of loyalty from you or else your mother is in danger.' The Jackal."

"We need to call the police at once," said Joyce with a quiet shaky voice. "It's some terrorist thing isn't it? Who is this Jackal person?"

"He's a leader of Hamas imprisoned somewhere in Israel just now, so I doubt this is directly from him. But it was sent by someone who knows about my past as a Muslim and an operative for Hamas. It's a threat meant to make me renounce my new faith, and force me to send money to Hamas. Even here, I am not safe from them."

"Well," said Joyce, grimly, "they have no idea who they are dealing with, and we are not giving in to fear. But we will be calling the police right now."

"And I will be calling my mother, right now," said Jake.

"Maybe you should suggest she stay with us for a while?" suggested Joyce.

"But if this package, which was sent locally, can get to me, who's to say she would be safe here?" said Jake thinking out loud. But by then his brain was already replaying in his head the horrible day when his brother was brutally murdered in Bethlehem. As he fumbled for his cell phone in his Nike jacket, playing basketball did not seem all that important any more.

27

The Invalid Scholar

ART WAS SITTING UP in bed, drinking his requested *vishne suyu*, his favorite Turkish cherry juice. With reading glasses on, he was scanning a series of photocopies of the now-recovered Papias papyri. With the help of his small portable lexicon, Art was happily translating the Greek text. Marissa hoped this project might jog his memory and at the same time take his mind off recent trauma in the cave behind the house of Papias. The light was filtering through the blinds in his little cubicle of a room, but Art was entirely back in his element, engrossed in things ancient.

Fleeting memories of what had happened to him before he went into the Plutonium corridor were beginning to emerge in his mind, one of which was recovering a papyrus, the first of the Papias scrolls. This memory had been triggered when Marissa brought the photocopies of all the scrolls to him this morning. Art finished writing in long hand his own Greek rendering of a paragraph on the photocopied scroll because it was in continuous script and it was easier for him to read this way, with the Greek words separated. It read:

> Τοσουτον δ επελαμψεν ταις των ακροατων του Πετρου διανοιαις
> ευσεβειας φεγγος, ως μη τη εις απαξ ικανως εχειν αρκεισθαι
> ακοη μηδε τη αγραφω του θειου κηρυγματος διδασκαλια,
> παρακλησεσιν δε παντοιαις Μαρκον, ου το ευαγγελιον φερεται,
> ακολουθον οντα Πετρου, λιπαρησαι ως αν και δια γραφης
> υπομνημα της δια λογου παραδοθεισης αυτοις καταλειψοι
> διδασκαλιας, μη προτερον τε ανειναι η κατεργασαθαι τον ανδρα,
> και ταυτη αιτιους γενεσθαι της του λεγομενου κατα Μαρκον
> ευαγγελιου γραφης. γνοντα δε το πραχθεν φασι τον αποστολον

αποκαλυψαντος αυτω του πνευματος, ησθηναι τη των ανδρων
προθυμια κυρωσαι τε την γραφην εις εντευξιν ταις εκκλησιας.

This passage matched quite closely what was reported in Eusebius, with
minor variants, and Art was working hard on his own translation of the
key bits. His rough translation read:

> And the light of piety/devotion illuminated the minds of those
> who heard Peter to such a degree that they were not satisfied with
> the once only hearing nor with the unwritten teaching of the
> kerygma/preaching but with all sorts of appeals they besought
> Mark, whose Gospel endures, being a follower of Peter, that he
> might leave them a memoir/memorandum in writing of the oral
> teaching which had been passed on through the Word, and they
> did not give up until they prevailed upon the man, becoming the
> cause of the writing of the Gospel called "according to Mark."
> And they say that the apostle [Peter], when he learned what had
> been done, it having been revealed to him by the [Holy] Spirit,
> was pleased with the earnest desire of these people, and the writ-
> ing was authorized [in response to/unto] the prayers/petitions of
> the churches.

This is a pious assessment of how the Gospel of Mark came to be written,
said Art to himself. And one good reason not to dismiss it is because of
another passage Eusebius cites from Papias, which Art now could confirm was almost a verbatim of what Papias had said, namely that

> The Elder [i.e. John of Patmos] used to say: Mark in his capacity
> as Peter's interpreter (*hermeneutes*) wrote down accurately as
> many things as he [Peter?] recalled from memory—though not
> in a chronologically ordered form—of the things either said or
> done by the Lord. For he [i.e. Mark] neither heard the Lord nor
> accompanied him, but later, as I said [he heard and accompa-
> nied] Peter.

Art had brought with him one of his favorite new books, *Jesus and
the Eyewitnesses,* by his friend and British scholar, Richard Bauckham.
He dealt with this very material in detail, validating the historical value
of Papias's comments. Papias was saying that Mark's Gospel indirectly reflects the eyewitness testimony of Peter himself, the leader of the Twelve.
The text does not claim Mark was an eyewitness of the preaching and
teaching of Jesus, but only that Peter was, and Mark was his interpreter
and scribe.

So engrossed in thought was Art that he almost didn't hear his phone ringing, but grabbing his backpack, which sat on the chair next to him, he found his smart phone and answered on the fifth ring. "Hello, this is Art the invalid scholar here."

There was a deep baritone laugh on the other end and then a familiar voice said, "Well, now, all these years I thought you were a valid scholar and now you are telling me you are in-valid? Surely not!"

"Kahlil, how wonderful it is to hear from you. It's been much too long. How are things in the navel of the earth, Jerusalem?"

"More importantly, how are you. Dr. Okur said you had another encounter with death."

"Yes, I almost managed to asphyxiate myself in an underground corridor. It's no one's fault but my own. And now I remember old friends, but not new ones. I remember my work in general, but I'm fuzzy about some of the recent events."

"Really, do you remember leaving open the door to the corridor?"

"Now that you mention it, I did do that, but it seems to have blown shut. But that doesn't entirely make sense in view of the fact that it was a very heavy creaky stone door. There certainly was no wind in the area."

Kahlil sighed. "If *my* memory serves, this sort of thing happened to you once before. Do you not remember how you were trapped in the Lazarus tomb? The culprit in that case is in jail now, I might add!"

"You are right, Kahlil! I'll have to think some more about all that. I can't remember if anyone was near the site that night. I have to talk to Marissa."

"Speaking of current events," said Kahlil, "Do you remember that you are going to need a tuxedo next week for Grace's wedding?"

There was nothing but silence on the other end of the line for a painfully long time.

"Art, are you still there?"

"Grace is getting married? Did I know about this before?"

"Yes, of course. You have known all the details from the beginning. You have supported her throughout her engagement."

"Oh dear," said Art. "This is more than a little upsetting. I remember Grace, but I don't remember anything about her being engaged."

"Well, then it is a good thing I called," said a worried Kahlil, "Because Grace would never forgive you if you weren't there for her big day!"

"No, I understand," said Art softly. "The doctor is releasing me tomorrow. Then I'm going to Izmir to recuperate for a few days. I wonder if I made flight plans? I'll have to check, but in any case you tell our dear friend Grace that I wouldn't miss her wedding for the world. Even an encounter with the underworld will not keep me away. And Kahlil, would you and Hannah meet me at the airport? I would feel better if I was with you two."

"Absolutely, just let me know when you are arriving. Meanwhile, please get well. We are praying for you, each in our own way," promised Kahlil.

"Thank you. When I get back, we can talk about the papyri, and the house of Papias," said Art as he rang off. What he had not noticed was Marissa standing in the room, waiting patiently for Art to finish talking.

"A wedding! In Israel? Are you ready for this?" asked Marissa with a surprised look on her face.

"It was a big surprise to me too! My friend, Grace Levine, is getting married next week. Apparently, I'm in the wedding! It's possible I already have plane tickets! One thing is for sure, I probably don't have a wedding gift anywhere!" And then Art got the funniest look on his face, and with a wry smile he said, "How would you like to accompany me to Jerusalem and then to the wedding—which I think is near Tiberias. Maybe my memory is coming back."

"Me?" said Marissa in a high shrill voice. "But what would I wear to a Jewish wedding near the Lake of Galilee! Besides, I wasn't invited!"

"I was thinking you could wear your archaeology garb—in which you look so fetching. A helmet would make a nice accessory. Or, with me being an invalid and all, you can come as my nurse."

"You really know how to persuade a woman," said Marissa blushing while they both laughed. But there was someone who would find this no laughing matter, and his name was Mehmet Ertegun.

~

Mehmet Ertegun had worked long and hard in the vineyard of archaeology, scratching and clawing his way to near the top of his profession. Like so many academics of his sort, however, enough was never enough, and he could never understand why he was always passed over for the plum archaeological assignments. In the case of Marissa Okur, he could just about endure playing second-fiddle, though he felt humiliated. But with the chance of winning her heart apparently slipping away, he had reverted to the more primal feelings of jealousy and a sense of entitlement. He, at least, was Turkish, unlike Art West.

Having been raised to think that Turkish women who performed traditionally male jobs were usually given those jobs solely because of political correctness not merit, he had to readjust some of that thinking when he discovered how skilled Marissa actually was. Yet in the end his academic admiration for the woman and her merits had lost out to his sexual desires, and so with his chances with Marissa on the wane, he resolved on a desperate attempt to get his "competition" out of the way, once and for all.

Having failed at the first attempt to eliminate Art West, where did that leave him? What if West figured out he was in fact trapped in the corridor to the Plutonium? Then what? Writing a memo to himself in his diary, Mehmet decided to stay the course at this dig for now. As a back up plan, however, he would ask for a transfer to the Laodicean dig. What he could not bear much longer was watching Marissa show a personal interest in West, who now cut a much more sympathetic figure. It really irritated Mehmet that his grand scheme had resulted in the opposite of the intended effect. Now, Marissa was even *more* interested in West than before! It just wasn't fair.

And the real insult had come this morning when Marissa announced that he would be needed to take over the dig for a week. For a second this made him feel elated and important, but when she explained that it was because she was going with West to a wedding in Israel, he realized he had accelerated a relationship he tried to snuff out! This left him seething, but he thought he had managed to hide this fact from Marissa, who had been distracted anyway and was paying little attention to Mehmet's body language.

"Oh, and one more thing Mehmet," said Marissa as she was leaving his tent at the archaeological site. "I am putting Dr. West in charge of deciphering the papyri we found, since he is the expert in that period's Christian documents."

There went Mehmet's chance to make some headlines with these finds. It seemed to Mehmet as if some divine hand had not only thwarted his attempt to do away with Art West, but now was going out of its way to give him the glory. If this was kismet, it was the kiss of death for Mehmet, or so he felt. Was he being punished for his sins?

Mehmet was a mildly religious Muslim, which is to say he did believe in fate, and so he pondered whether he had been destined to play this role and be thwarted at every turn, but this hardly made him resigned to his fate. No, it made him angry with Allah. In short, as Mehmet summed up things in his little diary entry, he was thoroughly miserable. Tonight he would seek consolation in large quantities of good Turkish beer. Drowning one's sorrows was always better than wallowing in them.

28

"Get Thee to a Nunnery"

JAKE WAS NOW FRANTIC to talk to his mother and sister-in-law. They still lived in Bethlehem and he now had a very good reason to suspect they were not at all safe. A threat, and indeed not a very veiled one, had been made against them. Jake knew that if he gave in to the demands of the persons who sent him the note, this still would not solve the problem. His family would always be in danger, and there was no way he was going back on his commitment to the Christian faith, nor on his commitment to play basketball. He had signed a nice contract which he had to honor. But since those options were eliminated, that left only one—get his family out of Bethlehem.

It was late in the evening when Jake finally got through to his mother. The line was crackling a bit, but nonetheless his mother's strong voice came through clearly. "*Salam aleichum*, Arafat residence."

"Mother it is me. Please sit down. I have some bad news for you." Jake's heart was beating at a rapid rate, and he was gulping in breaths of air to help him get out what he needed to say quickly. "I received a serious threat from someone connected to Hamas. They want me to give up basketball and my new faith, but actually the threat was against you and perhaps Issah's wife and children. The threat said that if I don't do what I'm told, they will harm you."

Mrs. Hagar Arafat listened quietly to this rapid stream of emotion-filled words, said a prayer and replied, "Son, if they know where to find me and Issah's family, where would you propose for me to go? If you are thinking I should come be with you, then surely that will not make this threat go away. How would I be safer with you?"

"But what can you do? Where can you go where I will know you are safe?"

Hagar thought for a minute and replied, "This is surely a providential nudge from the Lord, and I have a suggestion. I have often thought about this since you left for America. I would really like to dedicate the rest of my life to the Lord's work. There is not much for me here in Bethlehem, other than Issah's family and children. So I have been talking with Father Abbas here, as has Issah's wife. Suppose both I and your sister-in-law were truly to disappear—into a convent? Father Abbas says they would take us as workers in the cliff convent next to St. George's monastery in the wadi near Jericho. I would not take a vow of silence, so we could always talk, and you could come and visit some. And they say they would be delighted to have some children in their midst. I think we would be perfectly safe, as this convent is remote and semi-cloistered. No one would touch us there."

Jake was stunned by this revelation, "Mother, are you really sure you want to do this? You will be giving up a lot of your personal freedom."

"Son, I will not be giving up my freedom. I will be freely using it in a more profitable way."

There was a long silence on the other end of the line, and finally Jake said, "Mother, I think this does solve the problem at your end, but how soon can you move?"

"Well, as you know we live near the parish hall, and the church needs more space. I talked to Father Abbas about selling the house and property to the church, and he told me that would be feasible. I think we can accomplish all this within a week or so. Would that relieve your worries my son?"

"Yes, mother, it will be good to know you are in the protective care of both God and our church. And it reminds me, I must not make decisions based on fear rather than faith. I'm going to carry on and not honor this threat, knowing now it is highly improbable it could be carried out with you off the scene. I will call you again in a few days and see how things are progressing. I love you very much."

"And I love you too. Take this verse from Romans 8 to heart: "God works all things together for good for those who love Him and are called according to His purpose."

"You always have the right words, especially the right divine ones." And with that Jake sighed deeply, turned and saw Aunt Joyce smiling at him with relief written all over her face.

"You see, God will find a way to sort things out. The malice of men cannot trump the benevolence of God."

~

The Charlotte police had come in quietly without sirens blazing because the boxed up hand was not going to flee in any direction. Rather it sat stinking on the back porch, as Joyce West was not about to bring it into her house. Detective Richard Sears was a large man, built rather like a middle-linebacker, only with a softer middle. Standing 6'1" and weighing in at 220, he cut quite a figure even in his detective's rumpled suit. At this very moment he was standing in Joyce West's kitchen, taking notes as rapidly as his pen and right-handed scrawl would allow.

"So you're saying this just showed up on your back doorstep?"

"Yes, detective, that's correct. That's where those parcel post folks usually leave things. And the herd of cats living next door attacked the box before we could open it. Quite the hunters they are!"

Jake was sitting at the kitchen table, contemplating the decision his mother and sister-in-law had made. Suddenly, the detective turned his way and said, "Say, haven't I seen your face somewhere?"

"Yes sir, probably in the Charlotte Observer. I play for the Bobcats."

"Right! You're Jake the Cat Arafat. I thought I recognized that profile. So will we have a better season this year?"

"I sure hope so. Last year we lost every single game in the preseason, and then the season was not a lot better either."

"So, getting back to business here, do you have any known enemies in this town?"

"No, sir," said Jake. "But since I'm Palestinian there might be some prejudice. But the message in the box makes clear that it's one of my own people that sent this to me. They see me as a traitor to Hamas. I once supported Hamas, but I abandoned that when I became a Christian. They are also angry about my playing basketball, which they see as a decadent Western occupation. In other words, I have been branded an infidel. According to Islamic law, the punishment for theft is the loss of a hand, hence the hand in the box. They think I have robbed Hamas of much-needed funds by no longer helping them. They may even suspect I was partly responsible for the capture of El Tigre, a notorious operative who raised money and made plans for Hamas on a world-wide scale."

"And were you?" asked Detective Sears.

"Not directly, but he was caught because of the murder of my brother Issah, which in English is Jesus."

"You had a brother named Jesus?" asked the detective incredulously.

"He was very devout, a saint really, and he died trying to help me straighten out my life." At this Jake put his hands over his eyes as he had begun to tear up.

"Sounds like his namesake to me. So, just to repeat, you have no idea who could have sent you this locally?"

"No, but it has to be someone in contact with Hamas, and that means a Palestinian."

"Have you had any contact, even casual contact, with any Palestinians here in Charlotte."

Jake hesitated a moment, and Joyce jumped in "Yes! There's a Mediterranean Market over on West Boulevard where Jake gets some of his favorite Middle Eastern foods."

"Do you know any of the names of the people over there?' asked the detective.

"The man who worked behind the counter said his name was Ahmed."

"We will certainly question this man. Are you any relationship to Yasser Arafat?"

"Only distantly," said Jake. "The name Arafat over there is rather like the name Smith over here. It is very common, and just as you would not assume all the Smiths are closely related, you should not assume that to be the case with the Arafats."

"That is helpful, but do you know if there are other Arafats here in Charlotte?"

"I honestly do not know," said Jake. "I have been doing my best to leave my past behind and have a new life here."

"And what about your family at home?"

"I've notified my family and I believe they will be safe very soon," replied Jake beginning to tear up again. The gravity of this situation was really beginning to sink in.

"I certainly hope so. Through international channels we can help with that. Meanwhile, my team has some leads to follow, and we will be running tests on this box and the hand. We will want to know where that came from and to whom it once belonged! Meanwhile, I'm assigning an officer to watch your home. Please tell your coach what happened so they can increase security. Finally, due to the international nature of this case, we will notify the CIA and Interpol."

"My travel schedule with the team doesn't start for another couple of months so I promise to just go back and forth to practice."

"Very good. One more thing," insisted Detective Sears, "How exactly did you end up living here with Mrs. West?"

"If you want to hear that story, I think you had best sit down and have a cup of coffee and a Krispy Kreme doughnut!" exclaimed Joyce laughing.

"Thank you ma'am, if I wouldn't be imposing." said the detective grinning.

"Of course not," replied Joyce hospitably. But little did Rick Sears know that Joyce was a world-class talker. He would soon lose all control of his morning schedule. Rick was treated to a long discourse about Joyce's son, Art West, his archaeological work, his meeting of the Arafats, his presence at the baptism of Jake, and his invitation to Jake to come and live with his mother here. Catching her breath, Joyce poured yet more coffee and continued with, "I've got to ask you a good ole Southern question. Are you related to the Sears in High Point?" And as Jake quietly got up from the table and headed off to practice, they were off on a discussion in which Joyce asked as many questions as she answered. Clearly, the detective had met his match when it came to interrogation.

29

Sweating the Details

GRACE WAS FRETTING AS she read over her notes. What worried her was that this was such a public high profile wedding that she wanted things to go just right. She had never realized how complicated the planning of a wedding could be. Her rabbi had given her a little guidebook, and she was to follow it religiously, he had said, to the last detail. This is what worried her—what if she forgot a detail or two?

Marriage ceremonies in Israel are unlike most marriage ceremonies anywhere else in the world. For one thing there is no legal permission to have a civil ceremony; the rabbis are in charge of all Jewish ceremonies of any sort, and in fact an Israeli Jew is required to have his or her wedding ceremony according to the Orthodox way of doing things, with an Orthodox rabbi involved. Of course it is possible to take the Cyprus Express and get married elsewhere, since Israel *does* recognize the legality of marriages performed in other countries, but that does not much help those who do not have that kind of money, and though there was an initiative to break the hegemony of Orthodox control over wedding ceremonies in Israel, it would not come soon enough for Grace.

Within Israel itself this whole Orthodox approach goes back to at least the period of the Ottoman Empire, and left the performing of religious ceremonies in the hands of the religious authorities with the government basically staying out of the matter. This is also true in the Muslim and Druze and Christian communities in Israel as well. There is no going to the justice of the peace for secular Jews in Israel if they wish to be married, and some marriages are simply prohibited by law in Israel, in particular inter-marriage between persons of different religions. This is because when it comes to a Jewish marriage the chief rabbinate in Israel is the religious authority in charge of things, and they have mandated that Jewish weddings must be conducted according to the Orthodox way of doing things. The end of the process was when the Israeli Interior Ministry registered the marriage as legal.

As for the ceremony itself, it was not a matter of Grace and Manny writing their own vows and choosing this or that element to include in the ceremony. It all had to be done according to their rabbi's understanding of things, and he did not permit couples to write their own vows or add to the liturgy of the ceremony. Among other things, this meant that during the week before the wedding the bride and groom had to keep themselves separate, and indeed were expected to fast some, in preparation for the wedding itself. Part of the traditional theology behind the wedding ceremony is that a man is not complete or a whole person until he marries and 'the two become one flesh.' Then and only then is the man a complete or whole person. The wife may be viewed as his better half by some but the point is that they complete each other, and cease to be mere individuals having become a couple henceforth.

Before the wedding itself, the groom is not to see the bride, and they will greet guests separately. In a traditional wedding, the bride and groom are actually treated as if they are a king and a queen, with the bride sitting on a throne of sorts receiving her guests, and the groom standing and being toasted by his guests. In an Ashkenazic Jewish ceremony there is a tradition for the mothers of the bride and groom to stand together and break a plate. The point is to make clear the seriousness of the commitment. A vow once broken, like a plate once broken, is never quite the same again and can never again be fully repaired.

After the greeting of the guests, which in fact is the beginning of the ceremony, there follows the veiling of the bride by the groom. The point of this is not just modesty, but to emphasize that physical appearance is by no means the most important part of this relationship. The point is that what counts most about the person you are marrying is the soul and character of the person. The veiling ceremony itself also symbolizes the husband's pledge to clothe and protect his wife. The practice actually seems to go back to a certain reading of Genesis 29 where Rebecca placed a veil over her face before marrying Isaac. As was to be expected, the rituals reflect a patriarchal way of understanding the relationship. Some of this made Grace, as a modern woman, a little uncomfortable, and some she saw as a little archaic, but she decided she was not going to rock the boat here. After all, one only gets married once.

The wedding ceremony itself takes place under the famous wedding canopy or *chuppah*, and traditionally most such weddings are outdoors where a canopy can be put up. This is one reason why Grace had chosen the Capernaum synagogue ruin, as it had no roof, its only canopy being the sky itself, until the *chuppah* was put up—perfect. While Sephardic Jews tended to have the *chuppah* indoors, this was not the custom of Ashkenazic Jews. The open air wedding symbolizes that God is participating and blessing the marriage. He is looking on, so to speak. Sometimes Genesis 15:5 was seen as the background, where God promised children as numerous as the stars in the sky to the patriarch. The *chuppah* itself is a symbol of the home, particularly of the more nomadic or agrarian period of Jewish existence. We should think of the Feast of the Tabernacles where home would be a movable tent.

The Ashkenazic custom is that the bride and groom wear no jewelry under the *chuppah*, for what really matters is their mutual commitment to each other, not their material possessions. First the groom will be led to the *chuppah*, then the bride, by their respective parents. The bride circles the groom and then as the central part of the ceremony commences the bride will be on the right of the groom.

There are two cups of wine used in the wedding ceremony. The first cup accompanies the betrothal blessings, and after the blessings are recited, the couple drinks from the cup. Wine is a symbol of joy and fruitfulness in Jewish tradition and the *Kiddush* is the blessing over the wine for its sanctification. Marriage, which is called *Kiddushin*, is the sanctification of a man and woman to each other.

In a Jewish ceremony it is the vow of the man (and the giving of the plain gold wedding band which symbolizes the simplicity and purity of the relationship), along with the signing of the *ketubah* which makes the act official or legal. In the traditional Jewish ceremony it is the man only who gives the ring and makes the pledge. If the wife is also giving a ring, she does not do it under the *chuppah* but rather later. The giving of something valuable also indicates that by tradition the marriage act involves a property transaction. This is also evident from the haggling over the bride price (meant to show the great value of the bride) which traditionally takes place between the fathers of the bride and groom some time before the wedding ceremony as does the signing of the document which results, the *ketubah*.

Again the patriarchal elements of the traditional ceremony are clear. The groom takes the wedding ring in his hand, and in clear view of two witnesses, he declares to his wife, "Behold, you are betrothed unto me with this ring, according to the Law of Moses and Israel." The groom then places the ring on the forefinger of his bride's right hand. According to Jewish *halakah* or legal tradition, this is the central moment of the wedding ceremony, and the couple is now fully married at this point. The wife is given in marriage to the husband who makes pledges to her and weds her.

Whereas a Christian ceremony is basically over after the minister pronounces the wedding valid following the vows and ring exchange, by contrast there are several more important steps in the Jewish ceremony. After the giving of the vows and the rings comes the reading of the *ketubah* or marriage contract in the original Aramaic text. In a Jewish marriage, the groom accepts upon himself various responsibilities, which are detailed in the marriage contract, the principal obligations being to provide food, shelter, and clothing for his wife, and to be attentive to her emotional needs. The protection of the rights of a Jewish wife is so important that the marriage may not be solemnized until the contract has been completed. The document is then signed by two witnesses, and has the standing of a legally binding agreement. The *ketubah* is the property of the bride to protect her and she must have access to it throughout their marriage. The marriage contract is often decorated with beautiful artwork, and is meant to be framed and displayed in the home.

The reading of the marriage contract signals a break between the first part of the ceremony, *Kiddushin* ("betrothal"), and the latter part—*Nissuin* ("marriage"). At this juncture the Seven Blessings (*Sheva Brachot*) are now recited over the second cup of wine. The theme of these blessings links the groom and bride to their faith in God as Creator of the world, and redeemer of his people. These blessings are recited by the rabbi or other people that the families choose and wish to honor with the privilege of participating in the ceremony. At the conclusion of the seven blessings, the groom and bride once more drink some of the wine. Then, there is the breaking of the glass by the groom, who stomps on it. The breaking of the glass is said to be a symbolic reminder of the destruction of the temple in Jerusalem, and a reminder to follow the injunction of the Psalmist to put Jerusalem over one's highest joy, even the joy of getting married.

At this point, the bride and groom are taken to some private spot to have their first quiet moment together as a couple. This is called *Yichud*, and it is usually at this juncture that they break their fast and share their first bites of food together. This signifies the beginning of their normal life together. This in turn is followed by the proper festive meal for one and all, called the *Seudah*.

The *Seudah* is not only the time of the festive meal but of singing and dancing, and toasting the bride and groom. By custom, the celebrations continue on during the following week, hosted by family and friends in various places. After the wedding feast the *Birkat Hamazon* ("Blessing after the meal") is recited and the seven-fold blessings are recited once more. At this juncture the formal aspects of the process are over, though people will stay and celebrate as long as they like. These same seven-fold blessings are said at the end of each of the hosted feasts in private homes during the week after the wedding ceremony.

Looking over all of this, Grace felt overwhelmed by the commitment she was about to make and its public nature. Could they both really get through all of this without a misstep? Fortunately she now had a wedding planner to help with the protocol of the ceremony itself, and with the bridesmaids and groomsmen. They had even, with the rabbi's permission, added the biblical touch of the torch light procession by the bridesmaids from the *chuppah* to the celebration, to give the bridesmaids an important role to play. All looked to be in order on paper, but who knew what the day itself would bring? And that's what worried Grace the most. In some ways, getting through the wedding ceremony would be as much of a relief as a joy but she was, deep down inside, very excited about getting married.

30

The Game's at Hand

The fly buzzing around the forensic lab had successfully annoyed everyone that worked at the back of the police headquarters in downtown Charlotte near Marshall Park. No amount of room deodorizer could hide the fact that the hand really stank, as did the whole attempt at intimidation that led to its severance.

Thus far Dr. Mary Beth Watson, the short brunette forensics expert with the nose ring had made no headway at all on identifying the original owner of the aforementioned hand. No data base, national or international, showed any matches with any of the digits. Mary Beth had to hand it to the perpetrators; they had found a hand belonging to a person who seemed to have no recorded history.

More promising was the fingerprint she had lifted from the package itself. With enhancement she had almost a whole print of two fingers, but of course it could be the UPS delivery man. Still to be analyzed was the inside of the box, just in case there was a stray print from the person who placed the hand into the box. Mary Beth scratched her nose, wishing for a clothes pin to keep the smell from drifting up her nostrils, but she kept at the task. Someone wished Mr. Jake Arafat ill, and she needed to do her best to get to the bottom of things.

"So how's it going, my dear Dr. Watson?" said Rick Sears with a silly grin on his face.

"Well, Sherlock, I've learned a few things, but not nearly enough," replied Mary Beth pensively. "We know that the hands original owner was a male of Middle Eastern extraction, perhaps Egyptian, Syrian or Palestinian. His blood type was AB negative, rather rare. The instrument with which the dastardly deed was done was some kind of uber sharp hatchet or knife or cleaver. The medical examiner or the forensic pathologist in Raleigh will know for sure. It is unlikely that this hand came from a local morgue. I found a strand of hair on the hand, which is now out for DNA testing, and I hope to have some more results this afternoon. One more thing, the hand was severed at least five or more days ago, judging from the state of decay."

"Has anyone checked on whether there are any police reports from the past week indicating a person with a bandaged hand or a corpse with a missing hand?"

"Not my field," said Mary Beth. "Charlie is doing those searches."

"Fair enough. Anything else you want to tell me?" coaxed Rick.

"Yeah, we have two partial prints on the outside of the box. I still need to scan the inside of the box to see if there are other partials. Whoever did this seems to have been pretty careful."

"Hopefully not careful enough," replied the Detective. "The CIA wants copies of all the data, and then the hand itself!"

"They can have it!" exclaimed Mary Beth as she continued her examination. "But my exam is a work in progress. They will just have to wait!"

～

Ahmed Arafat admitted to his wife he was a bit nervous. He had never done anything quite like he did this week when he sent the severed hand to Jake Arafat. He was hoping it would either drive his cousin Jake to begin sending money to Hamas again, or at least make him think twice about continuing to pursue his basketball career. But the questions he was still asking himself boiled down to—How long should he wait to see if this threat produced any results? How long before he called Muktar in Bethlehem and told him to harass Jake's family? How much pressure would be enough to produce the desired results? Pressure affected different persons differently. He resolved he would wait at least a week to see what happened, and he would continue to have his son watch the Bobcats arena to see what players were coming and going from practice. If Arafat suddenly became a no show, he would know his efforts were beginning to have the intended affect. What Ahmed could not know was that he had left a tell tale sign of where that hand had come from, and the fickle finger of fate might well already be pointing in a quite unexpected direction.

~

Mary Beth always got a tingling sensation when she thought she was on the verge of a major revelation. And what she discovered inside the cardboard box just under the lid—a thumb and forefinger print which was *not* from the same hand as the prints lifted from the outside of the box—made all her nerve endings stand up and take notice. The outside of the box prints had in fact been traced to the UPS worker, one Clem Johnson, and so their relevance to the search for the perpetrator had been ruled out.

But clearly enough these new partial prints were not from the same hand, and when Mary Beth had scanned in the images of the prints into her computer data base, cross-referencing with the Homeland Security database that charted all those persons who had entry visas and green cards, something popped up on the screen almost immediately. Not a picture, nor a description, but a simple name and a Green card number—Ahmed Arafat. The only thing added on a line below was "Whereabouts Unknown. No Known Associates."

Not satisfied with this, Mary Beth did a database search of all residents and shop owners in Charlotte, and sure enough, though she could not find a residential address or phone number, she did find the following "Mediterranean Market, owner A. Arafat." Could this be a co-incidence? Mary Beth thought it unlikely, and so she rang up her now favorite detective, Rick Sears.

"Hey Rick, it's me again. I may have something crucial for you in the hand case, though in this case it's an example of the eye being quicker than the hand!" quipped Mary Beth. "I have made no progress on identifying the hand's true owner, but after careful microscopic scrutiny I have an identification of the source of two partial prints on the inside lid of the box that contained the hand—one Ahmed Arafat. I then checked our Charlotte data bases and discovered an A. Arafat who owns a Mediterranean Market over on West Boulevard."

"Excellent work Mary Beth. He's already on our radar—Jake Arafat shops at that very market! Meantime, keep working on that stinky hand. Have you checked the various biological mail order houses that ship body parts to labs around the country? I know there's one such company here in Charlotte."

"Nope, but I will look into it," replied Mary Beth, "We aim to please. And to do so, it's back to the forensics for me!"

"Go get 'em Dr. Watson," said Sink.

"Righto Sherlock, the game's afoot, or in this case a hand," and she could hear Rick laughing at the other end of the line as she closed up her Razor cell phone.

31

As Memory Serves

A RT WAS ON THE verge of fully recovering his memory. It had taken a few days, but already he had experienced a vivid dream in which he saw himself lying in the corridor to the Plutonium, and he remembered hearing a creaking sound above, as the door slammed shut. Someone seemed to have wanted to do him harm it would appear, for it would have taken a hurricane force wind for that door to simply to be blown shut.

Art had been released from the hospital the previous day, and after a little Internet surfing had found two tickets to Tel Aviv from Izmir at a reasonable price. "Nurse" Marissa was adamant about going with him, ostensibly because she had never visited Tiberias but also because her protective tendencies were already in motion when it came to Art. She did not believe that what happened to him had been a pure accident. For the next two days he and Marissa were going to pour over the photocopies of the Papias manuscripts and see what came to light on the first detailed scrutiny of the texts.

Sitting in a wicker chair with a high back, Art had out his magnifying glass and was carefully going over a passage first in the Greek then in his hand-written left-handed scrawl which had produced a translation as follows:

> The blessing thus predicted pertains, without [fear of] contradiction, to the times of the kingdom, when the just, rising from the dead, will reign, when even the creation, renewed and liberated, will produce a multitude of foods of all kinds from the dew of heaven and the fertility of the earth, just as the elders who saw John the disciple of the Lord remembered that they had heard

from him how the Lord would teach about those times and would say:

"The days will come in which vines will grow, each having ten thousand shoots, and on each shoot ten thousand branches, and on each branch ten thousand twigs, and on each twig ten thousand clusters, and in each cluster ten thousand grapes, and each grape, when pressed, will give twenty-five measures of wine. And, when one of those saints takes hold of a cluster, another cluster will clamor: 'I am better, take me, bless the Lord through me!' Similarly a grain of wheat also will generate ten thousand heads, and each head will have ten thousand grains, and each grain five double pounds of clear and clean flour. And the remaining fruits and seeds and herbiage will follow through in congruence with these, and all the animals using these foods which are taken from the earth will in turn become peaceful and consenting, subject to men with every subjection."

"Whoever said archaeology is boring and tedious? Here is a manuscript that has talking grape clusters!" laughed Art. "This passage, in a bit different form, is also quoted in Irenaeus, but now again we have more evidence the Church Fathers were faithfully quoting and using the Bishop's material. What is astounding about this passage is not so much the tradition about a messianic kingdom age, after Jesus returns, but the fact that Papias says that John got his millennial ideas ultimately from Jesus himself. This, for sure, would not have pleased Eusebius who wanted to cast aspersions on all the millenialists including John of Patmos. But what this also indicates is that John of Patmos had heard Jesus in person. This sheds an interesting new light on Revelation in general and on Revelation 20 in particular. Instead of John being the eccentric uncle amongst the NT writers, he turns out to be part of the mainstream, following the teachings of Jesus—a very intriguing and suggestive idea. Jesus himself would have been some sort of apocalyptic seer."

"Art, this is all very interesting speculation, but what will your NT colleagues say when they discover that you branded Jesus a chiliast or millenialist, someone who promises a future heaven on earth?" asked Marissa.

"I imagine some of them will think I am fifteen degrees shy of plumb, especially those who want to de-eschatologize Jesus. Trust me there are many who do not want to see Jesus as a prophet of the future. But once this Papias stuff is published, they will be in for a rude awakening, providing we have enough reasons to suggest that Papias knew exactly what he was talking about, and in fact had really talked to John of Patmos who was in turn someone who had heard Jesus' eschatological teachings either in person, or at least through someone like the Beloved Disciple—Lazarus in my view."

"Correct me if I am wrong," replied Marissa, "but you are talking about providing historical evidence that the Gospels were written by those who either were eyewitnesses or in direct contact with eyewitnesses, *and* you are talking about the notion that the portraits of Jesus as an exalted messianic and eschatological figure accurately reflect Jesus's claims and impact."

"Bingo!" exclaimed Art. "That's exactly what I'm going to say. Of course that contradicts not only liberal scholarly views, but also other religious views about Jesus—namely the various views commonly held by many Jews and Muslims as well."

"Don't say that too loudly around here," cautioned Marissa. "If Jesus did indeed die on a cross and believed he was doing so to save the world, or even more if Jesus in some sense presented himself as divine, then we indeed have a contradiction with normal Muslim claims about Jesus, or Issah, as Muslims like to call him."

During this whole conversation Art had been attentively listening to what Marissa was saying and was not saying, in short he was trying to read between the lines. "So Marissa, how is it you know so much about Christian beliefs about Jesus and the Gospels? Didn't you tell me you grew up in a so-called 'secular-Muslim' home?"

"Yes, I did. I also told you that my good English came from living in the U.S. for a considerable period of time."

"You did, and so . . . ?"

"Well," said Marissa coyly, "we've probably pushed this conversation as far as it ought to go for now. I'll get back to you on a future occasion." She smiled that beautiful enigmatic smile, and suddenly the Papias manuscripts seemed far less interesting than the woman sitting across the table. Art completely lost his train of thought.

32

How to Dry Clean a Menorah

AFTER BEING STUMPED FOR several days, Kahlil finally decided to obtain some dry cleaning chemicals from a shop in the Cardo. To clean the menorah he obtained a small feather duster, put a cloth over it, secured it with a rubber band and then sprayed the cloth with the cleaning fluids. He gently stuck the feather duster up into the menorah and twisted it around.

When Hannah emerged from the back of the shop, Kahlil had on his glasses and was intently detoxing the menorah so no one would get poisoned hence forth. As he gently pushed the feather duster all the way up into the stem of the menorah, suddenly he felt some resistance.

"There is still something in this menorah, jammed way up in the top of it!" exclaimed Kahlil.

"Take the duster out slowly and let's see if we can extract it," said Hannah while rummaging through a drawer to find her extra long tweezers. Kahlil laid the menorah on its side, and Hannah inserted her small, gloved hand up into the menorah with the tweezers and then felt around until she found something to grip. Ever so slowly she pulled her hand out of the menorah, being careful not to let go of the prize. When her hand emerged, she and Kahlil both let out a little gasp. She had a small crumpled piece of papyrus clamped between the ends of the tweezers.

"This menorah is just a cornucopia of surprises," said Kahlil. "In view of what was on the last papyrus, we need gloves on both hands before we unroll our find."

Hannah laid the tiny papyrus down on a wooden block that was on the working counter where Kahlil was sitting. Using two sets of tweezers, Kahlil very slowly pried open the crumpled papyrus. It was no more than two inches squared. Plain to see was a miniscule inscription, not in Hebrew, Aramaic, or Greek—but in LATIN!

Many years before, Kahlil had taken Latin at the British School in Jerusalem, never thinking he would ever have much use for that so-called dead language. What the one line inscription read was

DIVOTITODIVOVESPASIANIIUDEACAPTA

Kahlil rummaged around in his shop files until he found a picture of a menorah inscription in Latin for comparison. The picture showed a Jewish tombstone inscription from the Roman period.

Noting the similarities in the letters, Kahlil was able to translate the papyrus as follows: "to the divine Titus [son of] the divine Vespasian, [who] captured Judea". Suddenly, a light went on in Kahlil's brain and he got very excited. "Hannah, this inscription refers to the Jewish War when first Vespasian and then Titus besieged the city of Jerusalem, with Titus finally capturing it and carting off the plunder from the Temple and Herod's Palace to Rome. Remember the Arch of Titus in the Roman forum which we saw when we visited Rome once?"

"Yes, I remember," replied Hannah. "It was a rainy day, but we got good pictures of the arch from several angles. Let me fish them out." Pulling down a large photo album from a shelf above the workbench, Hannah flipped through a few pages quickly.

"Father, look at this picture of the Romans carting off a large menorah from the Temple, much larger than the one we have! But there is nothing preventing the supposition that they took smaller ones as well. And here is a close up picture of the inscription on the top of the arch of Titus."

"Yes!" exclaimed Kahlil. "See how the third line matches up with our little inscription on the papyrus fragment. It looks like someone put an identifier tag in the menorah, so people would know where it came from and who took it."

"You realize what this means, don't you father?" whispered Hannah in a voice full of awe. "We are about to give away as a wedding gift the oldest known menorah in existence, one which probably came from Herod's temple in the mid-60s AD." Total silence engulfed them. The enormity of the find eclipsed every item that had ever passed through their shop. Visions of temple plunder swirled around in their heads. In their minds, they watched this very menorah being carried through the old streets of Jerusalem, probably down the Cardo itself. Both of them sat down slowly as if weighed down by the ages.

"This does change everything," said Kahlil in an obvious understatement. "It is true that we will make our fortune by selling this to the Israeli museum here in Jerusalem. But I also know that I must report this find to the IAA. The Jewish people deserve to have this menorah. It is magnificent, isn't it, my dear," said Kahlil gazing lovingly at both his daughter and the menorah. Sighing, he continued with resignation in his voice, "Why do things have to be so complicated when you are dealing with antiquities? I just wanted to give this away as a wedding gift. There goes the surprise."

"Yes, there goes the surprise," agreed Hannah, "but at least our integrity will not be going with it."

"Right," said Kahlil, as he picked up the phone and began to dial the number for the IAA.

PART THREE

A Cliff Hanger

THE MONASTERY OF ST. George is Greek Orthodox, but through an interesting co-operation between the Roman Catholics and the Orthodox who share adjacent space at the Church of the Nativity in Bethlehem, there had developed a certain collegial relationship between

the Orthodox priests in the Church of the Nativity and Father Abbas in the adjoining Roman Catholic Church. Father Abbas had managed to procure for Mrs. Arafat, her daughter-in-law, and her grandchildren living arrangements in the famous monastery of St. George. In exchange, they would clean, cook, and provide for the monks of the monastery. The monks had been grumbling about the quality of food and services provided by their fellow male monks, and since in the Orthodox tradition priests could be married, there was no phobia about having women and children around the monastery. Indeed, Nicholas, the head of the monastery, was a married man himself.

The Wadi Qelt is a gorge paralleling the old Roman road from Jerusalem to Jericho made famous by the Good Samaritan. For those who have not made the journey up the Wadi Qelt from Jericho, past the Herodian palace ruins, the first occasion produces only awe when one turns the corner on the serpentine path on the west side of wadi. The monastery gives new meaning to the phrase, a cliffhanger.

The history of this monastery is interesting, not least because of its long association with Muslims in the area, and its service to Palestinians. Despite being called the Monastery of St. George by English-speaking people, it has an Arabic name:

This makes clear the monastery was not named after the reputed dragon slayer but rather after its most famous monk, Gorgios of Coziba. It was probably founded about 480 by a hermit monk named John of Thebes. who came here from Egypt. During the 6th century the monastery flourished, but it was destroyed by the Persians in 614 and abandoned. The present edifice was rebuilt between 1878 and 1901 in the village of Al-Khyader outside of Jericho. Both Jericho and Bethlehem are Palestinian towns.

The Church of St. John and St. George was completed in 1912 but the original chapel preserves a sixth-century mosaic pavement. Also in the chapel are the remains of the monks who were martyred in 614. The edifice has a Greek Orthodox interior, and the dome contains a portrait of Christ Pantocrator. During the Ottoman period in Palestine, some rooms were constructed in the adjacent convent to house the mentally ill of whatever religious affiliation. Since the priest in al-Khader was the only Christian inhabitant of the town, Saint George's Monastery attracted al-Khader's Muslims as it still does today. There would be no problem with Christian Palestinians who had many Muslim relatives working in such a place as this.

Like all such monasteries, there were distinctive features and religious festivals associated with this monastery. During the Feast of Saint George in early June, the bridle of Saint George's horse would pass over the bodies of visitors to prevent or cure any mental illness. More than anything else, this monastery was known as a place for curing the physically ill and caring for the mentally ill. Because of the difficulty of direct access to this cliff-hanging monastery, which no one could approach without being seen long before they ever arrived at its gates, it could be

said to be the perfect locale if one was seeking sanctuary from preda-
tors of various sorts. Yet it has attracted many tourists, not least because
legend has it that it is located next to the cave where Elijah stayed on his
pilgrimage down to Mt. Horeb.

The van pulled up in front of the house of Jake's mother, and she and
her family trundled down the stairs and into the vehicle that was being
driven by Father Abbas himself. Muktar, who was sitting across the street
watching from a little sidewalk café and drinking his Turkish coffee, had
no reason to think that the family was going any place special since they
were devout Catholics. Father Abbas had been seen to come and go from
this house with some regularity since the death of Issah the previous
year. Yes, they had small suitcases and school backpacks, but that was
all. Nothing to set off his radar that he would never again see the family of Jake Arafat. Indeed, if he had been more observant the previous
week, he would have seen a moving van load up most of the families'
belongings—under cover of darkness. The deeds of the two houses were
already signed over to the Catholic Church. The Arafats would not be
returning to this locale ever.

Muktar decided to call Ahmed. The phone rang for a while before a
woman picked up and in hushed tones said, "*Salam Aleichum.*"

Muktar replied, "*Aleichum salam.* This is Muktar. Speak up, woman!"

"There are police in the store talking with my husband just now,
and so I am very nervous. I do not trust these people."

"Police! That's never a good sign. What is wrong? Did Ahmed forget
to renew his business permit?" inquired Muktar.

"No, I overheard them talking about a hand. A real hand!"

"A hand? Please tell me that your idiot husband didn't do something stupid like threaten Jakov Arafat. Has he had any contact with the
man that you know of?"

There was a pause at the other end of the line, and then Ahmed's
wife said, "My husband sends many packages—food packages. There was
a box larger and heavier than most. I was told to call UPS to pick up the
box. It was addressed to another Mr. Arafat. I do what I am told. I am an
obedient wife."

Muktar could now overhear the increasingly heated conversation
going on in the store as Ahmed's anxiety level was rising: "I assure you,

that I would never send some strange object to Mr. Arafat, and I have not done so. He is after all, a distant cousin of mine from Bethlehem, and I wish him only the best."

"How then do you explain your finger prints on the inside of the package in which this hand came," questioned Detective Pierce, Rick Sears' partner, as he took the handcuffs from his pocket.

Ahmed's eyes widened. He blurted out, "How did you . . . ? There must be some mistake here! You can't arrest me! What about my store? My wife?"

"Mr. Arafat. There is no mistake. Put your hands behind your back. We are arresting you on suspicion of murder, for starters. Detective Pierce will read you your rights," said Detective Sears as he led Ahmed away.

At this point, Ahmed's wife dropped the phone, pushed back the beaded curtain, and slipped into the back room behind the Market. Shaking with fear, she murmured, "What has he done!? What has he done!?"

Muktar could still vaguely hear what was happening with Ahmed shouting "Stop, stop!" as they were leading him out, "You're making a terrible mistake!"

"No, Mr. Arafat, you made the terrible mistake. Hopefully, your lawyer will encourage you to tell us all about it downtown!" And then the phone went dead as Ahmed's wife retreated on her knees into the back room. More than one Arafat would have a change of address on that day.

34

Make No Bones about It

A RT WEST WAS BACK! And make no mistake about it, this Papias find was big! Art returned to the dig with vigor, and on this day was supervising a new trench into the scriptorium, so named because the manuscripts had been found in this room of the Papias house. It was mid morning and he and Marissa were digging side by side, hoping for some further revelations. They had been virtually inseparable since the hospital episode, and this had not gone unnoticed by Mehmet. No one had come to him and asked what he had been doing while Art went down in the corridor to the Plutonium, but he figured at some juncture questions might be asked. And so he had devised a devilish bailout plan.

While Marissa and Art were off to Israel, he would purloin the real manuscripts from the hotel safe. A bribe to the hotel manager should work. He had known Mehmet long before he knew Marissa, and liked him better than Marissa, not least because Mehmet would pay for his Turkish beer at night. He would then take the manuscripts to Ankara, see the government officials in charge of the digs and claim he had found these on the site. Next would come permission to have a press conference revealing the discovery, and a firm promise of resources for a translation and interpretation of their importance. Then finally, finally, Mehmet, who had labored in obscurity, would have the archaeological triumph of a lifetime, or so he told himself in his self-talk. What he did not know is that Marissa had already taken detailed photos of the manuscripts, and sent a full report to the supervisor of the dig at Laodicea. She promised that Professor West would translate and interpret the papyri. Professor Nisaturk had already responded that he looked forward to their report.

When the small spade hit something solid, but not as hard as rock, Art yelled out, "Halt! We've got something here, and we need to be careful. Time to go to hand trowels, brushes, and small buckets." Two

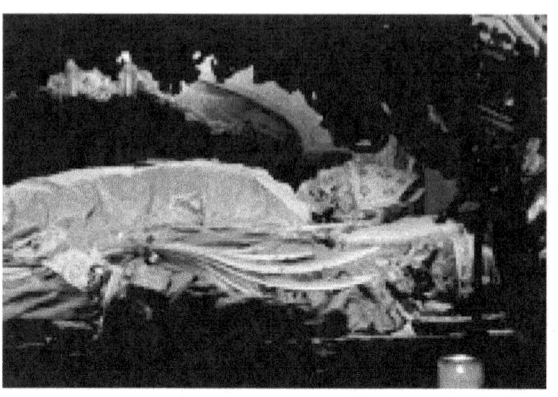

Turkish assistants came quickly with the required tools and set to work.

Art also got down on his hands and knees and began to dust off a protruding object in the dirt in front of him. Taking a little water from his bottle, he poured it on the protrusion and what he now saw produced a smile. It was the crown of a forehead, in other words, a part of a skull. "We've got a skeleton here," exclaimed Art.

"Indeed, so we have to be extra cautious at this juncture. We wouldn't want to disturb the rest of Bishop Papias, if that's who it is," added Marissa laughing.

Immediately, mental images of his trip to Milano to see the skeleton of Bishop Ambrose were conjured up in Art's mind. He remembered the shock of finding Ambrose in the crypt all decked out in his episcopal finery.

"Who knows?" said Art. "We may find him in his episcopal pajamas."

"Now you're being silly," said Marissa.

"No, really! Bishops were often buried in full regalia," said Art.

"Really? But did they even have such finery in the second century?"

"That I don't know. Maybe we are about to find out," replied Art with a bouncy assurance in his voice.

A good deal more careful digging, sifting, and brushing led to the revelation that there was indeed a skeleton laid out beneath the floor. This was not a total surprise, since Greco-Roman persons sometimes did bury their loved ones beneath the floor of the home, and kept their death masks in a cabinet in the house where they from time to time would

consult, or pay their respects to, the genius or spirit of the ancestor.

Art was down now at the far end of the skeleton, carefully brushing away dirt. What he came up with was a skeletal foot—with a slipper on it! Again his mind flashed back to the crypt under the Milano cathedral where he had seen the foot of St. Gervasius.

"Look, Marissa! These are no ordinary shoes, and these are no ordinary feet. Maybe we do have Papias himself right before us."

This thought led to a hushed atmosphere as Marissa and Art worked feverishly to uncover the full skeleton before dark. Meanwhile, Mehmet worked away at his potsherds and fumed in his neighboring tent. "Only one more day, one more day, and they will be gone for a while," he told himself. But what would tomorrow bring?

35

The Seven-branched Candlestick

KAHLIL RETHOUGHT THE ORDER of his phone calls, and decided to talk to Grace first, since he most wanted to please her in what was about to transpire. The phone rang only once and then Kahlil heard, "Yes? Who is calling please?" Kahlil recognized the voice as Camelia, Grace's mother, doubtless screening Grace's calls in view of the chaos leading up to the wedding.

"This is Kahlil el Said, Mrs. Levine. I think you will remember me?"

"Indeed I do. You're that tall dark and handsome Arab who looks like Omar Sharif, if I'm not mistaken."

"That's very kind of you," said Kahlil, not wanting to ruffle any feathers by correcting her about the Arab part. "Is Grace in?"

"Yes, she is. Please wait a moment." Putting the phone down she went quickly to fetch Grace, who was happy to hear from Kahlil.

"Grace, it's good to talk with you and I'll not keep you long, but I need your wisdom. It seems the wedding present which Hannah and I wanted to give you has proven to be more grand than I realized. Let me briefly explain. We were planning to give you a vintage menorah as a wedding present. Just how vintage, I had no idea until this morning. We found a little piece of papyrus in it which . . . maybe you should sit down at this point . . . dates to the Second Temple period. What I am saying is, we believe we have found a menorah stolen from Herod's temple by the troops of Titus!"

"What! If true, your menorah is worth millions! We have no such objects at present from the sacking of the Herodian temple! If it is genuine, then it will be about the most coveted artifact in all of Israel! If

140

anyone knew what was in your shop right now, you would probably not be safe!"

"Precisely! So would you agree with me that I should sell it at a reasonable price to the Israeli Museum? Would you also agree that I should use Dr. Cohen as my liaison in this transaction? Do you believe he will be amenable to my plan? He has already seen the menorah; however, he has no idea of its true significance. Do you want to be part of the authentication process—so close to your wedding and all?"

"Slow down, Kahlil! I have never heard you so excited. Yes, yes, and yes to all your questions! I would be thrilled to be part of this historic occasion. Even if I never hold the menorah, I would feel like it was an amazing wedding gift! I will call Sammy and apprise him of your most recent discovery. He can send a team to transport it to the IAA for safekeeping. I will personally see to the authentication. And then we will all approach the Museum and work out a fair deal for you and Hannah. I am so happy for you! And I'm so proud that you would make this artifact a part of our national treasure. Do you mind if I come over and have a quick peak at the menorah? I'd like to get a few pictures, and maybe one with you and me and the object itself, for future reference."

"Would you be so kind as to do that? Hannah and I would love to see you anyway. It seems like ages," said Kahlil.

"I'm on my way and calling Sammy on the fly. In the meantime, hold on to that menorah with both hands."

"Will do. Good bye, Grace," chuckled Kahlil. To Hannah he added, "I think she will really like her 'wedding gift.' Put on the coffee pot. Grace is coming over right now!"

Today would be a momentous day in the life of Kahlil and Hannah el Said. After a lifetime of struggling to make ends meet while pursuing their passion for antiquities, Kahlil and Hannah faced the prospect of no longer having to worry about money and their livelihood. There was a feeling of anticipation, a nervousness that usually accompanies big days in a person's life, and both of them were reduced to displacement activities to keep their minds off of what would transpire in the next twenty-four hours. Kahlil was happily counting ancient hand lamps in a glass case near the front of the shop for no good reason, and Hannah was actually double-checking their Jewish coin collection, making sure everything was in place. The menorah sat proudly on the counter, covered in velvet. All the doors were locked and bolted, until Kahlil came around the counter and undid them, having learned the buyers were on their way.

The two days following Kahlil's call to Grace were truly frenetic. Grace was overwhelmed at the site of the menorah. The IAA moved quickly to move the menorah to their facilities. Sammy and Grace worked quickly to authenticate the menorah. And today Dr. Samuel Cohen was coming to the antiques shop with Dr. Amir Genoor, the head of the Israeli Museum, who intended to make an official offer. In addition, Benjamin Gat from *Ha'Aretz*, a Jerusalem newspaper, was coming as well. Sammy promised him the inside scoop on this "sale of the century" item that would be the first Second Temple artifact of this magnitude ever recovered.

Grace and Manny had already stopped by the shop to see the menorah one last time, and give Kahlil their blessing on the sale before heading off to Tiberias. In conversation on the phone, Dr. Genoor had said that he was satisfied with the IAA's report of authenticity and that he was prepared to offer three million U.S. dollars. That much money, all at once, sent Kahlil's blood pressure out of sight. He meekly said he would look forward to dealing with Dr. Genoor. Kahlil could hardly think about

the rest of the day, which included: 1) going immediately to the bank, with Sammy and Hannah as escorts; 2) going to the airport to pick up Art and friend (name not disclosed); and 3) going to the rehearsal dinner all the way up in Tiberias. Hannah had already traveled to Tiberias twice this week. She certainly knew the way!

The shop bell tinkled, and before Kahlil could get around the counter in came Sammy with Amir Genoor close on his heels, followed by Benjamin Gat.

Kahlil, after greeting his distinguished guests, ushered them over to the counter. Kahlil looked at Hannah and then gently they removed the velvet coverlet from the menorah. Kahlil stood tall and announced in his full voice, "Gentlemen, I present to you the oldest known menorah in the world!"

There was an audible gasp as the three men came close to inspect the remarkable object, so beautifully formed and hand-tooled. Sammy, of course, had seen it before, but like someone looking at a Rembrandt, each time it commands awe. It was Benjamin Gat who spoke first.

"Whenever I see a masterpiece like this, it reminds me of how much of the artisanship of the ancients we have lost over the centuries. No one can make something this fine these days, at least not by hand. The intricate and detailed filigree work is just remarkable." And then he took three shots from three different angles.

Sammy rubbed his forehead and said, "Honestly, I missed this one altogether. I saw it earlier, but I was too intent on the manuscripts to pay much attention until Kahlil found the second papyrus. As it turns out, this is worth much more than the demon papyrus."

"Much more indeed," said Amir Genoor. "Culturally it is worth a king's ransom."

At this juncture, Kahlil neatly produced the small two-by-two-inch papyrus between two thin pieces of glass that were taped together. "Here are your *bona fides*, gentlemen. Study it all you like."

Sammy read the Latin inscription aloud. He then concluded, "There is no doubt that this papyrus is authentic and indicates the menorah is from the time of Titus, the conqueror and arsonist of Jerusalem. In view of its close similarity to the inscription on the triumphal arch of Titus in Rome, which depicts taking a large menorah out of the temple, I think we have as close to proof positive as one could want. Of course, this is not the menorah depicted in the arch of Titus, but it may have been modeled on that one. In any case, it is an exceedingly precious artifact."

"Right," said Amir Genoor. "And I am satisfied that the IAA did its job to authenticate the piece these past two days. Mr. el Said, I am prepared to offer you the sum of three million dollars US. How would you like your check written out?"

"Mr. Genoor, if it would not be too much trouble, could I ask you to all accompany me to the bank just down the Cardo from here. We can complete this transaction in the safety deposit box room there."

"Certainly," said Amir. "And speaking of safety, two of my security guards from the museum are waiting outside. With them also is my son, who works at the museum. He will take possession of the menorah and they will immediately ride back to the museum with the objet d'art, if we are ready for the transaction?"

"Yes," said Kahlil. "That will be perfect. But before we go, Hannah and I would like to just gaze upon the menorah once more. It has been in my possession these long years—as one of the family so to speak." A few pictures were then taken, and then Kahlil was ready to proceed.

Finally, with relief written all over his face, Kahlil left the shop in the company of three men, whilst three other burly men left through the Damascus Gate, got into an armored car, and sped off with an object cloaked in a large wicker carrier basket. The walk to the bank went without incident. Upon exiting the bank, the sun broke through the clouds above to shine down onto the white limestone bank. Kahlil felt as if God was shining down on this endeavor and giving it his seven-fold blessing, like the wedding blessing which would occur on Saturday evening when Grace and Manny were wed, like the light from a seven branched candlestick—a menorah.

Kahlil began to weep, standing in front of the bank, with the deposit slip in his hand. Hannah shielded him with a large hug. Wiping his eyes, he turned back to the three men, shook their hands, and said, "Thank you so much. It is hard to be old and have only a little means of support. But it would have been harder to keep the menorah from its people."

"Yes," said Amir, "but it is we who should thank you for taking such good care of this object for so long. To you we must say now *Shalom aleichem*."

Kahlil replied in kind, and realized it was surely time to get on the road to pick up Art and company. But for a moment he was lost in reverie, thinking through his life and how he had struggled to survive, to maintain his honesty and integrity in spite of temptations to cheat, as was readily possible in the antiquities trade. Allah had indeed been the rewarder of the honest man who walked humbly with his God. Suddenly snapping out of his train of thought and looking at his watch he said, "Hannah, Art will be landing in only an hour and a half!"

"Not to worry, Father. It will take a bit over an hour to get to the Tel Aviv airport, and besides, he has to get through passport control and customs to get his luggage. We have time."

"You are right as usual, daughter. I wonder who this mystery person is who is coming with Art?"

"We will soon know," smiled Hannah as they walked into the car park and prepared for the journey to Tel Aviv.

36

A Turkish Delight

MARISSA LEFT EXPLICIT INSTRUCTIONS with Mehmet to keep the digging going around the skeleton they had found. Thus far they had unearthed only about half of the skeleton, and they had found no other clothing items other than the slippers. Mehmet had simply agreed with Marissa and had made no protests about her leaving for a week, which she thought was a bit odd, but then Mehmet had always seemed quiet and secretive and hard to read anyway. She wrote it off as some sort of male-female tension thing.

The 5-hour drive from Pamukkale to Izmir would be more relaxing if the roads weren't so narrow through the mountains. As the jeep headed up the first mountain range past Laodicea, Art said, "Marissa, my dear, here is where I tell you we must do a little wedding shopping after lunch in Izmir. Not only do I need to get an appropriate present, which I am hoping you will help me find, I need to get a new suit. What about you?"

"Well, I know the perfect store where you can shop for a suit while I'm trying on dresses. Alterations can be done on the spot. Then I'll take you to my favorite antique shop—Meltem and I used to hang out there regularly to see what was new! If we don't find just the right thing, we will have to give Grace and Manny an IOU! Regardless, it will be a whirlwind shopping spree!"

"Sounds exciting. With you along, it could be yet another adventure!" said Art a bit bravely.

Marissa knew, deep down, that there was some positive chemistry going on here so replied softly, "Have you tried *tuza balik*—a fish baked in a large block of salt and served at the table? What I'm saying is, we could wrap up the day with a candlelight dinner along the Aegean shore. You're good company, and even more, by the way."

"That sounds so good. And pretty soon we ought to talk about the 'more,' some more," said Art.

Marissa was quiet for a minute and then said, "I quite agree." And then she leaned over from the driver's seat and gave Art a kiss on the left cheek. Turning to see his response, she saw the scarlet color creeping up the side of his face, and she wrinkled up her nose and laughed. She liked the innocence and transparency of Art. She could tell he was a bit shy, but that he really liked her. This could be interesting.

"Did you remember to move the Papias scrolls to a safer place?" asked Art.

"Of course, I did," said Marissa. "They are now safely ensconced in my personal safe, and nobody but me knows where that is. Even if there was a potential thief watching our every move, he would never guess where that safe is."

"Just out of curiosity, where is that safe?" inquired Art.

"I presume my secret is *safe* with you. It's hiding under a pile of Turkish Delight in a little shop in Pamukkale that a friend of mine runs."

"Sweet!" said Art. "You mean those shops right next to the hot springs bath with the Roman columns in it?"

"Precisely. The safe is under the counter, on top of which is every kind of candy imaginable, including Turkish Delight. Mimi locks the place up every night carefully because her own little safe is there as well, and all those shops have alarms anyway. And just to make sure, Mimi has an electro-magnet under the bottom of the case that makes it impossible to move any safe, so strong is the magnet pull. And I alone have the combination to the safe."

"Well barring an act of God, I feel better already. You are thorough. I didn't fully trust that hotel manager. He seemed a bit shady to me."

"I agree," said Marissa. "Oh, look at that beautiful valley. Some of the biggest farms are near Izmir. All the crops growing in so many shades— golden grains, red poppies, orange trees, green olives. I will miss this country even when I'm only gone one week!"

∾

When Mehmet arrived at the hotel around dinner time the manager was waiting for him. He had been off duty until five, and had not been party to things that had gone on at the hotel earlier in the day.

"Before we have dinner, I'd like to check on something that Marissa and I left in your safe, for sake-keeping, if you don't mind."

"Why certainly" said Mustafa, "I'll be back in a minute with whatever there is in the safe under those names." Mustafa was gone for five minutes while Mehmet waited in front of the counter. Then five minutes turned into ten minutes. Then ten minutes turned into fifteen minutes.

Finally Mustafa came back with a look of chagrin on his face, "I am afraid I cannot oblige you."

"Why not; there are some things in the safe are there not?"

"It seems that before Marissa left, she cleaned out her cubicle in the safe, and took the contents elsewhere."

"No, that cannot be true!" exclaimed Mehmet with a look of both anger and panic on his face.

"There is nothing in the safe right now that belongs to you two." There was an awkward pause and then Mustafa handed Mehmet a little wrapped up confection. "Here suck on this, and it will sweeten your disposition and provide a little consolation and compensation," said Mustafa and smiled. "Then we can go to dinner."

And as Mehmet unwrapped the confection he said, "Turkish delight, my favorite, but this is no consolation for the Turkish disaster that has just happened. That woman is trouble. Mark my words, trouble. And she is going to pay for this indignity. She didn't even tell me she was moving things, even though she left me in charge of the dig!"

"Women, what can you do with them? They are unpredictable."

"You said it. Let's go get drunk, after dinner of course."

"Sounds like a plan," said Mustafa.

And had anyone been watching they would have seen two glum Turks ambling off to the bar while chewing on Turkish delights. Some wounds in the gender wars even Turkish delight cannot heal.

37

The Spin Meister

MUSIC IS AN IMPORTANT part of any wedding, and perhaps as important to the festivities thereafter as well. Grace and Manny had diverse tastes in music, with Grace's ranging from classical music to jazz to Klezmer, while Manny preferred classic rock and blues, and so there needed to be some sort of compromise. They both agreed that no hip hop or rap should be allowed, although when their disc jockey, Raz Boyarin, played for them the following little dance number (sung and rapped to the tune of "Play that Funky Music White Boy") they laughed so hard that they were sorely tempted to include this "classic" by Two Live Jews as a bit of comic relief:

> When I was just a boychick,
> Couldn't wait to become a man,
> Had some problems with my Hebrew
> I really couldn't understand . . .

There was finally an agreement that there would be a little string quartet playing in the atrium of the Scots Hotel where the hors d'oeuvres would be served. On the opposite side of the atrium a small Klezmer band would play some traditional Jewish music. Within the rented dining hall, however, there would be a dance floor where Raz the DJ would supervise classic rock, soul, blues, and some jazz standards. He seemed very amenable and understanding about their musical dilemma and diverse preferences, and towards the end of the discussion he said, "Do you want me to throw in a few surprises here and there, like the number above by Two Live Jews? Maybe after the party has been going for a while, we can afford to loosen things up a bit?"

Manny looked at Grace who nodded and said, "Sure, but remember that we can't stand that rap stuff that's full of cursing, and we don't want to offend the more religious wedding guests. You must remember this is a wedding with lots of people attending, including Jews, Christians, and Muslims, so we have to do our best not to offend anyone but still have some fun."

"Right," said Raz, though he was thinking '*oy gevalt!*' "We will do our best to please of course." The truth was this gig was going to pay him double what he would normally make at a wedding, so he was highly motivated to please the customer.

And with that conversation, Grace and Manny had finally concluded all the pre-wedding plans and discussions, and were looking forward to the rehearsal dinner on Friday night, where they would have a chance to relax with the wedding party, and a few special guests who were coming from some distance—guests like Art West and whoever was accompanying him. Art had been coy about that when Grace had phoned him yesterday, and she figured she was in for a surprise. Just how big a surprise, she could hardly imagine.

The nearly five-hour flight from Izmir to Tel Aviv was so relaxing they both fell asleep until the pilot announced they were preparing for landing. As the plane descended over the coast, Art could see the archaeological site at Caesarea Maritima where he had spent some time examining the aqueduct and the theater of Herod. Excavations were continuing even in the July heat. Marissa was sitting quietly next to Art, not knowing quite what to expect next, but nonetheless quite excited. "So where did you hide the wedding gift we bought in Izmir?"

"I've got it right here in my large tote bag, and I'm guarding it with my life. How are you feeling about our adventure at this point?" asked Art."

"To be honest, I'm getting more apprehensive. Being off the dig right now means being away from my comfort zone! I've never been to a proper Jewish wedding! Grace is a professional, like me. Will she be taking Manny's last name?"

"Good question. I'm not sure, but I would expect so here in Israel since this is an Orthodox ceremony. Grace Cohen. That has a new ring to it for sure."

"Speaking of rings, I wonder what their wedding bands will be like."

"Gold, solid gold, and elegant I'm sure as the jewelers here in Israel are some of the world's best. But not ostentatious since they are supposed to be simple wedding bands."

"Well, that's a tough balance. You will have to explain to me what is happening during the wedding. Hebrew is not my forte."

"I'll do my best," said Art, and with that the wheels dropped down in preparation for landing. "It's almost time for you to meet Omar Sharif."

"What? I though Kahlil and Hannah were meeting us?"

"They are, but you will see what I mean shortly." And with that Art and Marissa arrived safely at Ben Gurion International Airport.

38

Sunrise at the Seashore

EARLY MORNING AT THE Sea of Galilee was incredibly beautiful. It was fascinating to watch the sun come up over the Golan Heights and then illuminate the lake where Jesus and his disciples so often fished for both followers and the creatures in the lake itself. Though the rehearsal dinner had gone until 10:30, and Art experienced a bit of fatigue coming from Turkey, he wouldn't have missed seeing the sun come up on the lake for anything, especially on a Sabbath morning when all the shops would be closed and almost all the sounds would be the sounds of nature, not of human beings.

The Scots Hotel was only a couple of blocks from the seashore up on a slight hill, and when Art got up there was a slight breeze blowing off the lake. Art thought about inviting Marissa to come with him on his walk down by the water side, but she was obviously exhausted after arriving in Tel Aviv, driving to Tiberias, and dealing with the rehearsal dinner. Dozens of introductions and scads of small talk had left her worn out. So Art decided to go it alone this morning, except for his old friend Kahlil who was also an early riser.

While waiting for Kahlil in the hotel lobby Art caught up with the news. There emblazoned on the front page of *Haaretz*, Israel's oldest daily newspaper, was an enormous picture of a menorah with the headline reading in Hebrew: MENORAH FROM HEROD'S TEMPLE DISCOVERED: FIND OF THE CENTURY. As Art stood reading the article, suddenly he felt a tapping on his shoulder and a deep soothing voice say,

"Wouldn't you rather hear the story from the horse's mouth?"

Turning, Art said to Kahlil, "Well of course. It's always better that way."

They walked down the driveway and crossed the shore road that led north by northwest around the lake bringing locals and tourists to Capernaum, Bethsaida, and other sites of biblical interest. Today was not the day to go exploring, especially since it was the Sabbath until sundown. Art and Kahlil walked down a pathway that led to the water itself and the narrow boardwalk that was along this portion of the shore at the Sea of Galilee. The sun was already beginning to beat down on the lake, cutting a golden path across the water.

"Well it is rather remarkable that Hannah and I had that menorah for thirty years in the shop, had been told it was maybe a second or third century item, and had never discovered the hollow inside of the menorah. It makes us look rather like amateurs," said Kahlil shaking his head ruefully.

"Not at all," argued Art, listening to Kahlil and the lapping of the water on the shore at the same time. Who would have thought that there might be a papyrus or two stuffed in the menorah. I'll wager neither of us has heard of such a thing, and I also have to say that I would love to know how both the demon papyrus that Sammy has, and the little other papyrus came to be in this item at all. If only those papyri could really talk—and answer questions! Answer me this: the little two-by-two identifier papyrus was the one crammed right up in the top of the inside of the menorah, right?"

"Quite right," said Kahlil. "The demon papyrus came out first, and was much bigger."

"Well, I can imagine a scenario in which the Latin papyrus was stuck up in the menorah not long after it was captured and dragged off by the Romans, as a sort of name tag. It would have been created by some scribe, because amidst all the chaos of the destruction of Jerusalem and the carting off of tons of booty, someone in Titus's entourage would have been in charge of cataloging things. The Romans were nothing if not meticulous and thorough about the records of their captured treasures."

"Yes, the little scroll is easier to account for, to be sure. But what about the demon papyrus? What do you make of that, especially when there was poisonous resin put on the thing before it was inserted into the menorah?" inquired Kahlil.

"I have a theory . . ." said Art

Interrupting, Kahlil added with a smile. "You usually do!"

"Well, check this out. We know that in the last third of the first century there were actually some Jews in Caesar's household. In fact there were some before the family of Vespasian began to rule the land. Vespasian is the one who pardoned Josephus and allowed him to take early retirement in Rome, having prophesied that Vespasian would be the next Emperor. My point is that there were Jews in the administration in Rome. Now some of them undoubtedly abhorred what had been done to the temple in Jerusalem in 70. Some of them despised polytheism and the notion that pagans had taken Jewish sacred objects like your menorah and had them on display in Rome."

"So you are saying this object went all the way to Rome, in Roman hands?"

"Right, exactly. And while in Rome someone decided to put a curse on the object while it was in pagan hands. Someone with access to the object stuck a curse scroll up in the menorah to protect it from pagan abuse. Remember that by the first century Jews had a robust theology of demons and the Devil. They certainly believed in curses."

"Right, but do we?" mused Kahlil. "I mean Agent Dershowitz almost lost his life from touching the poison on the papyrus while trying to preserve the thing."

"Well, we will leave that theological question for another day. For now I will just ask, does this idea make sense?"

"It makes good sense, but it does not explain how such a valuable object came back to Israel."

"That is a bit of a mystery. I can't imagine they just lost it!" laughed Art.

"Changing the subject a bit, let's talk about Marissa," said Kahlil. "You really know how to make an entrance with a lovely Turkish archaeologist on your arm, playing the role of your protective guardian after your near-death experience at a dig site! No soap opera could imagine such a scene!"

Art just laughed all the more. "Yeah, that was my plan all along, to stir up Marissa's compassion by nearly getting myself killed in a secret underground passageway. But seriously, what are your first impressions of her?"

"She is quite charming. Bright, attractive, not too young, not too old. Loves archaeology like you, and she certainly seems to be fond of you," replied Kahlil candidly.

"Yes, but there's just one problem," said Art.

"Don't tell me, let me guess," said Kahlil, "it's her religion, or lack thereof."

"Bingo," said Art. "I have been asking the Almighty about this for some time now. How could God bring someone special into my life that I'm certainly attracted to, and it appears to be mutual, and yet she is not a Christian! For me at least, that's a deal breaker."

"Well, don't be too sure about her religious persuasion, until you know it for a fact. You must have that deeper conversation at some point."

"I've been afraid of hearing the bad news that she thinks Christianity is something she could never embrace. I do know she comes from a secular Muslim family, not a devout one, and I do know she lived in the States for a while, which accounts for her excellent English."

"Well," advised Kahlil, "abide your soul in patience, and in any case, if it is Allah's will, things will work out, and those circumstances may well change several times before the matter is resolved."

Art just sighed and kept walking. They had come to a little seaside café where they served wonderful St. Peter fish caught right in the Sea of Galilee. "Shall we have a little breakfast by the sea before we head back to the hotel and the festivities of the day?"

"I thought you'd never ask," said Kahlil, "I am absolutely starving. We can reenact that famous last meeting of Jesus with his disciples here by the seashore by ordering some bread and fish cooked over an open charcoal fire!"

"Okay," said Art. "It's a good thing Marissa is not here, because then the reenactment might go a bit too far if she started asking, 'Art, do you love me more than these?' and I had to give a reply."

Kahlil looked at Art for a moment and then said, "My friend, whether today or tomorrow, soon you must come up with an answer to that question, you know."

Art just nodded and turning to his right said, "Waiter, can we sit at this little table right here by the shore? We want to order some breakfast." And the two friends sat down to break bread near where Jesus had communed with his disciples one last time.

39

And the Two Shall Become One

NOTHING WAS GOING TO transpire in regard to the Cohen and Levine wedding before seven when the sun began to sink over the Galilean hills to end the Sabbath. The day had been spent visiting friends new and old, and eventually getting dressed up for the big occasion. Grace and Manny rode in separate limos to Capernaum. At the same time a large tour bus from Jerusalem transported the rest of the wedding party and then the wedding guests down to the ancient synagogue. All was well arranged because the archaeological site closed right at five, the Franciscans being quite punctual, and at five thirty the wedding party was to arrive for picture taking. Father Jerome had made clear that, since there would be Sunday morning services in the church here, everything needed to be cleaned up before Sunday morning, which provided certain

 challenges to the wedding planner. But all had been managed well thus far, and Saturday had been a gorgeous day.

There was once more a light breeze, this time from the shore to the sea, and precisely at five thirty Manny and Grace separately watched as all the groomsmen and bridesmaids, and parents and siblings and cousins and aunts and uncles, all fifty some of them, poured off the bus and made their way through the bougain-villea-covered gates into the Capernaum archaeological grounds. The photographers had no problem finding picture-perfect sites for the next hour—Manny and Grace being photographed separately. Manny especially wanted to be photographed with the famous Greco-Roman carving of the ark of the covenant depicted sitting on a cart with a temple-like canopy over the top.

The synagogue itself was a magnificent ruin from whatever angle you viewed it, and few settings had more history behind it. The visible synagogue ruins dated back to the third or fourth century AD, but it had a far more ancient foundation beneath, which had led to the conclusion that this was the very location where the synagogue had been in Jesus's day. But on this day all the historical interest of the site would take a back seat to the celebration of a holy marriage between two prominent Jewish citizens of Israel.

By the time the bus had come and gone three more times (it held some fifty-plus passengers on each trip), the grounds were filled with as large a crowd as one would see at this site during the height of the tourist season. The place was buzzing with activity and excitement. The plan was to begin in the parking lot with a torch light procession to the synagogue itself, led by the bridesmaids, followed by the wedding party with the rabbi, and then the guests filing in behind them. There was a string quartet unobtrusively positioned towards the end of the walkway just inside the gate. Sparing no expense, a temporary amplification system had been set up so they could be heard from the parking lot all the way into the synagogue itself.

Comfortable folding chairs had been set up for everyone in the synagogue, which would be packed once everyone had entered and been seated. The wedding planning crew, being Jewish, hired secular Jews to work before five thirty to get everything set up in time for the wedding, since secular Jews had no problems with working on the Sabbath. It was quite impossible to set things up earlier on Friday or early Saturday, since tourists would be all over the site until closing time on Saturday. Such were the kinds of compromises made on a daily basis in Israel, both to be faithful to Torah and to deal with the exigencies of life.

Grace looked stunning in her pale yellow wedding gown and was already receiving numerous compliments, not least from Hannah.

"I have never seen any bride look so beautiful, if you don't mind me saying so," said Hannah.

"Of course I don't mind considering this bride is rather older than any other you have seen."

"Like a yellow rose in full bloom, and equally aromatic as well. What *is* that perfume?" demanded Hannah light heartedly.

"It is pure rose oil; a very special gift from Manny. But I also have a small bottle of Evelyn Rose from Crabtree and Evelyn with me. And we will surely need that perfume today! It's still hot out there, and those synagogue stones are radiating the heat."

Art stood with Marissa, who was wearing a floral print dress. Art had on a very neat gray suit with a deep maroon tie befitting his role as usher. Grace turned to them. "Art, have I told you I'm so thrilled you are alive for my big day!"

"Many times! I told you that not even the four horsemen of the Apocalypse could keep me away."

"Let's sneak in some talk time tonight. Topics should include menorahs and papyri—and Marissa being part of our crazy clan of archaeologists! Welcome aboard, Marissa."

"Thanks for having me," said Marissa truthfully.

After Grace left, Manny approached looking quite the part in his Armani tuxedo with black leather Gucci shoes shining in the sun. He too wanted to get to know Marissa. However, it was time for him to don the kittel, a white linen robe worn by Jewish men on special occasions to signify purity, holiness, and new beginnings. In fact, it was time for the ceremony to begin.

The torches were lit; the bridesmaids led the way; and before long all of the party and guests had processed to the synagogue. The veiling of Grace by Manny had been handled beautifully and there were murmurs in the crowd of approval and people saying, "so beautiful, so beautiful."

Manny had made his vow to Grace and placed the single gold band on her finger, right in center of the aisle at the front of the synagogue. The chuppah had been erected just off to the right side earlier so as not to block everyone's view while the veiling and vows were taking place. The reading of the marriage contract and the recital of the seven blessings by the rabbi had gone off beautifully, followed by the drinking of wine. Manny stomped the glass with such vigor that it shattered in all directions leading to a little laughter in the congregation.

Finally, as a special surprise, a little flower girl carried a cloth-covered object to Grace and Manny. Grace unveiled an elaborate birdcage, and she and Manny reached in and each took a beautiful white turtledove. On the count of three, they released them into the air, to the oohs and ahs of the crowd, for the birds first circled the synagogue in tandem and then flew off to the east towards the Sea of Galilee in perfect harmonized flight side by side. Camelia, Grace's mother, had been holding together rather well until this moment but she began to cry and said to herself, "Well, she is well and truly out of the nest now."

Since the festal dinner could not be held at the synagogue, the bride and groom processed out between two lines of bridesmaids holding their torches high. In the limo Grace was saying to Manny, "Well that couldn't have gone much better," and she gave him a big kiss. "You will have to use that suit some more, you look marvelous."

"Well, that can easily be arranged, but I guess I will not see you in that gorgeous dress anymore. What a shame!"

"Actually," said Grace, "it's a convertible like my car! The frilly lace and train come off, leaving a rather elegant evening gown, which I do indeed intend to reuse. So I'm expecting a lovely date in the future with my best beau!"

The reception and mingling in the courtyard lasted until dinner was announced at nine. When the bride and groom made their entrance into the hall everyone rose and applauded as the toastmaster said, "I give you Mr. Manny and Mrs. Grace Cohen!" Grace had earlier balked at being called Mrs. Manny Cohen, because, as she once explained to Manny, what that moniker Mrs. originally meant was "the mistress of." "I refuse to be your mistress. I insist on being Grace, your wife," she proclaimed. Manny chalked it up to pre-wedding jitters on Grace's part, and tonight he noted happily that she didn't seem to mind at all!!

One of Manny's old friends, a popular wedding speaker with a light touch, had been asked to say a few words about the couple. "I am Saul Levi and I must say I have hardly ever seen such a beautiful ceremony. But now that the two have been joined in marriage and have become one, the question is, Which one?"

This produced plenty of laughter in the hall and set the tone for the dinner. After a few more preliminary remarks, Saul invited Art to say the blessing before the meal—with the rabbi's permission and blessing of course.

Art went straight up to the head table and the little microphone stand and in a clear voice said in impeccable modern Hebrew, "Gracious God, the giver of all good gifts including bread from the earth and rain from the sky, we ask that you shower down your blessings on this beloved and lovely couple, Manny and Grace, on this night, and that you will unite them forever in your love. We give thanks in advance for the food we are about to partake, and ask that you would bless it to our good, and us to your service in your precious and holy name, Amen." And all present said Amen as well, even those who had not understood a word of what Art had said.

Grace smiled a big smile at Art and whispered, "Just perfect, just right."

And Art went and returned to his seat where Marissa waited and said, "You'll have to translate that one for me."

"No problem, but right now comes the toasting and roasting."

The convivial proceedings went on throughout dinner with little stories told about one or the other members of the couple, or both since they had been dating. As the meal ended, the band tuned up their instruments and the dancing began. Manny had picked one of his favorite songs, an old Journey tune entitled "Faithfully," for their first dance. As all watched and cameras clicked, Marissa leaned over to Art who had his eyes glued on Manny and Grace, and whispered "they make a lovely couple, and I have an idea."

Art, a little distracted turned to Marissa and said, "What? What idea?"

"I think we should stop pretending, announce that we are an official couple and see what God might bring next," said Marissa emphatically.

Art, totally taken off his guard, turned to Marissa and just stared as if they were the only two people in the room. Marissa continued quite calmly, "I have always been a woman who believed in the idea that 'you have not because you ask not' and so I am asking you Art West, would you be willing to date me exclusively? I don't want to play coy anymore. I'm tired of dating games. And I can't think of a more romantic setting than now to ask such a question!"

And then, and quite to his surprise the confirmed fifty-something year-old bachelor named Art West heard himself say, "Yes Marissa, I would like that more than anything else in the world. However, I'll be real nervous if you catch the bouquet!"

40

Aftermath

THE SOCIETY PAGE EDITOR of the *Jerusalem Post* was really miffed. The Cohen-Levine wedding was the biggest of the year, and she had been promised front-page coverage, but an even bigger story had trumped her moment of triumph. Plastered all over the front page of both the *Jerusalem Post* and *Ha 'aretz* was a huge picture of the menorah, and a full story about "the find of the new century." Fortunately there had been a link to the wedding story, namely that while the menorah's former owner remained anonymous, it had been stated that the menorah had come into the possession of the museum on condition that there was a plaque on its display saying this was placed in the museum in honor of Grace Levine Cohen.

After another day of wedding festivities, Kahlil and Hannah at long last took the vacation they had always dreamed about—to Istanbul. With them on the same flight from Tel Aviv was another pair who had also dumped their daily routines and duties—Art and Marissa. They had quietly announced to exactly four people—the el Saids and the Cohens—that they were now officially dating and contemplating the future. Mentally, Art reviewed their reactions:

Grace's had brightly said, "Mazel tov!"

Manny had blurted out, "See what it got me!"

Kahlil solemnly added, "My friend, it is long past time for this."

Hannah just gave Art a big hug.

As the Turkish Airlines plane landed at Istanbul airport, the four travelers got their belongings together and prepared to disembark, but once through security there was a surprise awaiting Art.

There standing on the other side of the barrier was his long time Turkish tour guide, Meltem, with a huge smile on her face. Her first words were, "I should have been the first to know you have fallen for a Turkish girl!"

And as the five of them got into the cab heading for the Galata Anemon Hotel, their favorite spot in Istanbul, new revelations began to pour forth from Meltem and Marissa about their youthful escapades. Hannah and Kahlil were enjoying this immensely. It looked like this was going to be an interesting holiday for one and all.

41

The Bones of the Bishop

MEHMET HAD BEEN BUSY since Marissa Okur left him in charge. He wanted to take full advantage of the time he had to enhance his status as a Turkish archaeologist. To that end, he set himself a deadline of three more days to get the alleged skeleton of Bishop Papias uncovered and the scriptorium room unblocked so that the press could do interviews and take pictures. Mehmet realized it was important to make sure this was not just in the Turkish language papers, but also in the one English language Turkish paper, the *Turkish Daily News*, because then it would be picked up by Reuters and other wire services. On Monday he worked steadily with his crew of helpers getting the site into the best possible shape and making it look presentable. Most of the skeleton was now visible above ground, so Mehmet had strung a tarp over the gravesite to protect the good Bishop who was going to be Mehmet's ticket to supervising a major dig.

Standing down in the trench itself Mehmet hovered over two workers who were using only small whisk brushes to avoid damage to the ancient skeleton. They had discovered no cross on the Bishop, but there was an interestingly little fish symbol resting in his palm. This comported nicely with what had been found on the lintel over the door into the scriptorium.

Specifically, Mehmet documented two fish, tethered or perhaps impaled on the bottom crosspiece of an anchor, and half way up the anchor a cross still etched in the stone but fading compared to the rest. Finally at the top of the anchor he noted a circle. Mehmet did not know his Christian iconography well enough to explain all the symbolism, but he had enough visuals to wow the biblically illiterate press.

"Be careful there," said Mehmet to one of the young workers. "We don't want the bishop to have any cracked bones before his coming out party."

As the work progressed it became clear that there was nothing left of the rest of the garments that had been left on Papias's body; only the slippers remained. This was enough, however, to indicate his importance, and with the scrolls, which Mehmet could refer to, but not show the press, as well as with the location of this site, Mehmet felt sure he could confirm this was indeed the famous Bishop Papias.

Mehmet decided it would be worth a little peak into the tunnel behind the scriptorium to see if there was anything immediately apparent there that could further add to the luster of his reputation. With the help of two student workers, he pried open the door and with his best and biggest flashlight shined a light into the darkness, scanning from right to left. Just inside the door and to the left he saw what Art had described, but had since forgotten about apparently—a chamber where Christians could have safely met and shared in their religious rites, maybe a very early underground church.

Of course, Mehmet did know all about the cave churches in Capaddocia, but this would be an example from a much earlier period, and Mehmet was stunned by what he saw. Here was an elaborately carved out vaulted ceiling arching over a room where perhaps a Eucharistic meal could be shared. Mehmet felt the thrill and rush of adrenaline when he realized the importance of this room. It meant there was a considerable underground church in this locale even in the early second century during the lifetime of Papias. He remembered learning in school about the Roman Governor Pliny who had written to Trajan the emperor in this same era asking what to do with Christians who would not recant their faith. Mehmet had a photocopy of that letter in his satchel.

Leaving the chamber and going back out to the scriptorium, Mehmet ordered his assistant to push the door shut again, and he headed to his tent. Filing through his papers he came on the relevant document in Greek with an English translation. In another source he had found a fine old classics scholar, William Melmoth, who had provided some notes. Pliny is writing to the Emperor Trajan in about AD 111–12.

> XCVII Pliny to Trajan:
>
> It is my constant method to apply myself to you for the resolution of all my doubts; for who can better govern my dilatory way of proceeding or instruct my ignorance? I have never been present at the examination of the Christians [by others], on which account I am unacquainted with what uses to be inquired into, and what, and how far they used to be punished; nor are my doubts small, whether there be not a distinction to be made between the ages [of the accused]? and whether tender youth ought to have the same punishment with strong men? Whether there be not room for pardon upon repentance?" or whether it may not be an advantage to one that had been a Christian, that he has forsaken

Christianity? Whether the bare name, without any crimes besides, or the crimes adhering to that name, needs to be punished?

In the meantime, I have taken this course about those who have been brought before me as Christians. I asked them whether they were Christians or not? If they confessed that they were Christians, I asked them again, and a third time, intermixing threatenings with the questions. If they persevered in their confession, I ordered them to be executed; for I did not doubt but, let their confession be of any sort whatsoever, this positiveness and inflexible obstinacy deserved to be punished. There have been some of this mad sect whom I took notice of in particular as Roman citizens, that they might be sent to that city. After some time, as is usual in such examinations, the crime spread itself and many more cases came before me.

A libel was sent to me, though without an author, containing many names [of persons accused]. These denied that they were Christians now, or ever had been. They called upon the gods, and supplicated to your image, which I caused to be brought to me for that purpose, with frankincense and wine; they also cursed Christ; none of which things, it is said, can any of those that are ready Christians be compelled to do; so I thought fit to let them go. Others of them that were named in the libel, said they were Christians, but presently denied it again; that indeed they had been Christians, but had ceased to be so, some three years, some many more; and one there was that said he had not been so these twenty years. All these worshipped your image, and the images of our gods; these also cursed Christ.

However, they assured me that the main of their fault, or of their mistake was this: That they were wont, on a stated day, to meet together before it was light, and to sing a hymn to Christ, as to a god, alternately; and to oblige themselves by a sacrament [or oath], not to do anything that was ill: but that they would commit no theft, or pilfering, or adultery; that they would not break their promises, or deny what was deposited with them, when it was required back again; after which it was their custom to depart, and to meet again at a common but innocent meal, which they had left off upon that edict which I published at your command, and wherein I had forbidden any such conventicles. These examinations made me think it necessary to inquire by torments what the truth was; which I did of two servant maids, who were called *Deaconesses*: but still I discovered no more than that they were addicted to a bad and to an extravagant superstition. Hereupon I have put off any further examinations, and have recourse to you, for the affair seems to be well worth consultation, especially on account of the number of those that are in danger; for there are many of every age, of every rank, and of both sexes, who are now and hereafter likely to be called to account, and to be in danger; for this superstition is spread like a contagion, not only into cities and towns, but into country villages also, which yet there is reason to hope may be stopped and corrected. To be sure, the temples, which were almost forsaken, begin already to be frequented; and the holy solemnities, which were long intermitted, begin to be revived. The sacrifices begin to sell well everywhere, of which very few purchasers had of late appeared; whereby it is easy to suppose how great a multitude of men may be amended, if place for repentance be admitted.

~

XCVIII Trajan to Pliny:

You have adopted the right course, my dearest Secundus, in investigating the charges against the Christians who were brought before you. It is not possible to lay down any general rule for all such cases. Do not go out of your way to look for them. If indeed they should be brought before you, and the crime is proved, they must be punished; with the restriction, however, that where the party denies he is a Christian, and shall make it evident that he is not, by invoking our gods, let him (notwithstanding any former suspicion) be pardoned upon his repentance. Anonymous informations ought not to be received in any sort of prosecution. It is introducing a very dangerous precedent, and is quite foreign to the spirit of our age.

After reading these two documents over carefully, Mehmet concluded that even in AD 111–12 it was conceivable, since there had been sporadic persecutions of Christians since the time of Nero in the 60s, that elaborate efforts might have been undertaken to allow Christians to worship their God in freedom. Papias may well have been one of the innovators of the underground church, for Mehmet knew that in ancient Bithynia Christians were still meeting in the open air, out doors. Here, in Hierapolis, it would appear they were more careful, and it was important to note that the access to this chamber was only through Papias's house.

Mehmet now had more than enough to create major headlines, and he was not waiting for Marissa's approval to go ahead with this little venture. In fact, he decided he would summon the press for tomorrow morning. Picking up his cell phone he rang the general number at the *Turkish Daily News*. "I need to speak to Mr. Turkoglu please." As he waited, he could already see his picture and name on the front page of the paper.

42

The Hand of Fate

Muktar was stumped. There had been no activity at the Arafat house now in many days. Could they have gone on vacation? Could they have figured out he was watching them? No one had come or gone from the house since he watched the family leave in the van last week. Muktar's followers had taken turns watching the house around the clock. How had these people vanished right before his eyes? He slowly realized he had been outwitted by Jake Arafat and his seemingly frail little mother. He also knew that Ahmed was in serious trouble with the law in Charlotte. Muktar started sweating his own involvement with Ahmed's crazy plot. This was all getting too confusing and too complicated.

Equally stumped was Dr. Mary Beth Watson, the forensics expert. While she had done exemplary work connecting the finger prints on the package to Ahmed Arafat, she was at a dead end connecting the hand's finger prints to any known human. Rick Sears dropped by to see how the tests were going and to remind Mary Beth that the hand should be shipped to the CIA soon. "Talk to the hand, the face is not listening right now. I have one more test to run."

Mary Beth had found some residue under the nails that looked kind of funky. Today she would finally find the time despite her case load to run a trace analysis. What she was to discover would stun not only the usually unflappable Dr. Watson herself, but quite a few others as well.

The dirt under the fingernails could not have originated in the eastern U.S. Indeed it was typical of the Mediterranean area. Furthermore, the chemical analysis of the hand revealed a kind of preservative not used in the U.S. either. It too had a Middle Eastern origin. Ringing up Detective Sears, Mary Beth wanted to report immediately.

"I've reached a conclusion and need your permission to pursue something."

"Shoot, what have you discovered?"

"This hand is not a U.S. hand; it has been in Israel and probably comes from there. Both the dirt and the chemical analysis point to this. I want permission to contact Mossad and have them run the fingerprints."

"Go for it. In the meantime we're making Mr. Ahmed Arafat uncomfortable, hoping to force him to say who sent him the hand."

"Perhaps working from both ends we can meet in the middle!"

"My thoughts exactly. Keep up the good work," and he rang off.

The sun rose very slowly in Wadi Qelt not least because the walls of the valley were so high. This was indeed the valley of the shadow. But instead of death, the Arafats were experiencing new life and new freedom from worry. Jake's mother had immediately taken to the task of cooking for the monks and their families. Meanwhile Naomi had stepped up to the cleaning tasks, and had organized the laundry operation into a much more efficient workplace. The head of the monastery, Father Jerome, had been praising them both all week, but this morning he was running down the hall to the monastery kitchen with some urgency calling out for Mrs. Arafat.

"Mrs. Arafat, you must come at once. For some reason you have a call from Mossad; an agent insists on speaking only to you. Please come with me." Turning to her assistant, Deborah, she handed her a stirring spoon for the soup, and then moved quickly out into the corridor towards the Father's office.

"Hello, yes, this is Mrs. Arafat. How may I be of assistance?"

"Mrs. Arafat, I am very sorry to inform you of a sensitive matter. It seems your son's tomb, on the top of the Mt. of Olives, has been desecrated, not by graffiti, the usual problem, but it has been opened and something taken out. In fact this seems to have transpired a good while ago, and we would not have known to even look had we not received an inquiry from the United States. In any case, there is no delicate way to tell you this, but in fact someone has cut off your son's hand and made away with it. The rest of the body is intact, but there was this theft of his left hand."

The silence at the other end of line was deafening, and so the agent said, "Did you understand me?"

"Yes," said Mrs. Arafat, "but what sort of barbaric person would do this? Was it not enough that Issah was brutally murdered, but now this!"

"Well, you have every right to be very angry, but we intend to get to the bottom of this. I just wanted your permission to dust the tomb for prints."

"Yes, of course, whatever you need to do. By all means do it. And keep me informed. And please have the tomb properly resealed when you are done, and call Father Abbas to sprinkle some holy water on it thereafter."

"Yes, of course," said the agent and hung up.

As she turned to go back to the kitchen, dazed and confused she said to Father Jerome, "Even here I am not immune to the hand of fate. Father could you please say a prayer for my family and me now. I am a bit shaken up."

"Of course, my child, just sit here in this chair across from me, and we will pray." Closing the door, Father Jerome began his petitions on behalf of the Arafats.

Part Four

43

An Impressive Press Conference

A RT WAS SURFING THE few channels provided on his TV in the Galata Anemon Hotel when all of a sudden he found something that got his full attention. It was barely seven thirty in the morning, but there was Dr. Mehmet Ertegun standing squarely in front of several cameras and saying, "We have here one of the great finds in all of Turkish history, particularly if we are talking about finds that illuminate the early Christian presence in this land. What you see before you was once the home of the illustrious early Christian Bishop Papias. Indeed directly below us are the very bones of Papias himself. We have found sufficient inscriptional evidence to confirm the identity of this skeleton. Notice the remains of a slipper on the foot. But that is only half the story." With the press following in his footsteps, Mehmet made his way to the house of Papias.

"Follow me as we open this door in the back of the scriptorium, turn on this large light, and you will see something very remarkable indeed. I present you with perhaps the very first Christian underground church!"

There was a murmur, even amongst the cameramen and jaded reporters who were all too used to people making extravagant claims, but this time the results lived up to the claims.

"Did you find this on your own, or were you helped?"

"Well, of course, we are always working as a team and I worked with Dr. Marissa Okur who has since left the site, but in the main the discovery of the skeleton and the secret chamber are my work."

At this juncture Art just exploded. Yelling as he ran from his room and down the corridor to where Marissa was staying, he bellowed as he knocked on her door, "Marissa, open up quick! Mehmet is in the process of stealing our thunder while we are gone!"

Throwing open her door, she stood there thunderstruck while Art raced past her and turned on Marissa's TV. They both stood stunned as Mehmet explained to the press about his great discovery of Papias and his little underground church.

"Why that little scheming snake!" said Marissa. "He must have been plotting this for some days. Did he even mention your name?"

"Nope, not even once, and he only mentioned you in passing, implying it was regrettable you had left the site."

This loud conversation carried out the door and down the hall to Kahlil and Hannah's rooms. Hannah was the first to open her door and head in the direction of the voices. She raised her eyebrows and blushed when she saw both Art and Marissa standing in front of the TV—in their pajamas! Looking at each other, and the look on Hannah's face, Art and Marissa laughed. Marissa said, "Hannah, it's not what you think! Actually it's worse! Look! My co-worker is having a news conference in Hierapolis, obviously without us! He's claiming full credit for the 'find of the century!'"

"Oh, well," said Hannah, "that explains everything—even the pajamas. So what will you do about this?"

"Well I have some ideas, but right now, I need to get dressed."

"Me too," said Art, "sorry for disturbing you. Let's rendezvous for breakfast in half an hour."

"Okay, I'll alert my father. Never a dull moment with you two!"

The morning tour and lunch would include the Topkapi Palace, the Blue Mosque, and Hagia Sophia. Meltem, however, had been called to substitute on a local tour for a guide who had gotten ill, so the four friends were on their own.

"Honestly, I had no idea Mehmet had that kind of nerve and scheming mind," said Marissa. "I guess I'm just too trusting."

"Don't blame yourself, Marissa," said Art. "I've had suspicions about the man for a while, and it's my fault for not sharing them. But when I saw on TV the little chamber church inside the tunnel, memories came flooding back to me. Remember the pictures on my camera that you showed me in the hospital—I'm sure they are dated." Whipping out his camera, he found the time-stamped digital pictures.

"See, right there. At least there's proof that I was in the chamber. But this leads me to a horrible thought—someone, and surely it was not an accident, closed that very heavy stone door on the chamber while I was climbing down to the Plutonium. Someone who did not want me to emerge alive and well. Who could that someone be? I can think of only one person—Mehmet Ertegun!"

After a long silence, Kahlil spoke, "If you are right, this is a grave matter. I know you are already in contact with the antiquities authorities concerning your role in the dig, but you will have to have substantial evidence before accusing the man of attempted murder. Perhaps you can confront him, but I doubt he will see you. Right now it is his word against yours. What evidence do you have?"

Marissa replied, "I would really like to confront him and not go through the police. For a traditional Turkish male like him embarrassment is almost worse than legal punishment. Besides, you are right, we have little evidence. When Art was trapped, it was late in the day and most of the workers had gone home. No one would see Mehmet skulking around."

At that moment, all four heads turned sharply. All thoughts of digs and death shot from their minds. Before them rising 180 feet into the sky was the Hagia Sophia. Their minds automatically began to fill with history dating back to the 6th century AD. Weightier matters could wait.

44

The Wonders of Istanbul

Today's trip proved to be a high moment for Hannah and Kahlil especially since Art and Marissa were more than adequate tour guides. The symmetry and precision of Hagia Sophia, dedicated to the Wisdom of God, and the immensity of the dome led to stunned silence for the four pilgrims. Today it is a museum, but in days gone by Hagia Sophia was a magnificent Orthodox Christian basilica, the center of the Church in Constantinople, as Istanbul was once called. For the four, standing in the nave was like traveling back in time to the mid-6th century when the Byzantine Emperor Justinian called for the erection of the largest church in the world and so it remained for one thousand years. Art and Marissa were separately thinking how lonely it is in a Muslim world to be a solitary Christian.

]

Few of the mosaics remain after hundreds of years of pillaging and destruction. One, however, stands out in the crowd—Christ Pantocrator—Christ Almighty or Christ Ruler of All.

All four appreciated the beauty of the Byzantine blue-robed Christ (blue being the color of purity) who seemed to be personally casting his blessing upon them.

Their next stop was the Sultan Ahmed Mosque, known by everyone as the Blue Mosque.

It seemed fresh and new compared to Hagia Sophia despite having been built in the 1600s. This was the height of the Ottomon period, which extended from 1299 to 1923 when democracy brought Turkey into the modern times.

Once inside, the four were compelled to be quiet for other reasons. Many had come in to pray—each upon his own prayer rug, each surrounded overhead by the magnificent chandelier. Quietly they examined the walls covered in the beautiful blue Iznik tiles that made this mosque so famous.

Outside, the call to prayer—the *adhan*—was being melodiously chanted from the minaret. Five times a day the *muezzin* reminds all Muslims that prayer is essential to daily life. More people hurried to the mosque stopping only for ritual ablutions at the outdoor water spigots. The four strolled around the courtyard and found venders with hot bread and cold drinks just outside the main gate—a refreshing break before heading on to the Topkapi Palace.

From the Galata district where they were staying they had seen the Palace in the distance. Now they were striding the grounds occupied by the Sultans for over 400 years. Such grandeur, and built before Columbus even sailed the ocean blue! They explored the palace grounds, a maze of gardens, fountains, and buildings housing the treasury, china, ornamental gowns, and so much more to tell the story of the Ottoman Empire. They knew they could spend days here but decided to get away from the tourists and sit by the walls overlooking the Golden Horn, the waterway separating the European side of Istanbul from its Asian side. "Imagine a city occupying two continents!" marveled Hannah.

The day was dashing, by which meant a late lunch at one of Marissa's favorite sidewalk cafes where they served traditional Turkish foods especially köfte, döner, börek and gözleme, not to mention Art's favorite the pepper dolma.

Of course Hannah and Kahlil often prepared some of these same items with slight variation in Jerusalem because the Ottoman Empire had left its cultural mark there as well. But the Turkish doner kebabs were the best anywhere. Pretty soon it was time to head back to the Galata district and their hotel for some quiet time before a late evening dinner.

Marissa had been somewhat preoccupied during the morning tour, not only because she had seen all these sights many times before, but also because she was thinking hard about how to talk to the ultimate supervisor of her archaeological work, Abdullah Koruturk. He was a fair man, but also a bit stern, and did not like to be manipulated in any way. Too many years of *bakshish*, or reciprocity conventions, had taken their toll on him.[1] So Marissa had to be careful how she approached this discussion, not least because both her co-worker and Abdullah were males, with rather typical male egos.

---

1. Bakshish: A Persian word for a gratuity. These gifts are demanded by all sorts of officials in Turkey, Egypt, and elsewhere in the Middle East, more as a claim than a gratuity.

45

Romantic Interludes

THE EXCLUSIVE RESORT ON the coast of Monaco, which Manny booked for the honeymoon, was known for its stellar service and even better food. The Chateau d'Marquis had been built in the fifteenth century for a French Marquis exiled from France for some undisclosed reasons. However, to take one look at the home, it hardly appeared that this gentleman suffered or lacked for anything while in exile. The mansion and its grounds were magnificent and the lawn went all the way down to the Mediterranean where an artificially constructed white sand beach was populated with beach umbrellas, recliners, a bar, and a dock with waiting sailboats. Manny and Grace were sipping sodas on the sparkling sands. Grace was also reading *The International Herald Tribune* when suddenly she sat up and said, "Oh boy, that can't be good!" to no one in particular.

"And pray tell what could perturb my beautiful bride on so glorious a morning as this?" asked Manny.

"Do you remember that Marissa is the head archaeologist overseeing the dig at Hierapolis? That's where Art was working also until he got hurt in the tunnel. Well, today's paper presents us with a man named Mehmet Ertegun who claims to have discovered Papias's bones and an underground Christian church connected to his house somehow. It looks to me like a case of 'when the cat's away, the mice will play.' There's no way Marissa authorized a press conference like this without being present. This guy seems to be taking credit or taking over or both, while Marissa is conveniently away traveling with Art. This does not bode well!"

Manny was only mildly interested in this whole matter, but since he was totally interested in Grace, he feigned shock and outrage. "Well that will never do; I hope she takes him to task as soon as she gets back to Hierapolis. For sure there will be some fireworks. Marissa Okur reminds me a bit of you—a take charge kind of gal."

"Indeed, and I think I can hear Art's blood boiling all the way from Istanbul."

"The only thing boiling out here in this sun is me. How about a quick dip in those azure waters over there my love and an afternoon sail?"

"I thought you'd never ask," smiled Grace, and they took each other's hand and walked into the water together.

It was clear how smitten Art had become with Marissa. Kahlil could see it; Hannah could see it; even Art knew it. Kahlil and Hannah had gone back to their rooms after the long tour. They wanted to rest up before dinner in the beautiful restaurant on top of the Galata Tower built in the 1300s by Italians from Genoa. With its 360-degree views of Istanbul it provided a beautiful setting for dinner.

Art was also resting, and barely heard a soft rap on the door. He opened it to find Marissa —and she wasn't smiling. "Arthur, how about you and I go for a little walk down to the park across from the Tower, please?"

"As you wish. Why do I have the feeling we are about to have a very 'serious talk'?"

Marissa just smiled enigmatically. "Shall we meet in the lobby in about ten minutes?"

It took Art no time to get ready for his date with destiny, or at least with Marissa, and his premonition that this was to be a religious discussion would prove to be right. It took no more than ten minutes for the two of them to walk down the sidewalk on a beautiful sunny day to the park where there were nice shade trees and benches. Art was apprehensive but still smiling, so greatly did the presence of Marissa affect him in a positive way.

As they sat down, Marissa took hold of Art's left hand with both of her hands, and looked right into Art's Carolina blue eyes. Her own chocolate browns seemed to bore holes into Art's head and heart, and then she began slowly. "Art you know I grew up in a secular, modern Muslim family. And, you also know that I moved to Boston with my family."

"Thus far, no surprises," said Art apprehensively.

"What you do not know is that while I was in Boston I made quite a lot of Christian friends, and ended up going with them to the historic Park Street Church."

"I used to attend that church once in a while when I was in divinity school actually," commented Art hoping to make a connection.

"I didn't just attend the church as an interested outsider. Through the ministry of Pastor Toms, I actually became a Christian." With this pronouncement she showed Art a small tattoo under her collar on the lower part of her neck—a tattoo of a cross.

Art sat in stunned silence.

"Before you get too excited, I must add how very difficult it has been for me to be a Christian at all, and pursue my career in archaeology in Turkey. In fact, if the government knew, I would have a very difficult time getting any job, let alone head of a dig. Being a woman was a big enough obstacle, but being a Christian woman would have been a bridge too far. I have not been a practicing Christian for a very long time. I don't talk about my background with anyone. There are days when I doubt everything, and can't find a reason to bother being a Christian. It would be easier just returning to the Muslim fold. I've got a lot to learn. I am nowhere near where you are in the faith!"

"Since this is the time for true confessions, in my job it's also hard to practice my faith—publically at least. If I'm in a Muslim country, it's illegal for me to proselytize. And when I'm traveling here it's nearly impossible to go to church, except when I'm in Izmir or Istanbul. I have a few Christian contacts there. Even in Israel I feel very much alone. My friends there are Jews and Muslims. Fortunately, I'm often accepted on dig sites precisely because I'm a Christian! I've been able to carry my Bible and other Christian resources without anyone thinking anything about my religion. It's just business to them."

They continued for another hour sharing the ups and downs involved in living out the Christian faith. They tried to find common ground and talk about the basics of the faith. Finally, Art said, "I think that if God has gone to all this trouble to bring us together, he can certainly work things out—if it's his will. Do you agree?"

"I do," said Marissa, "but I just don't see how right now."

"Well, maybe we could dig in Greece or Italy or somewhere where being a Christian is not an issue."

"I hadn't even thought about that possibility," mused Marissa.

"But maybe if we return and take over this dig in Hierapolis, the government will want you so much that they will have to accept you! The publicity alone should bring many more Christian tourists to Turkey and Pamukkale in particular!"

"Well . . . maybe," said Marissa doubtfully.

"In any case, first things first. You and I have some serious dating to do! And I would like to meet your family. And maybe my Mom will come over to visit Turkey and meet you. She's always wanted to visit the Middle East. We could be in for some really interesting times."

"Slow down! For now I would like to just sit here for a little while, be with you, and savor this moment." Art answered by leaning over and giving Marissa a truly wonderful kiss.

"You are just right for me right now," said Art. Melissa returned the compliment with further kisses. Even the casual passerby would recognize two people falling in love. Art and Marissa, in this moment, were quite happy to let the rest of the world pass them by. Indeed, they hardly noticed that a full two hours went by with them just basking in each other's gaze and conversation. Time to end the day with dinner at the Galata Tower.

46

Short and Long Distance Calling

WHEN THE PHONE RANG early and Detective Sears told Joyce he must speak with Jake at once, there was so much angst in his voice that Joyce knew this would be a difficult conversation. Handing the phone to Jake she simply said, "It's for you, dear, and it sounds important."

"Mr. Arafat, I have some rather grave news to report. In fact, it is grave robbing news. But first, are you aware that Ahmed, the shop owner over at the Mediterranean Market, is a relative of yours?"

"I honestly did not know that. Does that mean he is an Arafat then?"

"Indeed, but from Hebron, not Bethlehem."

"That explains why I've never met him; I have many cousins down that way, but we never visited Hebron mainly because my mother is a Christian. Plus, there are perennial troubles in Hebron between Jews and Muslims."

"Thank you for explaining that. But now I have to give you the really bad news. It seems clear now that your brother's tomb was opened some time ago. The severed hand belonged to your brother, I'm sorry to say! It was taken from his gravesite."

At this Jake gagged, ran to the sink and threw up while handing the phone to Joyce as he went by. She spoke into the phone saying, "What in the world did you just tell the boy that so badly upset him Detective?"

"I'm sorry Ma'am, but I had to give him some very bad news. I think it best that he tell you when he can." At this point, Jake returned to the phone to resume the conversation. Joyce found a quiet place out of earshot. The Detective began by asking about the safety of his family. Jake promised him that they were safely living in a monastery near Jericho. Mossad knew about their whereabouts and was keeping a distant watch on them.

"That is good news. Do you know someone by the name of Muktar Sayyid?"

"Yes," said Jake. "He was part of the group that held Art West, Joyce's son, captive in Gaza."

"Jake, I'm going to reconstruct what I think happened. Bear with me! It appears Muktar pilfered your brother's hand at some point and put it in preservatives, mainly salts common to the Middle East. He sent the hand, packed in dry ice we believe, to Ahmed. Together they planned to extort money or threaten you or both. You rightly understood the symbolism of the hand; they may have assumed that you would even recognize the hand. We don't know for sure. Ahmed is still sulking—not talking. We could use a confession, but I think we have enough evidence to convict Ahmed and bring in Muktar."

"Thank you Detective. All of that sounds real to me. By the way, what will happen to my brother's hand? Can it be returned to its gravesite?"

"That's the least we can do. We can ship it to the authorities in Bethlehem or to Mossad if you prefer. It can then be returned to the gravesite. One more final question, and you will have to forgive this one, but I must ask for the record. Are you still sending money to Hamas or do you have any contact with Hamas whatsoever?"

"NO, a thousand times no to your question—and I would take a lie detector test if necessary!"

"Yes, I believe you would! The Bobcats have agreed to have a body-guard shadow you for a while longer. It does not look like Ahmed was working with anyone else here in the States, so when we extract a bit more info from him, and if there is no one else involved, we will be able to set you free at least! I might add, we have done a little checking with the Bobcats and your story is sound. Michael Jordan seems to think highly of you."

Jake blushed and said, "I am glad to hear it. I love that game!"

"Yes, well, we've noticed," said Detective Sears and then he rang off.

Jake found Aunt Joyce crying on the porch. She knew something was wrong. "Well Aunt Joyce, that's not the way I wanted to start my day," said Jake turning towards a worried woman. "The hand was in fact my brother's! But it will be reinterred in Jerusalem." And he proceeded to tell her the whole story.

~

When Art finally called his mother, it was late at night for him but seven hours earlier in mid afternoon for Joyce in Charlotte. He knew it would be a very long, but important, call when she started telling him all about the seriousness of Jake's recent problems. From there she went into Detective Sears's life history; however, at that point Art had made a real effort to interrupt.

"Mom, I have some important news to share with you also—some good news I hope," said Art slowly and carefully to make a strong point.

"Yes? Have you discovered another archaeological find of the century in Turkey?"

"Actually, yes, but even that is not the subject of this call. Mom, I have found a special woman in Turkey."

There was a pregnant pause and then Joyce said, "Come again. I thought I heard you say you found a woman, which surely is not what you dug up in Hierapolis."

"No, Marissa Okur is very much alive. She is a leading archaeologist at Hierapolis. And I want her to meet you at some point soon."

"Well, why not? I'm free for dinner," said Joyce laughing.

"Sorry Mom, we already ate, but Marissa is here with me right now and would like to say hello!"

Marissa then came on the line feeling rather awkward and said, "Mrs. West, it is a pleasure to meet you—or talk to you. I have heard many wonderful things about you from Art."

"Greatly exaggerated no doubt," said Joyce, though secretly she was pleased with this opening salvo.

"I won't take up a lot of your time with Art, but I just wanted to say I am looking forward to really meeting you before long. Art and I chatted about coming to Charlotte in September if that's suitable."

"Any time will be fine, my dear. I'm retired and on no schedule. Anyone who can get my vagabond son to come visit me in Charlotte will be high on my list of favorite people. Then you can tell me all about yourself and your family. Where did you say you were from?"

Marissa glanced at Art with a "rescue me" look and Art took over quickly. "I will send you a picture of Marissa and me enjoying the sights and sounds of Istanbul. I took this picture in the park at Topkapi Palace. Have Jake help you with the technology—it will show up on your computer. Trust me." After more promises and pleasantries, Art hung up.

47

An Afternoon at the Museum

MARISSA OKUR HAD INDEED called Dr. Abdullah Koruturk, the Director of Antiquities in Turkey, very soon after the initial broadcast. They planned to meet late this afternoon at the Istanbul Museum where he kept a branch office. She told him it was rather urgent and had to do with the dig in Hierapolis.

The Istanbul Archaeology Museum was built to house the remarkable, so-called "tomb of Alexander" from Sidon, though really it was a replica of Alexander's actual tomb. This did not make it any less remarkable in appearance, though it lessened its historical allure to some degree. But while Art was showing Hannah and Kahlil around, Marissa went straight to the back of the building just inside the gates of the grounds to meet Abdullah.

After the usual greetings, Abdullah pointed to a chair opposite his desk. His office was very large, built during the early years when Attaturk was President, and it had a huge high ceiling and a grandeur to it all its own. It was easy to be intimidated in such a place, but Marissa had mustered up all her courage and began to speak.

"Dr. Koruturk . . ."

"Please call me Abdullah," said her boss rather surprisingly.

"Abdullah, we have a two-fold problem at the Hierapolis dig site. First, I must report to you that the press conference yesterday was *not* authorized by me. I never knew about it until it came on the TV. And I have reliable witnesses to prove that. Did you know about it in advance?"

"No, and frankly it caught me by surprise. I found out about it when a reporter from the *Turkish Daily News* showed up wanting comment at the very same time the news conference was happening. No one holds news conferences without clearing it first with me. The fact that you called yesterday to make this appointment was very interesting. Calls to Mehmet Ertegun have gone unanswered. That is why I am eager to hear your side of the story."

"Clearly," said Marissa, "I would *never* embarrass you that way. I was in the Galilee for a wedding, and then here in Istanbul, and I found out about the press conference plan only after coming here. Embarrassed is not the word. I was furious!"

"Go on," said Abdullah calmly.

"Second, I have no wish to shame the man, but Mehmet clearly wanted to steal all the publicity for this project and the work we have done. Not only did he say I had 'left the site' implying that I had little to do with the project, but also he left out our key consultant, Dr. Arthur West, a well-known archaeologist from the United States. He was there for another reason, which may be even more important than finding the home and skeleton of Papias!"

"What? You are saying there is more?" shot back Abdullah.

"Yes, indeed. We have three or four crucial papyri that were discovered in the scriptorium in the house of Papias that reveal new information about early Christianity, and confirm important things about its literature. The papyri, which you notice Mehmet hardly mentioned and with good reason because he has not studied them nor does he even have them, *are* the most important part of the discovery. Dr. West has been deciphering the papyri for us because his early Christian Greek is at the expert level, and there is much to tell. A press conference without some reference to these documents, now safely in a safe in Pammukale, I assure you, is entirely premature. Skeletons we have had before, and even underground churches we have had before, but significant Christian documents from the second century AD are something quite new!"

Abdullah was still looking down at his desk and taking notes. "Anything more you want to share?"

"I probably should not add this. I am no detective and have no solid proof. It is possible Mehmet attempted to commit murder!" Marissa blurted out.

Abdullah's head snapped up. His eyes widened. "Marissa, you are now on very shaky ground! Please explain yourself."

"I am saying that someone who didn't much like having a Christian scholar consulting on this dig attempted to seal Dr. West in the chamber behind Papias's house that leads down to the Plutonium. Art West was nearly asphyxiated by the gases in there. He was in the hospital for some days. The door to the chamber was shut by someone while West was in there exploring, albeit alone, which he realizes was a foolish thing to do. But I must stress that the heavy stone door into the chamber could not have closed itself or been blown shut. It weighs far too much."

"Marissa, these are serious accusations. Timing is everything. The police should have been called in long ago if you had such reservations," counseled Abdullah.

Marissa sighed. "As I said I am no detective. This was new ground for me. I can't prove that it was Mehmet or anyone else for that matter. But I know Mehmet was angry about West being handed the job of dealing with the manuscripts, as he complained to me about it in confidence. But I can prove nothing on this score, so I do not know what to do now. This has become more than a little problematic because now Mehmet is associated with 'the find of the century' and with Hierapolis, and he is seeking to make his reputation and become the face of this dig."

Abdullah quietly stared at Marissa for a long time mulling over all the information. He pursed his lips, touching them with his hands, which were in the folded prayer position, then sighed a deep sigh. "Based on what you have told me, and only on what you have told me, this is intolerable. I will try again to contact Mehmet. I will get his side of the story, of course; however, I will announce that I am taking full charge of the project, as is my prerogative. I *may* contact the local police to begin an investigation into your charges if you think that is necessary, but I will keep your name out of it for now. Let me clarify one thing. You are sure you did not leave the site permanently, turn over the project solely to Mehmet, or have anything to do with the press conference."

"I will stake my professional reputation and all I have done for archaeology in Turkey that I am innocent."

"Good. If you are innocent and he is guilty, then at best I will be sending him to the other end of the country. There is a tiny dig just beginning at the Simeon Stylites monastery outside Antioch up on the hill overlooking Syria. It is remote, and I think the chances are also remote he would find anything special there. *If* you are innocent, then you can have a proper press conference. *If* you are in the right here, then we will be back on the right track—right!?" laughed Abdullah

"Director, this is beyond even my best hopes of what would come from this conversation. If I may ask, please keep me apprised of your progress."

"I have much work to do on this matter. I have your number and I trust I will be able to reach you much easier than Mehmet apparently," said Abdullah. "What are your plans for now? I do not want you returning directly to the dig site until you hear from me."

"Along with Dr. West, I am acting as a tour guide for good friends from Jerusalem. But they will leave soon to Cappadocia, and we want to return to the Hierapolis area to retrieve and examine the papyri."

"Thank you for coming to me. It says much about your character, which is why I will entrust the papyri to you temporarily. However, they should be brought here eventually for safe keeping," said Abdullah as he arose to shake Marissa's hand, thus ending the meeting. As soon as she left, Abdullah was on the phone. And this time Mehmet answered amidst the background noise of clanking spades.

"Mehmet, this is Director Koruturk in the main office in Istanbul. I saw your press conference."

"Well, what did you think about what I have accomplished?"

Trying to keep the sarcasm out of his voice, he replied, "Remarkable, quite remarkable. But I need a full report from you—in person! Normally I am apprised of all finds at national dig sites *before* the news conference. So we have much to talk about. And I have a possibility to discuss with you about another dig."

"Oh, that is very good news," said Mehmet oblivious of impending disaster. "Thank you, sir. I have labored in obscurity here under that woman, Dr. Okur, and if not for my quick thinking I suspect that Westerner, Dr. West, would have leaked the news to the press and we Turks would not have gotten proper credit! "

"That is a very interesting assessment. We will discuss this in my office. It is a ten-hour drive, but I'm sure you will find a way to make it here by tomorrow afternoon late."

"I will be honored to visit you," said Mehmet.

"Informative," said Abdullah to the four walls of his office. "Mehmet certainly does not like Dr. Okur or Dr. West."

48

Suspects East and West

MUKTAR SELDOM BOTHERED TO shave any more when he got up in the morning. His wife refused to kiss him at that time of day anyway since his breath was so bad, and he therefore saw no reason to spruce himself up. The small house in which he lived on a back alley street off Manger Square in Bethlehem was only a short walk from the nearest little sidewalk café where the older men would sit, drink their Turkish coffee or apple tea, read the Palestinian newspaper, gripe about the general situation, play a game or two of checkers or backgammon, and then trundle off to work or home again. Muktar Sayyid was well known to this crowd, and his support for radical Hamas politics was equally well known. Some Palestinian Christians who frequented the same café would clear out when they saw him coming, as they were not looking for an argument to start their day.

On this morning, however, there was a new face at the Aziz café. It belonged to a young tanned man wearing a black bomber jacket. He sported a new beard, several days' worth of growth, and his jet-black hair was luxuriant. With his face stuck behind a newspaper it was not possible to get a full impression, but he was sitting off by himself minding his own business and sipping an espresso. No one troubled him.

Muktar barely noticed the man, as he was half asleep and his guard was down. He walked up to the counter and was greeted by name by the shop owner.

"So what will it be today, Muktar? The usual?"

"Why not?" said Muktar, "I am a man of regular habits."

Suddenly a third voice broke into the conversation from behind Muktar and said, "And it's precisely those regular habits which have just cost you dearly." The man with the new face said to the shop owner, "Just mind your own business. I am an undercover police officer." He quickly flipped out his Mossad credentials.

When Muktar attempted to shift his weight a bit to get a look at the man behind him, the officer grabbed his left hand which dangled by his side and handcuffed Muktar to himself.

"You're coming with me now, Mr. Sayyid," whispered the officer. "My partner is waiting for us in the car."

"May Allah strike you dead," said Muktar as he spat on the ground. A white panel van drove up quickly, and Muktar was shoved inside, followed by the officer.

"I knew it would come to this someday," said the shop owner to no one in particular. The regulars lifted their heads hoping for more, relief written all over their faces.

"If you keep sticking your nose into a beehive, eventually you'll get stung badly." At that the regulars sagely nodded their heads in collective agreement. They too had grown weary of Muktar the troublemaker who, despite all his big political rhetoric, had managed to improve none of their lots in life even a little bit.

"Mossad, no less!" informed the shop owner. At that, the regulars were finally impressed!

～

Back in the U.S., Ahmed Arafat was still in custody since no one had posted his bail. By now his story was coming unraveled. He had been shown proof that his fingerprints were inside the box. With Detective Sears staring holes into him, Ahmed had admitted receiving the package from a "friend" in Palestine.

"And did you know what the contents of the box were?" asked Rick.

"I knew it would be some body part, and the most appropriate one to send a thief is always a hand," replied Ahmed sheepishly.

"More to the point did you know whose hand it was?" pressed the Officer.

At this Ahmed hesitated and then said, "I knew Muktar was planning revenge on another member of the Arafat family who was seen as a traitor."

"You mean Issah Arafat, who was brutally murdered last year in Bethlehem—right? How exactly is it revenge when someone has already been murdered? Isn't his death enough?"

"Well, his family was still among the infidels so there were other family members who needed a warning about Allah's justice."

"And you saw yourself as the personal emissary of your version of Arabic justice?"

"Well each man must do his part for the cause," said Ahmed boldly this time.

"Even when it involves desecrating a grave and a dead person? Even the radical Imams frown on that—do they not?"

"Desperate times call for desperate measures," retorted Ahmed.

Though the detective had extracted enough information to send this case to the lawyers, he himself had one more twist to add to this drama. "I am pleased to announce to you that Muktar, your partner in crime, is now in the custody of Mossad. So I have to ask, Shall I send you back to face the justice of Mossad, or would you prefer the justice of us folks in America?"

Ahmed began to sweat and realized that he was unlikely to escape the noose, which was tightening around his neck. "Oh by all means I prefer American justice," he pled.

"How ironic since you have been lambasting it as the worst in the world while you have been incarcerated here. You better hope that we believe in justice and fairness far more than you do—you sick son of gun." And with that the Detective handed Ahmed back to his jailors.

49

Traveling To and Fro

O N THE SAME HIGHWAY, on the same day, but going in opposite directions, two cars passed each other and had they but known to look, they would have recognized the passengers in the other vehicle. Dr. Mehmet Ertegun, driving his small Turkish car, left Hierapolis/Pammukale in the pre-dawn hours and was driving hard on northbound roads by way of Usak, Eskesihir, and Yalova to catch the ferry across the Strait to Istanbul for his appointment with the Director. Coming in the exact opposite direction in a rental car were Marrisa and Art. Kahlil and Hannah were by now flying to Ankara to explore the region of Cappadocia. Very different thoughts were on the minds of all these travelers.

Mehmet was thinking about a promotion as director of some new dig in Turkey, and could hardly wait to talk to Director Koruturk about the matter. Marissa and Art were enjoying a countryside drive and feeling rather carefree now that the director was dealing with Ertegun. They were looking forward to getting back to Hierapolis and spending some quality time examining the Papias papyri.

Mehmet arrived in Istanbul quite weary after the very long drive, and checked into his small hotel near the Istanbul Museum. After freshening up and putting on his best suit, he climbed the hill to the gate at the entrance to the Istanbul Museum expecting this to be a triumphant day for his career.

After entering the Museum office complex, a secretary asked him to sit and wait until the Director was free. After forty-five minutes of nervous thumb twiddling, Mehmet was summoned into the Director's palatial office.

"Please have a seat," said Abdullah rather sternly as he himself rose and began to pace the floor. "I saw your press conference, and must say I was taken by surprise by it. Explain again why you did not notify me first before calling the press?"

Immediately Mehmet was backpedaling. "I am sorry, sir. In my excitement I forgot to give you a call, which in my understanding was just a formality in any case."

"Really? Just a formality to consult with the Director of Antiquities, your boss, the man who funds your dig, before you call in the press? I should think not Dr. Ertegun. We have to be very careful what we say to the press, as our reputation is on the line. Finally, I noticed that you said almost nothing about the papyri discovered at the dig in Hierapolis."

Turning red, Mehmet said, "You have heard about those?"

"Indeed, Dr. Okur has discussed the papyri with me, before going to the press I might add. I am wondering why you felt you had the authority to call a press conference without either her knowledge or mine?"

And now Mehmet began to stretch the truth and even lie. "She left me in charge of excavating the skeleton of Papias and since I was in charge she would expect me to make such decisions on my own. She would surely have supported the press conference. And besides she had left. I did not know when she would return. I felt the matter could not wait."

"The matter could not wait? The matter could not wait until Dr. Okur returned? You made it sound as if Dr. Okur had permanently left the dig—you knew she would be gone for only a week. It would seem that the only reason the matter could not wait is because you wanted to steal the limelight from Dr. Okur and perhaps from Dr. West, whom I gather you don't much like. Did you really expect Dr. West to leak the information to the press as you suggested? It seems that you are the one who leaked the preliminary, and incomplete, findings to the press."

And now Mehmet knew that the director had been recently talking to either Marissa or Art or both. He slunk down in his chair, now fearing the worst.

"Tell me, Dr. Ertegun, is this version of the story more accurate than the one you gave me on the phone?" Mehmet was glum and silent. "I will take that as a yes. By the way, what part of Turkiye are you originally from? Is it not the Hatay province?"

"That is correct," said Mehmet meekly.

"Then you will be pleased to know that I am transferring you to ancient Antioch on the far southern coast to work on the ruins of the Monastery of St. Simeon Stylites the Younger. You will discover I have provided you with help when you arrive. You will need to talk to Aziz in our office in nearby Antakya!"

"Thank you, sir," said Mehmet, but he had a bad feeling about this.

"Before you start on your very long drive from here to there, let me give you this warning. If I ever discover you had anything to do with the near demise of Dr. Arthur West, anything at all, your career is over, and indeed you will be prosecuted for attempted murder. So if I were you, I would mind my own business, keep my nose in the dirt there in Antioch, hope for some significant results, report to me regularly, and do not call any press conferences in the future without my approval. Have I made myself perfectly clear?" asked Abdullah hovering over the shrinking and sulking form of Mehmet in his chair.

"Very clear," said Mehmet in almost a whisper.

"You may consider yourself lucky to still have a job at all. Now get out of my office and out of my sight and start heading east."

Mehmet did not reply but simply picked up his hat and left quietly, closing the door behind him. His day of triumph had turned into a day of disaster.

50

The Demon Papyrus Revisited

THE HONEYMOON HAD COME and gone and Grace Levine Cohen was now back in her office at Hebrew University quietly examining the photocopy Sammy had sent by fax of the demon papyrus. There was something unusual about this papyrus and its script, but Grace couldn't quite put her finger on it.

Phoning Sammy at the IAA headquarters Grace drummed her fingers on her desk waiting for Sammy to pick up. "Sammy Cohen here."

"Well this is the first time we have had a Cohen to Cohen chat!" said Grace.

"Welcome to the priestly clan of Cohen, and again congratulations on your marriage. The ceremony was wonderful and fortunately the weather cooperated. No sudden squalls on the Sea of Galilee that day! How can I be of service, Grace?"

"Sammy, this script on the demon papyrus is a bit too perfect. Maybe it was copied from something else; I can't put my finger on what. But it leads to the question of whether you did any radiocarbon dating?"

"Not yet. We need a very good reason to do that considering the time and expense. Are you thinking maybe that it's from a much later period than the menorah itself?"

"Yes, that's precisely what I'm thinking. Is it possible to test both papyri that were found in the menorah?"

"It is possible. Accelerator Mass Spectrometry tests use much smaller samples, are more precise, but are naturally more expensive. We have to send out the samples and the results are returned in about one month. Meanwhile I will have my best technicians look more closely at the papyri. We really haven't had time to study it yet. There may be clues as to age that we missed the first time around."

"I think this find is worth the effort," said Grace. "Let me know what you decide." After more banter about the wedding and even the honeymoon, Grace signed off, picked up her tote bag and headed for her little sports car. Her plan was to enjoy coffee and lunch at Solomon's Porch, and then to spend the afternoon showing wedding pictures to Sarah. The drive was a short one, and parking was difficult, but finally Grace found a spot behind Ben Yehuda Street near the back entrance to McDonalds—Sarah's competition. She walked down the narrow alley to Ben Yehuda, turned the corner and discovered a line of customers extending right out the door. Sarah was doing a land office business at Solomon's Porch! Since she had an appointment with Sarah herself she squeezed into the shop and headed up the stairs to her usual perch in the window overlooking the busy street below. A waitress appeared saying, "Miss Sarah will be with you shortly; what can I bring you?"

"How about a white chocolate mocha—tall—and the *Jerusalem Post*," requested Grace.

"Sure. Back in a minute," said the waitress and she set off as quickly as she had appeared.

In less than five minutes Grace was enjoying a coffee cup full of mocha with whip cream on top. The morning paper seemed to have few revelations of interest to Grace, though she did notice the brief mention of some archaeologists down south of Jerusalem who thought they had found a piece of pottery with paleo-Hebrew script dating to the monarchy period. If so, this would be the oldest such piece of Hebrew script thus far found. "We shall wait and see," said Grace to herself. Another five minutes drifted by and then Grace heard, "Well girlfriend, you look mighty tan and neat. I guess honeymoons agree with you?"

"Any time you go to a resort in Monaco, and you can't have a good time, well, there is something seriously wrong with you. Yes, it was just great, and I have the pictures to prove it, so have a seat. But let's order since I am famished, having skipped breakfast," suggested Grace. "You seem to have really turned the corner businesswise with this shop Sarah. Mazel tov!"

"Thanks Grace," replied Sarah with a sigh. "Believe me, it has been an uphill struggle in so many ways, but we seem to be winning. We have outlasted some of the American chains, though I'm still competing with

McDonalds with their new line of so-called 'designer premium coffees.' We, however, seem to be the coffee shop of choice on this side of town. I've hired new servers."

"Which, considering the economy, is a nice problem to have," replied Grace.

The waitress emerged from below with an order pad. Reubens for both were promptly written down. Grace then brought out a stack of wedding proofs from which she had to pick no more than fifty for her final wedding album. But for now the girls happily pored over pictures, selecting some and nixing others. Two hours slipped by easily, and then it was time for the drive back to Tel Aviv where, she suspected, Manny was waiting for a home-cooked meal.

Early the next morning, the phone rang. "Well your woman's or scholarly intuition deserves full marks," said Sammy. "My team spent the afternoon doing their own analysis of the Latin papyrus and they feel certain it is first century. But closer inspection of the demon papyrus suggests that it is not. They believe it only has the appearance of age, and may even be twentieth century. We may still have it sent off for analysis, but it appears we paid for either a late copy or, worse, a forgery. I hope it isn't the latter!"

"Wow! I wouldn't have guessed it was that recent, but that means the papyrus has to do with the more recent history of the menorah. What exactly do we know about that?"

"Well, all we know for sure is that Kahlil el Said bought the menorah in the seventies apparently from Yigael Yadin, but I will need to check back with him to see if his memory can conjure up any more details. I have a copy of the file as does the Museum."

"My intuition is tingling again. Do you suppose that this piece could be some of the WWII booty looted from synagogues in Europe? Do you suppose that maybe a Jew involved in the Holocaust put that scroll in the menorah?"

"That's one idea. We will need evidence to support or refute it, but I will start by talking with Kahlil again. I think he is back from his Turkish tour."

"Whoever created this papyrus and then added the magic poison dust wanted its owner or possessor dead, I would wager."

Sammy promised to get back to Grace and then rang off.

"Some mysteries just keep getting more complex," mused Grace. "I wish Art were around."

The Church of St. Papias

MARISSA AND ART DROVE through the countryside for two days visiting small villages and just enjoying the scenery and food. Sometimes lunch was at a roadside stop where fresh fish were pulled from the owner's pond, immediately grilled to perfection, and served on picnic tables. The director called to confirm that Marissa had the go-ahead to return to the dig site and begin work again. He promised that Mehmet would never set foot on the property again. They also agreed to drop the inquiry into Mehmet's alleged plot to get Art out of the way. With multiple projects needing attention, Marissa and Art agreed that the first order of business in Hierapolis would be to carefully exhume the skeleton. It would go to the little museum in Hierapolis for the time being. Further, they must document the house, scriptorium, church, and underground chamber. The final, long-term project would be to decipher the papyri.

On this first morning back, Art and the workers pried the stone door at the back of the scriptorium wide open. Fumes could now readily escape and some natural lighting could penetrate the darkness. Lights and cameras on tripods could now be brought in so that a full photographic record could be made of the underground church chamber to the left of the corridor that led down to the Plutonium. Once that work was completed, then Marissa, with the director's approval, would call the press and give them access to the church itself, with Art explaining its significance. They would also, as a sort of tease, tell the press there was much more than a skeleton and a chamber found. This way the media coverage would not get ahead of the systematic scholarly work, and the archaeologists would be prepared for whatever questions that might arise.

Art had been scurrying in and out of the chamber taking pictures from this and that angle and making notes all morning. Marissa had been dealing with the skeleton and the clean up of the room where the skeleton had been found. Art had also been working on the lintel with the word ΙΧΘΥΣ and the remarkable Christian design on it. At lunchtime they rendezvoused to discuss progress.

Over what the English would call a Ploughman's Lunch—bread, cheese, pickles, salad, but apple tea rather than apple cider—they gushed about the morning's work. Art said, "You've got to see the chamber! There's a long low table with two benches on either side. This was surely a place where meals were eaten and perhaps even the Lord's Supper in the context of the meal. In short, it's a dining room. But in another area, we have more of a meeting room complete with what looks like an altar in the back. Early Christian worship, with aid of candlelight was probably held in there. I guess you could call it an early purpose-built church."

"In that case," piped in Marissa, "let's call it the Church of St. Papias. What I'm wondering is how they combated the fumes that must have been in there. I'm ordering oxygen masks so that we can lead an expedition down the steps to the bottom. Maybe there is a door to the Plutonium chamber that was closed to seal off the fumes. The director will be visiting soon. I can get him to bring the equipment. In fact, he may be up for the adventure also. It must be boring being behind a desk all day!"

"And I am thinking once bitten, twice shy," laughed Art. "I'm still having nightmares about that staircase. And did I ever tell you the story about the Lazarus tomb when . . ."

Marissa interrupted with a big smile. "More than once! Maybe we should leave you behind on this one!"

"Okay," said Art. "Why would Christians in any case build a stairway down from their meeting place into the Plutonium? Could it be because they were pneumatics who still believed in the living voice of prophecy? Maybe some of their ideas about prophecy were learned from the prophets of the Temple of Apollo here? We know that Christians filled in the front entrance from the Temple of Apollo to the Plutonium in the 4th century to make clear that the pagan gods were dead and gone."

"Well, that makes some sense I suppose," said Marissa. "In any case, no one, and I do mean no one is going down those stairs without a mask and oxygen tank."

"Right chief, you're the boss of this dig."

"And don't you forget it and go freelancing like Ertegun," laughed Marissa, "or someone will be sending you to the boondocks for insubordination."

Art made a silly face and said sarcastically, "Oh I wouldn't think of freelancing! That would be totally out of character."

The banter went on back and forth for a minute or so more, but secretly both were thrilled to be working with each other, and without a shadow hovering over either one of them, for the time being.

52

The German Connection

KAHLIL HAD SETTLED BACK into his antiquities routine, and even though he now had millions in the bank from the sale of the menorah and the papyri, he had no intentions of quitting his day job. When the phone rang this particular afternoon, Kahlil was busy cleaning some brass objects with brass polish. "El Said Antiquities, how can I help?" said Kahlil in his famous baritone.

"You sound like Darth Vader this afternoon," said Sammy joking.

"I should hope not. What can I do for you?"

"We are hoping to track down more information on the menorah. Your records and memory show that you bought the menorah from Yigael Yadin. There is nothing else in the file to indicate otherwise. And there is nothing in the file to indicate where he got the menorah. We guessed it was from a dig site somewhere. Now we need to do some detective work and figure out just where! Grace has some interesting ideas but I'll surprise you with those later."

"I have been trying to remember that day so long ago. My memory is not what it used to be obviously. And in those days I had local helpers who were hardly as good as Hannah at keeping records. Give us both some time to look further through records from the 1970s to see what we can find. But I make no promises, my friend."

"Whatever you can do—I will wait patiently to hear from you one way or the other," promised Sammy. "I would like to have lunch with you soon so that you can regale me with stories of your tour through Turkey. It is certainly high on my list of places I must explore. Everyone tells me I should get out of the office more often, but I think they are just tired of looking at me!"

"Vacations are good for the heart and soul," counseled Kahlil. "I will call you as soon if I find anything useful."

Kahlil called Hannah, explained the situation, and the two of them set off on another exploration of sorts—through dusty files long since stacked away. Days later they hit the jackpot. A small letter from Yadin was tucked into the wrong folder. Kahlil must have read it so many years ago that its memory had totally faded. Then he gave it to a clerk who was less than accurate in his filing abilities. But there it was—a handwritten note claiming that Yadin had not found the menorah at any particular site. Quite the contrary. The menorah had been given to him by a European dealer, not a local individual, to be sold in Jerusalem and that dealer had gotten it from a German with an odd name—Schickelgruber—Edmond Schickelgruber—from Passau, Germany.

Sammy was sitting in his office when Kahlil called and related what he had found in the files. Sammy seemed very subdued. "Do you have any idea who Edmond Schickelgruber was?"

Kahlil replied, "No, should I?"

Sammy quietly replied, "Being Jewish, I know this history in some detail. I believe that Yadin received the menorah from a dealer who got it from none other than Adolph Hitler's younger brother! Hitler was born Adolph Schickelgruber and his family moved to Passau from just over the Austrian border when he was very young. Edmond would have been three to five years younger than Adolph and he grew up entirely in Passau. It was thought that he died of measles as a youth, but there were no death certificates or burial records anywhere to confirm this, so there have always been speculations that he survived. I guess we now know that he lived to a ripe old adult age, unless this man was simply posing as Hitler's brother, but why would anyone in their right mind pretend to do that after WWII and the Nuremburg trials? That makes no sense."

"So you are saying that this menorah may have been Nazi booty, stolen from some European synagogue at some point?"

"It is certainly possible. I doubt we will ever know where this alleged Schickelgruber got this particular menorah. And this makes the demon papyrus all the more interesting. Was there some Jewish person trying to poison the owner of this menorah?"

Kahlil was quite shocked by this revelation, and even feeling somewhat guilty for taking money for this menorah. He said to Sammy, "I bought this in good faith, not knowing what you have just told me. I feel a little strange about having sold the menorah for such a sum now. I have no desire to keep blood money of any sort."

Sammy reassured Kahlil, "As you say, you dealt in good faith, and you had no idea who the seller really was, nor do we still know for sure where this came from. But now that we have a clue, I intend to begin to research the matter, starting with the evidence of synagogues in and around Passau in the 1930–40s. In the meanwhile, as your name has not been made public in the sale of the object thus far, we will keep it that way. I can imagine that some reactionary Jews might blow up at the notion of a Palestinian Arab making money off a Jewish menorah that had been stolen by the Nazis. That's one too many negative associations for some. Some stories are better left untold. I am your friend, Kahlil, and we must continue to work side-by-side in this divided city. I have no desire to stir up resentment or wrath against you. This menorah has an illustrious origin. We may not need to reveal all its history."

"Shokrun," said Kahlil, "I feel a little less uneasy now." And as he hung up he said to Hannah, "You are not going to believe who once owned that menorah!"

53

Arrival in Antioch; Hermeneutics in Hierapolis

A NTIOCH ON THE ORONTES was most certainly off the beaten track and barely in Turkey at all. Sitting right on the Syrian border, one had to want to go there. While it was a thriving metropolis in the time of Peter and Paul, today it was a city of no particular modern distinction, its fame resting entirely on its ancient Christian and Greco-Roman history. When Mehmet arrived in Antioch completely worn out from the long drive from Istanbul, he went straight to the tiny office of Aziz on the main street. The door was open and flies were buzzing over a plate of half-eaten kebab. Mehmet stepped further in and heard a toilet flushing. Out marched Aziz, a little man wearing dark trousers with suspenders.

"Yes?" said Aziz.

"I am Dr. Mehmet Ertegun. I was sent by Dr. Koroturk to supervise the new dig at the monastery just on the edge of town."

"Ah yes," said Aziz, brightening up. "I saw you on TV just this past week. Congratulations. I guess you plan to make more history here in Antioch?"

"Perhaps, with your help," said Mehmet trying to ingratiate himself.

"My younger son, Sharif, will be your assistant and I have been authorized to give you a set of tools."

Going to the back of the building, Aziz came back huffing and puffing carrying two small spades and a pick. "My older son, Omar, will be expecting you tomorrow morning. He has studied archaeology and is quite knowledgeable about the site and its long history. I personally will show you the way."

"And this is all the assistance I will have?"

"Yes, that's all there is in the budget you see, but then this means you get all the glory with whatever you find!" smiled Aziz.

"You are joking, right?' said Mehmet indignantly. "I am a pottery expert from Istanbul University. I do not dig. I analyze. We will need several strong men if there is digging to be done!"

"I am so sorry but that is beyond our means. You will have to discuss the budget with the director," said Aziz calmly as if he knew more than he was letting on. "Omar is quite capable of helping you dig, and he is a good lad. Oh, I am also sorry to inform you that you will be boarding in the smaller hotel down the street, the Scimitar, not the Grand Hotel."

"Let me guess, because of the budget," said Mehmet.

"You are a quick learner!" smiled Aziz feeling fully in charge of this situation. "So welcome to Antioch. Here is your voucher for the hotel and the meals there."

Mehmet snatched the papers from the hand of Aziz, crammed them into his pocket, took the tools and marched out the door without the usual amenities. He threw the spades into his trunk and grumbled too loudly, "I swear I will kill that woman if I ever see her again." Aziz heard this clearly from an open window.

≈

The skeleton had been nicely laid out in a lengthy container in the back of the Hierapolis Museum. The notion of an airtight container, like those provided for the mummies in the Cairo Museum, had been suggested, but at the moment there were no funds or real need for such an extravagance. The lintel or beam with the inscription had also been taken to the museum for safekeeping. Already a debate was being carried out between Marissa and the antiquities director concerning two options: an upgrade to the Hierapolis Museum or a new room at the National Museum in Istanbul to house the whole Papias collection. Marissa was pleading the case for keeping it local by suggesting that if it was properly publicized the exhibit could pay for itself, enticing many more tourists to the Denizli Province.

Meanwhile, Art, now ensconced in the tent that once belonged to Mehmet, was pouring over copies of the manuscripts. The originals, of course, were now at the Museum—cool and dry. Art decided that the proper title for Papias's five-volume work would be, *The Exegesis of the Lord's Sayings* (Κυριακῶν Λογίων Ἐξηγήσις), mainly because this is the way Papias himself began the work. Papias saw himself not only as a conveyor of the sayings, but also as their interpreter. This morning Art was comparing what he found in Eusebius, and what he found in the scroll in front of him about the authorship of the earliest Gospel, Mark, and then what is said about Matthew's Gospel. He concluded that on the whole Eusebius had simply quoted Papias directly, while interjecting his own commentary at some points. The Greek which Art copied out in his own hand in order to separate the words that were all run together in the Papias scroll read:

καὶ τοῦθ' ὁ πρεσβύτερος ἔλεγεν· Μάρκος μὲν ἑρμηνευτὴς Πέτρου γενόμενος, ὅσα ἐμνημόνευσεν, ἀκριβῶς ἔγραψεν, οὐ μέντοι τάξει τὰ ὑπὸ τοῦ κυρίου η λεχθέντα ἢ πραχθέντα. οὔτε γὰρ ἤκουσεν τοῦ κυρίου οὔτε παρηκολούθησεν αὐτῷ, ὕστερον δὲ, ὡς ἔφην, Πέτρῳ· ὃς πρὸς τὰς χρείας ἐποιεῖτο τὰς διδασκαλίας, ἀλλ' οὐχ ὥσπερ σύνταξιν τῶν κυριακῶν ποιούμενος λογίων, ὥστε οὐδὲν ἥμαρτεν Μάρκος οὕτως ἔνια γράψας ὡς ἀπεμνημόσευσεν. ἑνὸς γὰρ ἐποιήσατο πρόνοιαν, τοῦ μηδὲν ὧν ἤκουσεν παραλιπεῖν ἢ ψεύσασθαί τι ἐν αὐτοῖς.

"And the presbyter would say this: Mark, who had indeed been Peter's interpreter, accurately wrote as much as he [Peter?] remembered, yet not in order, about that which was either said or done by the Lord. For he [Mark] neither heard the Lord personally nor followed him, but later, as I said, Peter, who would give the teachings according to the form of chreiai, but not exactly in a [rhetorical] arrangement of the Lord's logiae, so that Mark did not fail by writing certain things as he[Peter] recalled them from memory. For he had one purpose—not to omit what he heard or falsify them."

περὶ δὲ τοῦ Ματθαίου ταῦτ' εἴρηται· Ματθαῖος μὲν οὖν Ἑβραΐδι διαλέκτῳ τὰ λόγια συνετάξατο, ἡρμήνευσεν δ' αὐτὰ ὡς ἦν δυνατὸς

"But concerning the Gospel of Matthew, he said this—that Matthew on the one hand in the Hebrew/Aramaic dialect compiled [in an ordered arrangement] the logia (sayings) but each interpreted as he was able."

Fascinating reflections recorded by Eusebius, were also found virtually verbatim in the Papias scroll before him, but Art noticed that towards the bottom of the column there were a few further comments by Papias:

Now this Mark, was the one called John Mark, whose mother had a house in Jerusalem. While he had been a sometime companion of Paul and Barnabas, his real service to the Gospel came in being Peter's interpreter towards the end of Peter's life, and then the recorder of Peter's memoirs, in shorter form and according to the rules for expanding chreiae into narrative. Unlike the case with Matthew's Gospel, Mark chose, for the most part, not to interrupt the narrative with collections of sayings of the Lord. While Peter had tended to speak in Aramaic to the Jews, Mark, whose Greek was better, served as the translator and interpreter for Peter while he was in Rome. When Peter's memoirs were first taken down by hand, they were in Aramaic, and required translation and interpretation. It was Matthew who had compiled the Aramaic sayings of Jesus in an ordered arrangement, which only those who knew Aramaic could interpret. This was not a full Gospel, but only a collection of Jesus's main sayings and parables.

This passage was fascinating, and provided new and important light on the Gospels of Mark and Matthew. Among other things, it suggested that Mark's Gospel had been composed in Greek in Rome on the basis of Peter's Aramaic memoirs, while the so-called Q material is what Matthew had compiled in Aramaic. This explained many things, not the least of which was the evidence for Semitic interference in Mark's Gospel and his occasional citing of Aramaic phrases, but always with translation for his listeners who evidently knew Greek but not Aramaic. What followed this passage was a confirmation of what had long been suspected was Papias's views about the Fourth Gospel:

I have not been fortunate enough to meet the apostles themselves being born too late and in a different part of the Empire, but I did indeed learn from the elder John who taught me many things, and himself knew both the apostles and other eyewitnesses. For me the living voice of that John was the most important thing. From him I learned about the apocalypse and the millennium. He was not to be confused with John the apostle, who was one of the Twelve and who had been martyred earlier on as Jesus said he would be, thus fulfilling prophecy. And there is yet a further confusion which John the seer explained to me, namely the mystery of who the Beloved Disciple was, who was neither of the two Johns. I shall say more on this later, but here it must suffice to say that it was the elder John who assembled the memoirs of the Beloved Disciple, forming them into a Gospel after that Disciple whom Jesus loved had unexpectedly died in great old age. This is

how it came to be that that Gospel was called John's, even though
he was only the editor and interpreter of the Beloved Disciple, not
the originator of those traditions. The testimony of the Beloved,
in both his Gospel memoirs, and in his famous sermon, had influenced John the seer in his later writings when he wrote to the
churches near Ephesus once overseen by the Beloved Disciple.
Most importantly, even today one can see the memorial stele
in Ephesus to both the elder John the prophet, once exiled on
Patmos, and also the Beloved Disciple, who was not named John,
but rather Eliezer or Lazarus.

Perhaps nothing Art had ever discovered so moved and excited him
as this extended testimony about the origins of three of the canonical
Gospels. Here was firm evidence that an eyewitness testimony had been
included in all three of those Gospels either indirectly (as in the case of
Mark's Gospel based on Peter's testimony), or more directly by the inclu-
sion of Matthew's compilation of Jesus' sayings in the First Gospel, or
by the presenting of the full testimony of the Beloved Disciple, a Judean
eyewitness, whom the world knew as Lazarus. Here was more confirmation for the theories he had presented in Jerusalem two years before. The
Gospels were not anonymous tracts written too late, and too loosely, to
present us with eyewitness testimony. Indeed, as Luke himself affirmed
in 1:1–4, the Gospel writers were very careful to consult the eyewitnesses
and the original preachers of the word, some having had the privilege of
knowing them personally. Further, in the case of the Fourth Gospel we
have a person who was an eyewitness of Jesus's Judean ministry himself
as the source of the vast majority of the Fourth Gospel.

Marissa slipped quietly into the tent through the door flap behind
him and gave Art a kiss on the cheek.

"My, that's a first for me!" smiled Art returning the favor. "I think
the mystery of the origins of the earliest Gospels, at least in three cases,
is just about solved!"

"Wow," said Marissa with her arms around Art's neck, "and all this
before lunch. I am so impressed. It leaves little to do after lunch."

"Are you ever wrong about that," replied Art. "But a good start has
been made. As it turns out Papias is the key link back to John the Seer
of Patmos and through him to the Beloved Disciple, and the link forward to Polycarp and Ireneaeus, who may have been his understudies.
Furthermore, he seems to have known Philip the Evangelist's prophesy
ing daughters who also finished life right here in Hierapolis. They had

many tales to tell as well. Could it be that they all settled here because it was a place famous already for prophecy, what with its Temple of Apollo and Plutonium?"

Marissa shrugged her shoulders. "It might explain the connection between the Papias house and the Plutonium. Speaking of the latter, I think we should send a team down the stairway to see what's at the bottom? The oxygen tanks and masks arrived this morning on the supply truck. We should soon find out what further revelations the Plutonium might offer. I think the director is in Laodicea right now, but he is scheduled to come our way very soon."

"Let's hope it produces no more prophetic dreams about meeting Alexander in Hades," replied Art. "Let's have lunch and light the torches!"

The Synagogue of Passau

I N THE GERMAN CITY of Passau there still stands a pilgrimage church called the Church of St. Salvatore, built before the Lutheran Protestant Reformation in 1479 under the patronage of a powerful Prince-Bishop named Ulrich III. It is the only remaining medieval building in the city that is still intact. Before Bishop Ulrich laid the cornerstone for this church, Ulrich expelled Jews from Passau, after the trial of several of them for supposed desecration of some Eucharistic hosts. In fact the church was deliberately built right where a synagogue previously stood, and indeed over its remains. The final demolition of the synagogue seems to have included confiscation of its treasures.

Relying on the online work of Mitchell B. Merback who studied the matter in some detail, Sammy Cohen discovered that the new church was built either "on the site [of]" (*an der Stelle*) or, in the words of the famous broadsheet created around 1498 to commemorate the events, "from" the Jewish synagogue (*auß der juden synagog*), [and] dates to the earliest phase of the shrine's career. Secularized in 1803, sold off to become a saltpeter factory (!) in 1811, repurchased and renovated by the Bishop Heinrich von Hofstätter in 1861, damaged and again closed after 1945, the church now stands empty, confounding city planners, who cannot find a viable use for it, and tourists, to whom the building is sometimes pointed out, by local tour guides, as Passau's "former synagogue."[2]

2. This is a citation from an expanded version of a lecture given in April 2004 at the Society of Architectural Historians in Indianapolis by Mitchell B. Merback. The expanded lecture is available online under the title "The Vanquished Synagogue, the Risen Host, and the Grateful Dead at the Salvatorkirche in Passau" which can be found at http://peregrinations.kenyon.edu/vol1-4/articles/merback.pdf. The quotation is found on p. 8.

As a result of this investigation, Sammy conjectured that the menorah was taken from this medieval synagogue and passed to the church. However, the church after WWII stood empty, and its relics and artifacts were sold off. It was Sammy's thought that Edmond Schickelgruber had come into possession of the menorah during the hard times in Germany after WWII and many years later had brought it to Jerusalem. This would mean that it was not some sort of Nazi booty stolen from a synagogue, but possibly simply bought in Passau by the brother of Hitler. What then to make of the demon papyrus?

Sammy hypothesized that the papyrus had been inserted into the menorah prior to the sale to Edmond, perhaps to put a curse on the family that spawned the most famous anti-Semite in history—Adolph Hitler. And, as Sammy knew, there was irony in this, since it appears likely that the record showed that Hitler had some Jewish blood in his veins. The evidence is circumstantial, but seems convincing.

Getting out his old scrapbook on Hitler and his family, which the Cohens, who had emigrated from Germany to Israel before the war, had kept, Cohen found this entry:

1837:

June 7, Alois (Adolph Hitler's father) is born illegitimately from the 42-year-old Maria Schickelgruber, most probably to the 19-year-old heir of the Jewish Frankenberger family of Graz. (Maria had been employed by the Frankenberger family in Graz as a sewing-maid at the time she fell pregnant).

- Maria receives financial support up until Alois' birth, which now terminates with a lump sum payment.

- Alois' entry in the parish baptismal register leaves the name of his father *blank*.

- Maria Schickelgruber subsequently marries a Johann Georg "Hikler" [Hiedler], who later dies before her son, Alois, begins his career as an Austrian customs officer.

Whatever else one made of this, there is clearly an attempt to cover up the origins of Alois. Whether Adolph and Edmond knew this full story or not, and it appears likely they did, the Cohens had vowed to keep the story known, as Sammy's now deceased father had spent a good deal of his adult life after WWII as a Nazi hunter. This was a story that would not go away. But why would Edmond have a dealer sell the menorah in

Jerusalem—using Yadin as a co-between? Perhaps no one would ever know since the man was surely now dead. But whatever else one could say, the menorah had somehow come back to the right and the righteous hands through the most roundabout and unlikely of routes—through the hands of Adolph Hitler's brother in the 1970s and then through a mystical Muslim! Oh what a subtle web God sometimes wove, his wonders to perform.

After some thought and prayer, Sammy decided not to tell Amir Genoor about the background story of the menorah. It might unnecessarily and unfairly put the searchlight and heat of an investigation on Kahlil, who had been an honest merchant in Jerusalem for many years, and from whom the Museum and the IAA had benefited on numerous occasions when he had turned over or sold them artifacts, depending on their provenance and date.

Sammy remembered a time in the 1990s when Kahlil donated a precious Jewish oil lamp from the first century AD Burnt House museum, which had been stolen from the latter and sold to Kahlil under false pretenses and with a false date. Kahlil asked nothing; he simply called Sammy and turned it over in compliance with the Israeli law about precious artifacts that post-date the late 1970s. This was a contact and source Sammy did not wish to lose through unfair publicity. Still, it made the story of the menorah and its recovery worthy of an Indiana Jones movie script. "Maybe someday this story can be told, but not today, not now, and not while Kahlil and his daughter still run an important antiquities shop in Jerusalem," he said to himself. But now he could turn his attention to the demon papyrus, and ask the question, what sort of 20th-century Jew still believed in demons and curses? Who would put this in a sacred object like a menorah? "We may never plumb the depths of that mystery," said Sammy, scratching his head. "It's time for me to take a break, and get some lunch at Solomon's Porch."

55

Getting to the Bottom of Things

THE STEPS DOWN INTO the Plutonium were built of large stones, and someone had gone to a lot of trouble, a long time ago, to install them. The stones were not carved out of the natural rock, but appeared to be dragged in from elsewhere and laid in place. Art watched closely as their best assistant, Hakan, led a small team down the stairs. A cameraman borrowed from the Laodicean site followed Hakan closely. Others carried lights. All were properly fitted with oxygen masks. This was a big day, and standing with them was the director of the Laodicean dig— Besim Aksoy.

Aksoy was a tall man in his early 60s. His distinguished career in archaeology included work at the famous Ephesus and Miletus sites near Kushadasi. He had taken note of Marissa's work particularly at some of the Hittite sites around Hattusha, and had recommended her for the supervisor's task here at Hierapolis. This confidence was now paying dividends and reflected well on Besim also.

"You realize of course," said Besim, "that once the full scope of what you have discovered here, especially in regard to the manuscripts, gets out, it should increase the tourism particularly among the Christians. Hierapolis could become more famous than Laodicea, despite all our work over there."

Art replied, "Right now Christians are more familiar with Laodicea thanks to all the interest in the end times, than in a bishop of the second century. You are being too modest about your remarkable work at Laodicea."

"Thank you, Professor West," replied Aksoy, "but we shall see what we shall see. In any event all this is good for Turkish archaeology—very good indeed. Now if the government will just allot more funds to our work."

"If only," sighed Marissa.

The men had nearly disappeared out of site down to the bottom of the staircase. Marissa and Art could smell very faintly the gas seeping up from the Plutonium. Suddenly there was some loud discussion at the bottom of the steps, though it was indecipherable from this distance. Hakan was seen climbing with some dispatch back up the stairs. When he reached within five steps of the top, he stopped for a moment, out of breath. Taking off the mask he said to Marissa, "There is certainly an entrance into the Plutonium down there. In the chamber there is a niche carved out of the native stone presumably where the priests could sit before emerging to offer their prophecies. The gas seems pretty over-whelming, so I have no idea how they stayed down there for any length of time. It must have been shut tight while the Christians were here! The cameraman is busy taking pictures and shooting film. There are some bones down there, probably human remains. But I wanted to ask if we should shut the stone door down there on our way back, and block off the gas for now?"

"Dr. Aksoy, what do you think?' deferred Marissa.

"We don't want to seal the chamber just yet. We will send at least one more team down there to go over every inch of the lower chamber. Graffiti is easy to miss. The bones should be removed and dated. For now, let's just close the door down a bit. I agree with Hakan that eventu-ally the Plutonium must be closed and even sealed, especially if we want tourists to come and see this underground church. In fact, I'm going to suggest we put up an iron gate with a padlock at the top of the stairs, so there will be no more attempts to go down into the Plutonium. Better safe than sorry. Besides, someone could fall down those stairs. We don't want to be dealing with that!"

"Yes," said Art, "I totally agree. And we will have to build a ramp or walkway to bring tourists down into the Papias house and this chamber. Under those conditions, I can easily see bringing tour groups here."

The sound of the door creaking triggered in Art's mind the simi-lar sound he heard when he was trapped on the stairway weeks before. Putting the horrors of that moment out of his mind, he mused, "I am thinking that the House of Papias must have formerly been the house of a priest. Whatever you say about the Christian prophets here, they did not need a noxious gas to inspire them in their prophecies, and were unlikely to descend to that chamber to get in touch with the Holy Spirit. During their day, that door was closed tight!"

Marissa had a thought. "This means that the little carved notice in the stone at the back of the scriptorium saying 'to the Plutonium' was there before Papias ever arrived in this place. He must have bought the house, and then discovered the chamber and the stairs, and over some years Christians must have carved out the chamber for Christian use. The letter of Pliny to Trajan suggests indeed that there were occasional or sporadic persecutions during the time Papias was writing his Exegesis of the Lord's Sayings, and so I suspect the scriptorium and the chamber became a Christian refuge where the church met in such times. The problem was a growing one because of the refusal of Christians to pledge allegiance to the Emperor through worship in the Emperor cult, and there is evidence of the cult here. Notice who built the big gate out there near the Necropolis—Domitian! Patronage like that from an Emperor almost always set in motion reciprocity, in the form of honoring and worshipping the Emperor, in the early second century."

Art picked up that train of thought. "But what brought Christians to this city in the first place? Why had Philip's daughters settled here? Perhaps we will never know, but my suggestion would be this: the charismatic and prophetic movements of Christianity, of which Papias seems to have been a part, as were Philip's daughters, did look for places where the populous was receptive, indeed eager to hear about new prophecies, even prophecies about the end of the world. Hierapolis, the city of priests and prophets and indeed many Jews, was naturally such a place, hence the growth of the Christian church here in the late first and early second centuries AD."

"Professor West, this is a very interesting hypothesis. I wonder if we could ask you and Marissa to present us with a lecture at the Istanbul Museum at the end of the digging season. I am sure the Director would be delighted with this, and if you both gave the lecture it would show the spirit of co-operation now extant in Turkish archaeology," said Besim.

"Of course," said Marissa as Art nodded. "We would be honored to do that in August. But there is much more to document, photograph, and analyze before we call the press and give a public lecture."

"True, but I will go ahead and set things in motion," Besim promised.

As they were emerging back into the scriptorium Art quipped, "At least now, no one will ever say that working at this archaeological site stinks."

Besim did not catch the play on words, and seeing the quizzical look on his face, Marissa explained as they emerged into the sunlight.

"I see," said Besim. "Perhaps a little humor makes the hard work a little easier," he smiled.

"I guess it's a testimony to the fact that when Allah made archaeologists, he obviously had a sense of humor," said Marissa, and they all had a good laugh.

56

All Quiet on the Eastern and Western Fronts

S TANDING ON TOP OF the windy hill, a hill that his small car had barely been able to climb, Mehmet surveyed his new domain. A scowl came upon his face. Omar emerged from the car and started lugging two shovels up the hill to the monastery entrance. Two guards, smoking Turkish cigarettes, were chatting about the new

developments. The sun was rising higher over the Syrian territory just on the other side of this hill, and off to the right a horse was grazing on the tall grass which had grown everywhere around the neglected site. Sure enough, according to tradition, Mehmet could see a central column where Simeon Stylites the Younger (or Simeon the Stylite, AD 521–97) sat and preached to attract other ascetics to his monastery. Indeed, the word *stylite* is Greek for pillar. Simeon the Elder (390–459) was the more famous of the duo, but he lived near Aleppo over the border in Syria. Historians claim he climbed upon his pillar in AD 423 and remained there until his death 36 years later! Icons depict both of the saints.

Simeon the sequel apparently spent his whole life, even as a young boy, living in one or another tower which he had built for himself. Towards the close of his life Simeon occupied this pillar upon this mountainside near Antioch on the Orontes called the "Hill of Wonders" due to the miracles performed here. Some referred to the saint as Simeon of the Admirable Mountain. Despite all this, in Mehmet's mind he was investigating a second-rate Christian saint.

Mehmet found this whole neglected scene both depressing and inexplicable. What would lead a man to sit on a pole for years? It was a type of piety he in particular could not quite understand. And there was still the seething anger in his heart about his "promotion" to dig supervisor, which was really a demotion, sending him to one of the most remote places he could go and still be in Turkey.

Mehmet had read up the previous night on his computer what one historian had written about the original Simeon and Byzantine stylites in general. Edward Gibbon in his *History of the Decline and Fall of the Roman Empire* describes Simeon's existence as follows:

> In this last and lofty station, the Syrian Anachoret resisted the heat of thirty summers, and the cold of as many winters. Habit and exercise instructed him to maintain his dangerous situation without fear or giddiness, and successively to assume the different postures of devotion. He sometimes prayed in an erect attitude, with his outstretched arms in the figure of a cross, but his most familiar practice was that of bending his meagre skeleton from the forehead to the feet; and a curious spectator, after numbering twelve hundred and forty-four repetitions, at length desisted from the endless account. The progress of an ulcer in his thigh might shorten, but it could not disturb, this celestial life; and the patient Hermit expired, without descending from his column. (Vol. 4, Chap. 37)

Try as he might, since both Simeons, like Mehmet, had been of Arab extraction, Mehmet could muster no sympathy for these men, except for their apparent dislike of women. That he could understand. Omar was standing near a grove of olive trees impatiently waiting for orders. "Where shall we start?" he asked, prodding Mehmet out of his reflections.

"Let's start around the central column in there. Who knows? Maybe we will get lucky." But the guards who overheard this just chuckled to themselves and turned away. In their view Mehmet had no chance of striking archaeological gold here. He had been placed up on a remote hill, like Simeon Stylites the Younger on his column. The sun would soon beat down on the site. All was quiet on the eastern front of Turkey.

∾

Jake and Joyce's life was returning to normalcy. Jake was still followed by a bodyguard, also named Jacob, who looked like a Greek god chiseled out of marble, being 6'4" with bulging muscles everywhere and yet with flat abs from all the sit ups he did each day. Somehow the two Jakes had become friends, with the bodyguard even happily going to church with Joyce and Jake. Practice with the Bobcats had gotten more intense, and in the first pre-season game, Jake posted a remarkable seventeen points and ten rebounds, which caught the eye of the *Charlotte Observer* sports reporter once again. Another flattering article entitled "A Star on the Rise" was published the next day. Joyce and Jacob enjoyed watching this exhibition game, with Joyce asking the other Jacob question after question about the fine points of the NBA game and how it differed from college basketball.

"Well, let's think about three things. First, the pro game is 48 minutes long as opposed to 40 minutes in college ball. Secondly, in the NBA one gets six fouls before fouling out, as opposed to only five in college ball. Finally, the 3-point line is further out for the shooters in pro ball."

"I see," said Joyce, "so the pro game requires more fitness and skill, it would seem."

"Yes indeed," replied Jacob, "in fact most every player was the star of a team in college and a college All American, but now he plays against whole teams of All Americans. And yet, professional basketball with its eighty-two-game regular season does not inspire the same passion and loyal following that ACC basketball does in general. The season is just too long, and sometimes teams play listlessly for considerable stretches of the long season. Jake is going to have to learn to pace himself, even though in Tel Aviv he played a sixty-game schedule. He's more ready to play than American college players usually are, but still not up to the stamina level of NBA veterans."

"My, he really does need to exercise and eat right, doesn't he," marveled Joyce.

"Absolutely," said Jacob. "I work out with him at Gold's Gym, and he's in good shape, but he still doesn't eat quite right during the playing season."

"Okay," said Joyce, "I need to learn more about feeding an athlete."

"I know you will," said Jacob smiling. "I think I'll be relieved of my duties soon. Now that Ahmed is in custody pending trial, and his wife and family have closed up the Market and fled back to Palestine, I'm expecting a new assignment any day now."

"We will miss you, and you must come over for dinner some night," said Joyce. "We want to thank you for watching over us." And to the outside observer, the life of Jake and Joyce seemed quiet, perhaps not as quiet as the silence of a monastery on top of a Turkish hill, but nonetheless a satisfactory peace had descended upon their lives.

57

The Anonymous Trust Fund

KAHLIL HAD BEEN CONTEMPLATING for some time what he was going to do about all that money, and having consulted with Hannah,
he made a decision. He was going to fund Art West's digs but he wanted
it to be a surprise. He had called Grace for advice on how to pull off a
surprise of this sort with Art West. Her response was, "I don't know, but
we would like to chip in and help fund that work as well. I will talk to
Manny. His lawyers will have some bright ideas I'm sure."

Today Kahlil sat back with another cup of Turkish coffee and rethought the matter on his own. Maybe he could set up a biblical archaeological trust fund. The bank then would inform West that "you've got
funds" and he would be able to draw on them for his work in various
countries. With the cooperation of this or that Lands of the Bible government, and the assurance of funding, Art might be able to choose dig sites
not previously claimed; for instance, the unexcavated area at Colossae
in Turkey. Kahlil could picture Art's face when he discovered he didn't
have to raise funds for his summer archaeological work. As a professor,
he got paid to teach throughout the school year, not to go traipsing all
over foreign parts digging. This independent source of funding could be
a huge blessing and a relief all in one.

After many calls to Grace and with the help of Manny's lawyers,
Kahlil and Hannah settled on depositing one million dollars into a special account at Wells Fargo Bank in Charlotte. Mr. Richard Character, an
old friend of Art's from college days, would manage the fund. Kahlil and
Hannah both went to their local branch of the Eretz Israel Bank to make
the final transfer.

"How can I help you both today?" the manager said racing over to serve Kahlil and Hannah as they entered the bank lobby.

"We need to do a wire transfer of some funds to an account in the United States," replied Kahlil.

"Certainly. Let us go into my office. Where will we be sending the money?"

"Wells Fargo Bank in Charlotte, North Carolina," replied Kahlil promptly.

Sitting down in the office of the manager in a large comfortable chair, Kahlil settled in for a considerable wait, but in fact the matter went much smoother than anticipated.

"What is the number and routing code for the bank account please?' said the manager.

Kahlil handed over a piece of paper with the relevant data, which the manager typed into the computer program.

"And the amount from your account we are transferring?"

Hannah replied confidently, "One million U.S. dollars, or 3.75 million shekels. I believe that covers the rate of exchange this morning."

"Hannah is very good with these figures," replied Kahlil smiling.

The bank manager gulped and said, "So much, but as you wish." He hated losing this much capital so quickly.

Kahlil and Hannah waited for the signal that the money had been sent. "We are through with this transaction," said the manager. "Is there anything else I can do to assist you?"

"You have been most gracious," said Kahlil. "*Shalom.*"

"*Aleichum shalom,*" said the manager as Kahlil walked out of the office.

Later in the day when business hours were waning in Jerusalem but waxing in the eastern U.S., Khalil's cell phone alerted him by playing a Coltrane jazz number which Hannah had purchased for him at a ringtones website. "*Salam aleichum,*" said Kahlil.

"Good day to you as well," said Richard Character, who was not sure what Kahlil had just said. "I want you to know that the money is safely stored in the account. I will call Art West now to inform him of his big surprise, if you wish."

"And you can do this without giving in to pressure, should he insist on knowing where it came from?" said Kahlil a bit worried.

"Of course, sir. I've been a banker a long time and I can assure you that I can handle our mutual friend!" assured Richard.

"Thank you so much," said Kahlil, and there was a strong feeling of contentment that settled into Kahlil's heart at that very moment, and a big smile crossed his face. "Not so random acts of kindness are as much a blessing to the giver, as to the receiver," he said and he began whistling the tune on his phone as he headed down the road to the Damascus Gate for the daily walk that Hannah claimed he so needed to take.

≈

Art was hovering over his photocopies of the Papias papyri, and occasionally stealing a glimpse over at Marissa as she sat on the other side of the tent analyzing the still photographs of the bottom of the stairwell to the Plutonium. "Someone sure did want to get down to that Plutonium, and it is hard to believe so much work was put into that stairway just so a priest could occasionally get high on the gas fumes and be a pseudo-prophet. There had to be something else going on, surely."

"If so, we will probably never know what it is" said Art.

"You're no fun! Where's your spirit of adventure?" chided Marissa.

"You know what they say about curiosity—it almost killed the Art."

The cell phone on Art's belt put an end to this conversation. He flipped the phone and suddenly heard the Carolina fight song—"I'm a Tar Heel born and a Tar Heel bred and the day I die I'm a Tar Heel dead, so it's rah rah Carolina, lina, rah rah, Carolina, lina . . ."

Art interrupted, "Okay, I pledge my allegiance to the alma mater. Did I somehow forget to send my pledge to the alumni fund?"

"Greetings Art, this is your old friend, Richard Character."

"Dick! This is a pleasant surprise. How about them Tar Heels last year winning the National Championship?"

"Yeah, it was great. Sorry you weren't here to see it. We could have had courtside seats."

"Well, the work of a Bible scholar is never done."

"I'm glad you mentioned that. I'm calling to tell you that someone must love you a lot, because you now have a fund set up in your name for the sole purpose of doing archaeological work. You, Art West, are the beneficiary of a one million dollar trust fund."

"JUMPIN' JEHOSHAPHAT!" cried Art scaring Marissa out of her wits.

"I don't know about Jehoshaphat jumpin' for joy but you should be," said Richard recognizing the reference to 2 Chronicles 20. "God has indeed delivered you from worrying about bills."

"This is miraculous deliverance! And to whom do I owe endless thanks? There must be a catch; there are always strings attached," said Art with some caution creeping into his voice.

"The donor insisted on being anonymous, so my lips are sealed. Therefore, there can be no quid pro quo in this case."

"Come on man, give me a hint. Who is behind this?" whined Art.

"Sorry, no can do. All I can say to Art the archaeologist is, Can you dig it!?'

At this Art dropped the cell phone and just started laughing hysterically. After awhile Art recovered his composure and glanced over at Marissa. Quickly, she whispered, "I want full details on this, or else I'm forced to think you've been back in the Plutonium!"

Art held out his hand to make her hush for a minute, and then had the presence of mind to ask, "In all seriousness, how do I access this fortune?"

"I will act as the administrator of the trust fund here in Charlotte. We can keep in touch easier by e-mail. Naturally, you will have access to the account and pass code. All receipts will be faxed to me for review. Only dig-related expenses will be accepted and I will e-mail the contract to you. Read it carefully. I will balance the books and take care of the taxes, et cetera. The Bank of Wells Fargo is working for you now. Use the money wisely—a million dollars is exciting but it doesn't go as far as it used to, remember. The next time you are in Charlotte, we will have dinner together—on Wells Fargo's expense account!" Art was in too much shock to catch up on other news, so the two of them signed off.

Art sat back in his chair and said to Marissa, "Obviously, those who wait on the Lord shall have endless serendipitous moments. It seems I now have a trust fund with one million dollars in it for the sole purpose of doing archaeological work. Now who could have done this?"

"Well, it's in a Charlotte bank. Did your mother start his fund?"

"Not a chance. My mother doesn't have that kind of money."

"Maybe it's that famous basketball player you told me about?"

Art thought about this for a moment and replied, "No, he doesn't make that much money yet. We can speculate for hours I guess. Meanwhile, my dear, we must go out and celebrate even if we can't claim the dinner on our new expense account!"

"Wonderful! A chance to dress up! I know a great restaurant in Denizli if you aren't tired of Turkish food by now."

"Just let me finish translating this little bit of what Papias is saying about the millennium."

"Fine, but it better not take a millennium to finish it. I'm already hungry." They returned to the Pamukkale Grand Palace to shower and change for an enjoyable evening doting on each other. Art West had had more dates with Marissa in the last two months than he had had with anyone in the last twenty years—and he was loving it.

58

How Can Anyone Ignore a Menorah?

THE ISRAELI MUSEUM WAS chock full of antiquities of different peri-ods, but it had surprisingly few ancient menorahs. In fact, it had only two—one from the early Middle Ages and now the so-called Herodian menorah. The latter was under tight security in a special exhibit room, which required a separate ticket costing sixty shekels or a bit less than twenty dollars. Clearly Amir Genoor intended to have the menorah pay for itself rather rapidly.

In the foyer, Genoor was talking with Benjamin Gat about the remarkable object and Gat was asking, "Are you saying this Herodian menorah was right under our noses for who knows how long? And the demon papyrus that came out of it is a modern imitation of an ancient scroll? Do we know anything about the recent history of the menorah prior to it landing in Kahlil el Said's shop?"

"Nothing of consequence that I know about," said Amir. "In any case, we have it safely here now and there are no disputes about ownership. The menorah has already created an enormous buzz around Jerusalem. I mean just look at that line at the ticket counter! We will soon recoup what we spent to get it and more. Don't you think it is a nice touch to have the Latin papyrus displayed directly across from the menorah pro-viding the *bona fides* that it is from Herod's temple?"

"Yes, that's well done and leads to a logical traffic flow. First they see the menorah; then they see the proof it is from Herod's temple."

Amir noticed one visitor who whizzed right by the menorah and was staring intently at the Latin papyrus. Genoor leaned over and whis-pered to Gat, "Now what kind of person takes a cursory look at that incredible menorah, and then stops and spends all his time examining a two by two inch papyrus? How do you ignore a menorah like that?"

"Why don't you ask the man?" suggested Benjamin. "I'm sure he won't mind. He looks the studious sort."

Approaching the short, thin man with the gray handlebar moustache, Amir Genoor politely said, "Excuse me for interrupting. I am Amir Genoor, the curator of this museum. I couldn't help but notice you zipped right past the menorah, and have been standing here studying this papyrus intently. Why does it fascinate you so?"

"And I am Professor Widdrington from the classics department of Oxford. Do you have any idea what you have here in this little piece of papyrus?"

"It's a first century papyrus which identifies where that magnificent menorah came from," explained Amir.

"Quite so," said the Professor, "however, this is now the earliest extant piece of Latin script from the Flavian period and it proves beyond question that Titus actually plundered the temple in Jerusalem. Now it is a fact, not just a claim."

"I had not thought of that. So you are saying that this little papyrus is doubly valuable? Indeed it has a value for students of the classics and Roman history just as much as it does for Jewish history."

"Exactly. It provides us with the intersection of the two. And here surely is one of the earliest uses of the phrase *Judea Capta*, later to appear on coins and the arch of Titus in Rome," replied the Professor emphatically.

"Yes, we could see that the inscription on the papyrus is a virtual duplicate of the second line of the heading over the arch of Titus."

"So you can see my fascination. Titus could claim all he wanted that he treated Jerusalem with clemency, but in fact his men plundered the Herodian temple. And perhaps you know the famous legend about that?"

"There are several, I believe. Please tell me which one you have in mind," urged the curator.

"The story goes that the Roman legions, after so lengthy and difficult a siege, got into the Temple and began setting things on fire before they recovered all the gold in the treasury. The gold began to melt, so intense was the heat, and seeped between the huge Herodian stones. It was the greed of the soldiers, not their lust for revenge, which caused them to leave 'not one stone on another' as Jesus had predicted apparently. They toppled all the stones of the temple itself, going after the gold."

"Your version would explain why only the retaining walls and platform under the temple were left standing, hence our modern Wailing Wall. Normally Romans would have nothing to do with destroying a temple—it was bad luck in their view. Nobody wants to make the gods angry!"

"Just so," said Professor Widdrington. "Might I have permission to take a couple shots of the papyrus?"

"I will allow that," said Amir. "Do you wish to photograph the menorah as well?"

"No, thank you," replied the Professor. "Judaica is not my field." And as the little professor was walking away, Amir said to Benjamin, "You've heard of over-specialized academics? This is a good example."

"To that, I can only say, Amen," agreed Benjamin, and the two men wandered off towards the main entrance, shaking their heads.

59

Safes Are Not Always Safe

IT HAD TAKEN SIX long weeks for Art and Marissa to assemble all the necessary data and pictures to get ready for the big press conference in Istanbul. The latter half of the summer fairly zoomed by, including the hottest spells. Now the time had come for packing and heading north by northwest to Istanbul, where they had booked a week's stay at the Galata Anemon Hotel. Art decided to do nothing with the archaeological trust fund until digging began once again next May. Marissa applied for permission to christen the Colossae site with its first spadework, and Abdullah told her that he would expedite this request with Art as a consultant. Because Marissa was listed as the lead archaeologist, the $50,000 fee for foreign teams was waived.

As time marched on, Art and Marissa had grown closer and closer. Even eHarmony couldn't have made a more perfect match. The clincher for Art had been when he discovered Marissa was indeed a Christian, even if circumstances had made her very reserved and cautious about her faith. All of the really valuable finds of the season had been transferred to the Hierapolis museum, where Papias was now housed in a glass case under lock and key. Also locked up was the entrance to the church chamber and the Plutonium. Director of Antiquities Abdullah Koruturk finally visited Hierapolis and declared that no more was to be found in the Plutonium. Marissa and Art were feeling good about leaving the site of Hierapolis behind. In the spring, the site would be spruced up for the new tourist season. The Museum and its guides would be in charge.

For security and preservation reasons, Abdullah Koroturk decided to remove the Papias papyri to the Istanbul museum. Art and Marissa were tasked with escorting the papyri to Istanbul personally. Art felt like an emissary of Bishop Papias going on pilgrimage to Constantinople, the ancient name for Istanbul. Of course the city had not become the Christian town of Constantinople until after Papias's time. But still Art was thinking in terms of the continuities of Christian history in Turkey. They were looking forward to the trip back to Istanbul and since he was viewing it as a pilgrimage, Art and Marissa had agreed to stop in Iznik, ancient Nicaea, where the great Christological council met under the watchful eye of Constantine in AD 325.

It had been beastly hot in Antioch all summer, and Mehmet Ertegun had turned as brown as a roasted chestnut in the relentless sun that beats down on top of the knoll where the monastery was situated. Though there had been some minor finds of Christian crosses and priestly regalia, nothing newsworthy was uncovered, and the resentments over what had been done to him had only built up to a white hot heat as the summer blazed on. Mehmet kept in touch with what was happening at Hierapolis by means of his loyal assistant, Hakan, who continued to work quietly at the site after Mehmet left. To Mehmet he had reported the investigation of the Plutonium, the documentation of the underground church chamber, and the moving of the skeleton to a museum. He had also given a heads up to Mehmet two days in advance that Marissa and Art were leaving for Istanbul with Marissa's small safe.

This last notification had sparked a plan, a desperate plan in Mehmet's angry heart. He would intercept them at some point, force them to hand over the little safe, and then take the papyri to an antiquities dealer in the capital city of Ankara. He would sell them for a nice price, and then disappear as a wealthy man. Clearly, his archaeological career had taken a nosedive into oblivion from which he would be unlikely to recover. He blamed both Art and Marissa alone for his current situation. Packing up his dusty, open-aired car, he cashed in all his vouchers, checked out of the Scimitar Hotel, and headed west. He would spend the first night in Gaziantep or Konya, but he would drive relentlessly to be sure to catch up with his now archenemies. A further phone call from Hakan, after Mehmet started off, provided additional help, as Hakan had seen the map that Art had marked planning the route to Istanbul. He told Mehmet they had decided to stop in beautiful Iznik by the lake, a romantic spot. This made Mehmet's blood boil even more. From Iznik it was a simple drive to Yalova from which one could take the ferry to Istanbul. While eavesdropping, Hakan heard Marissa make reservations at a new hotel on Iznik Lake, so Mehmet had no need to go to Hierapolis. He was on his way to Iznik.

Iznik had long been on Art's list of places to visit. He had heard wonderful things about the quaint little town with its remarkable Roman walls, gates, monuments, theater, and the little Hagia Sophia church. His friend Mark Wilson, an intrepid traveler, biblical scholar, and tour leader extraordinaire had raved about the place saying, "You must stop in Iznik.

Not much left of Constantine's summer palace and Senate house on the lake, but plenty of other things to photograph there. Today the city is also famous as the center of the Iznik tile industry."

The drive to Iznik was a bit difficult but uneventful. Marissa and Art arrived late in the afternoon. There are no major highways into Iznik, and the two-lane road over hilly terrain was packed with trucks and hairpin turns. They enjoyed a late supper while watching a beautiful sunset on the lake. The fresh grilled vegetables served at this time of the summer were delicious, and went great with Art's new favorite, the paper thin bread made on a large iron convex griddle—yufka ekmeği—a phrase he couldn't yet pronounce.

The Hotel Nicaea was brand new. The manager apologized because the keycard system was not working correctly. In fact, Art and Marissa quickly discovered that their room keys could be used on all the rooms! Fortunately, there were few guests this night. Marissa said, "No one but us knows that the safe is safely tucked away in the wheel well for the spare tire, so we can leave the safe outside where, paradoxically, it will be safer!"

Art nodded because he was too tired to argue. After kissing Marissa goodnight, he went to his room after dinner, took a cold shower, and fell quickly into a sleep, which involved vivid dreams due to the evening's spicier than usual food.

In his dream he was Peter, as in Acts 10. A tablecloth filled with all sorts of different animals was laid down, but Art kept saying, "No Lord, I'll just eat the dolma, thank you; that meat might be tainted or spoiled." To which the Lord replied, "Get up at once, and go down to the street for someone is waiting there." Dreams don't have to be logical, but the dream was so vivid that Art finally got up. Putting on his pants and a jacket, Art went down to the lobby at eleven and out the front door, saying to the man at the counter, "I'm going for a little walk by the lake in the evening breeze. Back soon." The man smiled, waved and pretended to be interested. Art was back in less than fifteen minutes, and now he felt comfortable enough to go back to bed. Having put his mind to bed, his body could now quickly follow.

Mehmet had abandoned his plan to intercept Art and Marissa by car. He was no James Bond after all. Now in Iznik, he bided his time in patience, waiting for Marissa and Art to arrive at the new hotel. He would wait until after midnight to put his new plan in action. He even knew that Marissa hid the safe under the chassis of the jeep because Hakan had watched her put it there at the site. Marissa never imagined that she was being watched or that it would even matter if she was. Mehmet was gone!

But Mehmet was closer than she thought. If the safe was with the car, great; if he had to sneak into their rooms thereafter to get those scrolls, so be it. Mehmet had a keycard as he too had checked into that new hotel!

When the clock struck midnight, Mehmet got up from his bed, went down to the lobby and on out the door without even making eye contact with the evening clerk whose job was to watch the desk and entranceway. Fortunately, however, the jeep was out of the clerk's eyesight. This should be easy; he would have his revenge. Marissa would not get away with shaming him. He would outwit her.

Iznik was a small town, and this hotel was on the far edge of the lake away from civilization. The parking lot was both small and very quiet. No dogs barked; no cats yowled. Only the noise of the frogs and the gentle lapping of the water could be heard. The beam of Mehmet's penlite was weak but it had enough life to illuminate the safe. Crawling under the rear end of the jeep Mehmet saw the safe in the wheel well, right where Marissa had kept it before, just next to the spare tire. It was easy to open the snaps and remove the safe. For time's sake, Mehmet realized that the smart move was to take the whole safe and leave as quickly as possible. In his eagerness to extract himself from under the jeep, he bumped his head badly—blood started trickling down his face. Dragging the small safe in one hand, he let out a small curse. But no one was there to hear it. Having paid for his room on arrival, he was free to leave. He would be well on the way to Ankara before those two lovebirds even got up, much less found out that the safe was missing. How simple it had been to trump Dr. Okur. Allah must have been with him this night, he thought, exacting a sweet bit of revenge for wrongs done against him.

60

The Light Dawns

MORNING CAME FAR TOO early and too quickly for both Marissa and Art. A continental breakfast kept them going as they toured the city sites especially the Roman Walls and the Hadrianic gate. The Iznik Tile Museum highlighted dozens of different Byzantine patterns, and tile replicas were available in the museum store—great for Christmas gifts. Having seen the real tiles decorating the Blue Mosque, Hagia Sophia, and Topkapi Palace, they could appreciate the time and effort that went into making the intricate tiles in Byzantine times. Marissa and Art enjoyed a light lunch at a café near St. Sophia church, walked down by the lakeside, packed up, paid their bill, and were ready to head for Yalova, to catch the late afternoon ferry to Istanbul. "I'd come here again," said Art. "What a charming little town."

As they got into the jeep and began to pull away, Marissa's keen ears heard some flapping, under the jeep. Screeching to a halt after driving only a block, she hopped out and looked under the back of the jeep and saw the metal straps hanging down. "No, this can't be! Someone has stolen the safe!" Art leapt down; looked underneath the jeep; and said, in a much too matter of fact tone, "You are absolutely right."

"And why are you not as terribly upset about this as I am," accused Marissa, who began to cry. "Don't you realize this will be a big humiliation when we have to explain it to Abdullah?"

"I had some prior warning that something like this might happen. I had a dream!"

"Excuse me, but that line was copyrighted by Martin Luther King Jr."

Art laughed. "I'm glad you can make a joke while you're busy being frantic, but do you want to hear about the dream or not?"

"This better be good, and it better be relevant."

"I had a repeat of the famous dream of Peter in Acts 10 when he sees the tablecloth with all the animals on it."

"Come on Art, what has this to do with a missing safe and documents!"

"Just hang in there. Remember how the dream ended with a command to go downstairs, as there was somebody down lurking below? I took that as a warning from above, and I went down and I swapped out my own photocopies of the scrolls for the genuine articles! I figured if a thief was going to steal the safe in the middle of the night, there was a fair chance he wouldn't open the safe or pause in the pitch black to examine the contents of the safe ultra carefully."

With this disclosure Marissa leapt up into Art's arms and began kissing him over and over. "My hero!" she yelled.

"Actually, all credit goes to God for the colorful dream, or we really would be wailing and gnashing teeth about now. But as the Bard says, 'All's well that ends well.'"

~

The drive to Ankara was hot, even though a fair bit of it from Eskesehir had been super highway. Mehmet had been in a buoyant frame of mind, thinking of the money he was about to make. He drove into the outskirts of Ankara, called an antiquities shop, and asked them to wait patiently for his arrival. He would make it worth their while, he promised. He began to have visions of large piles of Turkish lire in his head. Just before arriving at the shop, he used his tools to jimmy the lock so that it would readily open. "Now I'm ready to make some money." Getting out of the car, and placing the safe under his arm, he sauntered into the shop with the confidence of a cat that had just swallowed the long pursued canary.

"Greetings," said Mehmet. "I am Dr. Mehmet Ertegun and I have something very special for you today."

"Ensh'allah [As God wills]," said Yildiz, the shop owner, who was already eyeing the broken lock on the safe. Not a good sign, he thought.

Opening the safe quickly, Mehmet extracted the rolled papers. Now in the full light of day he noticed that the paper was not aged. In fact, it looked lily white. Not a good sign, he realized.

"Oh, noooooo," said Mehmet, as he carefully unrolled the papers as if they were ancient manuscripts. To his horror he was looking at photocopies—good photocopies—but worthless photocopies. Slowly he looked up into the face of the antiquities dealer who was now sneering at him. Somewhere in the distance a bell was urgently tolling. He was reminded of Donne's famous words: "Therefore, do not seek to know for whom the bell tolls; it tolls for thee."

61

The Calm before the Conference

THE GALATA ANEMON WAS by now used to seeing Art West in town, since he had stayed there many times over the years. On this day, he was kicking back up on the roof garden with Marissa, enjoying a grand overview of the old city, the Galata Bridge, and the Golden Horn, one of the many water channels that can be found on all sides of Istanbul. A study in opposites, in Istanbul the East and the West meet—the Orient and Occident. The juxtapositions are often striking. At the same restaurant you can see a woman completely veiled sitting next to a man in an Armani suit who is sitting next to a man in a tie dyed T-shirt who is sitting next to a girl in a mini-skirt who is sitting next to a man wearing a fez. One will be smoking a water pipe, one will be drinking a dry martini, one will be listening to an iPod full of Turkish rock music, one will be playing a traditional Turkish stringed instrument. It's a place of all sorts of outrageous extremes.

Art was drinking his favorite Turkish cherry juice while Marissa was nursing a frozen margarita. His Power Point was prepared complete with an embedded film depicting the descent into the Plutonium. But the heart of his presentation would be the discussion of the three Papias papyri. He was mulling over the order of things.

"Shall I lead with the story of Papias himself, or with some of the more daring details about the archaeological finds?" Art asked Marissa.

"People love a story, so tell the story first and give them a more personal context in which to hear about the dig and its findings," replied Marissa. "Don't forget I am going to talk about the archaeological work there in general first. You can concentrate on the scrolls and their meaning and significance."

"You have the personal touch, and I am beginning to wonder how I ever did so well before I knew you. I tend to be oblivious to those factors, a bit too subject matter focused."

"You just needed a good woman in your life," smiled Marissa.

"Amen to that. For too many years I had no idea what I was missing."

"Remember that we have to call Grace about the lecture next week. Let's give her a call," said Marissa, as she reached into her bag, grabbed Art's cell phone, and tossed it to him. He despised the things and, even more, despised carting them around, so his had found a safe home in the bottom of Marissa's bag.

"It's ringing," announced Art. "Hello? Grace, is that you."

"You were expecting maybe the Pope at this particular phone number?"

"Only if it is a Jewish Pope!" retorted Art. "You know the famous joke about the Pope and the rabbi?"

"No, but I am afraid I am about to," replied Grace with a chuckle in her voice.

"The most famous rabbi of Jerusalem was invited to the Vatican to meet with the Pope. While in the Pope's chambers, he noticed a red phone and asked the Pope about it. 'That's my hotline to God.' The rabbi asked politely if he could make a quick call. The Pope said, 'Be my guest; it's a long distance call, however.' The rabbi promised to reimburse the Pope for the expense. Later the same year the Pope visited the rabbi in Jerusalem. In the rabbi's house he noticed a red phone. The rabbi said, 'You should recognize that, it's a hotline to God.' The Pope then asked to use the phone and reassured the rabbi he would leave money for the expenses. 'Oh that won't be necessary,' said the rabbi. 'From here it's a local call!'"

There was a pause and then laughter at the other end of the line. "Corny, but I like that one. Is that why you've called me—because I'm closer to God?"

"No, Marissa and I are sitting atop the Galata Hotel wondering how marriage was suiting you so far?" replied Art.

"So far, so good. We seem to be quite compatible, and quite unwilling to give up our workaholic ways as well, so we find we have to carve out time for each other intentionally. Does that perhaps apply to you and Marissa?"

"Not yet at least—but I'll keep that in mind. Tell me though, what has happened with the menorah and the papyri Kahlil told me all about while we were there?"

"Glad you asked," said Grace. "I cut the ribbon for the new special exhibit at the Israeli Museum. They put up a plaque saying that the menorah was bought in my honor. Turns out that the most expensive menorah in the world was going to be a wedding present from Kahlil and Hannah. Now the demon papyrus turned out to be a modern copy, so it's remaining in the IAA's hands for further study, but the tiny Latin papyrus which identified the provenance of the menorah is nicely displayed opposite of the menorah."

Art was impressed. "Excellent! On another front, Marissa and I are about to give a major lecture at the Istanbul Archaeology Museum on what we found in the Papias House in Hierapolis. We would like you to come and be part of the presentation."

"If you're not kidding, I would enjoy that. I need to have some woman-to-woman time with Marissa to reveal to her all your hidden flaws. So when is this lecture?"

"It is scheduled for two weeks from today at four in the Alexander sarcophagus room of the museum. Can you make arrangements to get here?"

"What's the use of having a Lear Jet in the family if you never get to use it?"

Art turned to Marissa and said with his hand over the phone, "Grace can come to the lectures. She could introduce me, and the director could introduce you. How does that sound?"

"No problem. How about we have a brief panel discussion after the lecture along with the Q and A time?" queried Marissa.

"One more thing, Grace. Are you up for kibitzing about the lecture in a panel discussion afterwards? Naturally I'll send a copy of the lecture to you so you can bone up on Papias."

"Sure. I can write off the flight as a business expense. Having a plane does not mean free fuel and a free crew," replied Grace.

"You always were more savvy about the business end of things," said Art. "Should I reserve you a room here with us at the Galata? We can go out to a nice dinner thereafter and we will stuff you with dolma, which means 'stuffed' in Turkish anyway."

"Why not?" said Grace. "I'll meet you at the hotel for a light lunch and then we can head to the museum. There are a couple of things like the Jerusalem Temple Warning Inscription that I would like to study while I am there. You know the one I have in mind which says 'No outsider shall enter the protective enclosure around the sanctuary. And whoever is caught will only have himself to blame for the ensuing death'?"

"I've seen it many times on the third floor of the museum, and I'm sure the Museum curator and the Antiquities Director would both be glad to work with you," said Art with enthusiasm. "We will look forward to hosting you soon." And as he hung up, he said to Marissa. "Now that is one flexible friend."

62

Impressing the Press

THE WEATHER HAD BEEN impeccable as Grace flew out of Tel Aviv at 6:30 AM in Manny's private jet. All had been arranged, and she would zip through passport control paying her $20 visa on the spot. She decided to get a three-day visa. She and Manny were planning a party at her new house the next weekend. Camelia, with Grace's help, had settled in nicely at her new beach flat just down the road from Manny and Grace's. She and Manny's butler would attend to the party details. Camelia was enjoying this new role as mother-in-law in charge, at least when asked to do so!

The flight of some 1138 kilometers would take about five hours from take off to touch down, depending on how fast the pilot chose to fly. Sure enough, by 12:30 Grace found herself in a cab heading to the Galata Anemon in time for lunch with Art and Marissa as promised. Gabriele Stein from *The Jerusalem Post* had been invited to join Grace to cover the lecture and archaeological finds. They chatted mainly about the ups and downs of politics in Israel.

Meanwhile, at the Museum, all the major press corps had been summoned and Abdullah Koroturk promised major revelations about early Christianity in Turkiye at the lecture. It had been stressed that this would be a public lecture, not a press conference, and the press would have to wait their turn to ask questions until the panel discussion had concluded. The lecture was being staged as an academic event, not a media circus.

When Grace arrived, her bags were whisked up to her room, and she was escorted by the concierge to the roof garden where Marissa and Art were waiting.

"I was starting to get bored with all the household stuff," complained Grace lightheartedly. "Thanks for giving me a chance to escape for awhile. So Tiger, are you read to deliver the goods?" she asked Art.

Marissa with a quizzical look on her face said, "Tiger? But Art is a pacifist."

"A fighting pacifist, an apologete who can argue his case with tenacity," explained Grace.

"This will be a new facet of Art to study," said Marissa, to which Grace replied "Wait until we have our little woman to woman chat later this evening."

"I think I'll be going to bed early tonight," joked Art.

The lunch passed by all too quickly, with much chatter as Art and Grace caught up with each other, and Marissa from time to time asked judicious questions. Truth be told, she was a little intimidated by Grace who was clearly a strong woman and a top academic. What Marissa really wanted to know was how Grace was balancing this with a marriage.

Art had had the foresight to plan ahead for a cab, and it arrived precisely at 2:30, which would give the three of them the time to look around the museum for a bit. Art and Marissa met first with Abdullah's assistant so they could make sure the presentation would go smoothly.

The trip up three flights of stairs to see the Jewish items left the three of them a little breathless. This museum was definitely too old to be handicap accessible, and the third floor lacked air conditioning as well, which led to few visits in mid-afternoon. Nevertheless, there were things worth seeing. Art pointed out the interesting small altar to "nameless gods" like the altar Paul saw in Athens mentioned in Acts 17. He then showed Grace the famous "warning inscription" from the Herodian temple telling Gentiles in Greek to keep out of the inner courts or else face death on the spot:

> No outsider shall enter the protective enclosure around the sanctuary. And whoever is caught will only have himself to blame for the ensuing death.

By 3:20 Art, Marissa, and Grace headed to the Alexander Sarcophagus room. Even on the third floor, one could hear the crowds coming in below. Some 500 chairs had been set up, but this was a free public lecture and it soon became apparent to Abdullah that more chairs would be needed. Museum employees scurried as he barked orders. Those who could not attend today would be able to see the telecast in the evening. Following the lecture, panel discussion, and question and answer session, there would be an invitation-only reception across the courtyard in the Ishtar Gates building, as Art called it.

When the clock reached the top of the hour, the Alexander Sarcophagus room was packed with an eager audience waiting to hear new revelations about early Christianity. Christianity was not a subject much taught at schools or universities in Istanbul, not even from a scholarly point of view. The intellectually curious found this a new terrain worth exploring. Because of Art West's connection with the Lazarus tomb finds last year, the press was also eager to be the first to report a grand new finding.

Abdullah Koroturk walked to the little podium that had been erected in front of the Alexander sarcophagus. The track lighting had all been focused on the lectern there on the podium. To the right and at an angle had been erected a large projection screen, and an image projector had been strategically placed some thirty feet from the screen. Art had been handed the clicker for the presentation and had a lavaliere mike on the lapel of his nice tweed jacket that he was wearing. Marissa had made sure he was properly coiffed, and that his famous red bowtie was straight. Abdullah welcomed the crowd in Turkish and explained that henceforth this presentation would be in English, and that the first person they would be hearing from was Dr. Marissa Okur, the director of the dig at Hierapolis/Pammukale.

"Good afternoon friends. It is indeed a pleasure to see such a large and enthusiastic crowd here this afternoon. We have some exciting things to tell you about, and we would simply ask you hold all your comments or applause until Dr. Marissa Okur and Dr. Arthur West have completed the presentation. Following that there will be a short panel discussion and then we will open things up for a brief period of time for your questions. To begin with, let me introduce Dr. Marissa Okur, the chief archaeologist at our site in Hierapolis now known as the Home and Church of Bishop Papias. Dr. Okur has been a distinguished archaeologist for over a decade now and was put in charge of the excavations at Hierapolis, an important Greco-Roman and Christian site. She is also known for her work on the Lion Gate at Hattusa, which confirmed that this indeed was one of the most crucial cities of the Hittites in all of Anatolia. Today she will be enlightening us about some surprising finds at Hierapolis. I give you Dr. Marissa Okur."

There was sporadic applause. Many were expecting Mehmet Erte-gun to speak. Most were not expecting a woman at all. Marissa just delved into her subject.

"It is a pleasure to present these new finds to you. And I know you will enjoy the many slides of never-before-seen areas of our excava-tions at Hierapolis. We have known for a very long time that Hierapolis was an important Greco-Roman city. Its necropolis is large for its day. Many important persons were buried there including some prominent Jews—here you can see a Jewish tomb of the period.

"People then, as now, came to the healing hot springs of Hierapolis, today called Pamukkale; however, ironically many of them died in the process. Our initial task at Hierapolis, the city of priests, was to see if we could find the priestly homes. We predicted that they would be near to the famous Temple of Apollo with its very famous Plutonium. Here it is alleged the priests descended under the earth, inhaled sulphur and carbon dioxide fumes and came forth prophesying. We found a house not ten yards from the temple, which includes a manuscript room at the back of which was a wall with an inscription, 'to the Plutonium' as can be seen on the screen now. What we did not expect, indeed, what caught us completely by surprise is that this home, which had one time apparently housed priests, had become early in the second century the home of a very famous early Christian, Bishop Papias.

"How do we know this was his house? We not only found various papyri in the scriptorium or library of this house which were authored by him, we found him!" The series of pictures of Papias set off loud murmurs throughout the audience. "Yes that is the good Bishop himself laid to rest with his episcopal slippers on!

"Now, let me take you on a little walk through the scriptorium of Papias, by his chambered church, and down to the Plutonium." As the short movie showed up through the Windows Media Player, Marissa continued. "There you can see the remarkable chamber on the left, where we believe Christians held underground worship services, and here is the stairway down to the Plutonium. There's just one problem. Toxic sulphur and carbon dioxide gases permeate the area. Now you can see the bottom of the stairs, and the large room of the Plutonium itself. The ancients believed Pluto or Apollo would inspire them if they went into this chamber, and they then could come out and prophesy. Thus Hierapolis was indeed the city of the priests and prophets too, for priests could be prophets and prophets could be priests in the Greco-Roman world.

"We continued to work diligently throughout the summer. We hope you will all journey to the Hierapolis Museum to see the remains of Bishop Papias. The work on the manuscripts is ongoing and Professor West will tell you about that and other matters. What I would want to stress to you is that Turkiye is rich in all kinds of history, including Christian history, and we will all continue to be enriched the more we learn about our past. Thank you very much for being such good listeners."

The applause rang through the hall for several minutes and Abdullah allowed it to die down before he stepped up to the microphone and said, "Thank you, Dr. Okur. Now it is my pleasure to welcome Dr. Grace Levine Cohen, a Professor of Epigraphy at Hebrew University and long time friend of our second speaker. She will introduce Professor West. I give you Professor Cohen." Yet again, there was polite but brief applause.

"It is an honor and a pleasure to be in your beautiful cosmopolitan city," said Grace. "Istanbul is truly the great crossroad between east and west. Even your presenters today symbolize the friendship between east and west." This produced some approving nods.

"For many years I have known Dr. Arthur West as a friend and colleague. We have worked and taught together, and it is no exaggeration to say he is one of the top biblical scholars in the world, not to mention an expert in biblical and early Christian archaeology. It is in this latter capacity that he appears before you today. As you came in you were handed his simplified curriculum vitae. A cursory glance will show he has enjoyed a remarkable career lecturing and writing. So, without further ado, will you join me in giving a warm welcome to Dr. Arthur West." This time the applause was considerable, and went on until well after Art settled himself at the podium. He allowed the applause to die down naturally and then he began clicking the mouse.

"Turkiye is a remarkable country with a rich heritage from many historical periods. Our topic highlights a man who lived only one hundred years after the turn of the era, from about AD 80 until the middle of the second century. Throughout this period he lived here in Turkiye—a native son of a land which was then part of the Roman Empire. He grew up in the western part of Turkiye, went to school in the western half of Turkiye, and like most of those in this region, his spoken language was Greek. That he was well educated for his age is clear from the fact that he could read and write, something only about fifteen percent of the residents of the Roman Empire could do; in fact, his Greek is very good. I have enjoyed reading through some of his scrolls of late. I am referring to one of the most famous of second century Christians, Papias, Bishop of Hierapolis.

"Papias may well have deemed himself a person born a little too late. He was not alive when Jesus walked the earth, and was only a young man when the last of the eyewitnesses to the life of Jesus were dying out. If you look at the screen to your left you will see a papyrus he wrote which has the title 'The Exegesis of the Sayings of the Lord.' Here Papias tells us of encounters he had with someone called 'the elder/old man John.' This elder John, though perhaps not an eyewitness of Jesus, apparently knew those who were. This John was part of a living chain of tradition going back to Jesus himself. Papias tells us not only that he was interested in the living voice and living testimony of persons like John who had known the eyewitnesses, but also that he had inquired about the Christian sources written before his time.

"Scholars have known for some time about Papias, and even though not one of his five volume work survived, we know about his writings because he was frequently quoted by later Church Fathers such as Irenaeus and Eusebius. Our knowledge of Papias and his writings has been indirect until now; that is, until the diligent work of your own Professor Okur to whom full credit must be given for discovering the skeleton and house of Papias, the scriptorium and the papyri of Papias, and finally the secret underground church of Papias [click went the mouse]. As you have seen this hidden room was linked by a stairway to the ancient Plutonium underneath the temple of Apollo

"In my judgment what is most important about Professor Okur's discoveries are the manuscripts which I can now announce are *the earliest Christian manuscripts still extant from antiquity.* It is true that there is a small piece of the Gospel of John which dates from about this same period, but here we are talking about three entire scrolls written somewhere around AD 111–12. Understand I am not saying these documents were the first Christian documents. Indeed not. But I am saying these are the earliest extant copies of any Christian documents that we have.

"For the study of earliest Christianity these scrolls are extremely important. Let me show you for example one bit of one of these scrolls. I will provide both the Greek and an English translation.

καὶ τοῦθ᾿ ὁ πρεσβύτερος ἔλεγεν· Μάρκος μὲν ἑρμηνευτὴς Πέτρου γενόμενος, ὅσα ἐμνημόνευσεν, ἀκριβῶς ἔγραψεν, οὐ μέντοι τάξει τὰ ὑπὸ τοῦ κυρίου η λεχθέντα ἢ πραχθέντα. οὔτε γὰρ ἤκουσεν τοῦ κυρίου οὔτε παρηκολούθησεν αὐτῷ, ὕστερον δὲ, ὡς ἔφην, Πέτρῳ· ὃς πρὸς τὰς χρείας ἐποιεῖτο τὰς διδασκαλίας, ἀλλ᾿ οὐχ ὥσπερ σύνταξιν τῶν κυριακῶν ποιούμενος λογίων, ὥστε οὐδὲν ἥμαρτεν Μάρκος οὕτως ἔνια γράψας ὡς ἀπεμνημόσευσεν. ἑνὸς γὰρ ἐποιήσατο πρόνοιαν, τοῦ μηδὲν ὧν ἤκουσεν παραλιπεῖν ἢ ψεύσασθαί τι ἐν αὐτοῖς.

"And the presbyter would say this: Mark, who had indeed been Peter's interpreter, accurately wrote as much as he [Peter?] remembered, yet not in order, about that which was either said or done by the Lord. For he [Mark] neither heard the Lord personally nor followed him, but later, as I said, Peter, who would give the teachings according to the form of chreiai, but not exactly in a [rhetorical] arrangement of the Lord's logiae, so that Mark did not fail by writing certain things as he[Peter] recalled them from memory. For he had one purpose—not to omit what he heard or falsify them."

περὶ δὲ τοῦ Ματθαῖου ταῦτ᾿ εἴρηται· Ματθαῖος μὲν οὖν Ἑβραΐδι διαλέκτῳ τὰ λόγια συνετάξατο, ἡρμήνευσεν δ᾿ αὐτὰ ὡς ἦν δυνατός

"But concerning the Gospel of Matthew, he said this—that Matthew on the one hand in the Hebrew/Aramaic dialect compiled [in an ordered arrangement] the 'logia'/sayings but each interpreted as he was able."

"These fascinating reflections which we already knew from Eusebius's quoting of Papias, were also found, virtually verbatim in the Papias scroll. But there were also some scholia by Papias at the bottom of this papyrus as you can now see on the screen.

> Now this Mark, was the one called John Mark, whose mother had a house in Jerusalem. While he had been a sometime companion of Paul and Barnabas, his real service to the Gospel came in being Peter's interpreter towards the end of Peter's life, and then the recorder of Peter's memoirs, in shorter form and according to the rules for expanding chreiae into narrative. Unlike the case with Matthew's Gospel, Mark chose, for the most part, not to interrupt the narrative with collections of sayings of the Lord. While Peter had tended to speak in Aramaic to the Jews, Mark, whose Greek was better, served as the translator and interpreter for Peter while he was in Rome. When Peter's memoirs were first taken down by hand, they were in Aramaic, and required translation and interpretation. It was Matthew who had compiled the Aramaic sayings of Jesus in an ordered arrangement, which only those who knew Aramaic could interpret. This was not a full Gospel, but only a collection of Jesus' main sayings and parables.

"Scholars have long suspected that Papias's chief source of information about the origins of the canonical Gospels was this elder or elderly John he keeps talking about. This finding of Papias's own handwritten scrolls confirms this conclusion, and makes evident as well that it was John of Patmos, the John who wrote the book of Revelation whom Papias had known. The following passage from Papias is not found in any of the later Churches Fathers, and is being revealed here to the world for the first time. Please read along with me.

> I have not been fortunate enough to meet the apostles themselves being born too late and in a different part of the Empire, but I did indeed learn from the elder John who taught me many things, and himself knew both the apostles and other eyewitnesses. For me the living voice of that John was the most important thing. From him I learned about the apocalypse and the millennium, and other documents which he himself wrote, namely some letters included in the apocalypse. He was not to be confused with John the apostle, who was one of the Twelve and who had been

martyred earlier on as Jesus said he would be, thus fulfilling prophecy. And there is yet a further confusion which John the seer explained to me, namely the mystery of who the Beloved Disciple was, who was neither of the two Johns. I shall say more on this later, but here it must suffice to say that it was the elder John who assembled the memoirs of the Beloved Disciple, forming them into a Gospel after that Disciple whom Jesus loved had unexpectedly died at a great old age. This is how it came to be that that Gospel was called John's, even though he was only the editor and interpreter of the Beloved Disciple, not the originator of those traditions. The testimony of the Beloved, in both his Gospel memoirs, and in his famous sermon, had influenced John the seer in his later writings when he wrote to the churches near Ephesus once overseen by the Beloved Disciple. Most importantly, even today one can see the memorial stele in Ephesus to both the elder John the prophet, once exiled on Patmos, and also the Beloved Disciple, who was not named John, but rather Eliezer or Lazarus.

There was a gasp from some in the audience, for even those who knew a good deal of the history about Ephesus and Mary and John would be surprised by this revelation, especially the Greek Orthodox present for the lecture. Art continued.

"Now the actual importance of what I have just shared with you needs to be stressed. The earliest Christian Gospels, which were written during the lifetimes of the eyewitnesses of Jesus, were not anonymous documents, and were not composed by those who wrote too late to be in touch with the eyewitnesses. To the contrary, they were either written by eyewitnesses or by those who knew the eyewitnesses and relied on their testimonies. It is somewhat ironic that scholars have tended to view the Fourth Gospel, called John's, as the least historically trustworthy. As Papias confirms, it was written by someone who knew Jesus, who was a close friend of Jesus, and who took care of the mother of Jesus, and so on.

"The real and crucial importance of Papias is that he provides the link to the past, which makes clear that the eyewitness testimonies about Jesus in the earliest Gospels are just that. They cannot be ignored as if they were documents written much later and by those who had not known Jesus or the eyewitnesses. To the contrary, Mark's Gospel was written by John Mark but was based on the memoirs of that great leader of the first disciples of Jesus—Peter. Matthew's Gospel includes collections of Jesus' sayings which Matthew himself recorded in Aramaic. Later, they were translated into Greek. John's Gospel included and was based on the testimony of the Beloved Disciple, whom John of Patmos knew. What then of Luke's Gospel? Luke was not an eyewitness. He was a sometime companion of Paul. What he tells us in the opening verses of his Gospel is this,

> Inasmuch as many took in hand to arrange an account about the facts that have been fulfilled among us, just as those who were eyewitnesses from the beginning and who became attendants of the word delivered them to us, it seemed fit for me also, having followed all things from the first, to write to you accurately, in order, most excellent Theophilus, so that you might know the secure basis concerning the words which you have been instructed.

"In other words, Luke too had been in contact with the eyewitnesses and had checked his source material with their testimony. This leads to an important conclusion. *Papias was right! He confirms that the canonical Gospels were the most ancient testimonies about the life of Jesus, and were reliable ones as well. He had this confirmed to him by John of Patmos himself, who had known at least one of the eyewitnesses, the Beloved Disciple, and had learned from him.*

"Let me sum up then the importance of this for Turkiye, and of this you should be truly proud. Turkiye was one of the cradles of Christianity and today it is one of the most important lands of the Bible, which archaeology continues to demonstrate. It provides us with historical evidence about the origins of monotheistic religions—the religions of Moses, and Jesus and Mohammed. You should be proud that it was here in Turkiye where more confirmation of biblical truth came to light in these very summer months. Just as you have long been proud of Konya and its tradition of Sufi mystics, so now we have a true story to tell you about Christian prophets and mystics from not far from Konya but from an earlier time. These prophets lived and learned and loved and died in Hierapolis/Pammukale. Papias as a prophet like John of Patmos foresaw for us all a better day for this world, a day much like your President Attaturk once said was desirable and to be longed for—a day of prosperity and plenty on the earth, a day of peace and understanding on the earth, a day when God will dwell with all his creatures on earth, a day when we will all be one. May it be so, even in our lifetimes. Amen"

After the final words sunk in, thunderous applause erupted. Row after row of the audience stood and applauded vigorously. Art turned scarlet red. Marissa, Grace, and Abdullah came up to stand beside Art. Then a table and chairs were brought forward so the four scholars could all sit on the podium and discuss this stimulating lecture.

To the ordinary observer this may have seemed like just another day and just another lecture, but Abdullah knew better, and he was smiling. Here finally he had found not only a woman scholar who could inspire other women to pursue such important archaeological work, but also a Christian scholar who knew how to talk to all sorts of persons including Muslims without belittling their beliefs. Here finally were two people that the Turkish government could work with who would help them interpret their many Christian ruins responsibly and accurately and help them attract many more Christian pilgrims to beautiful Turkiye. This augured well for the future of the Turkish tourism industry.

Abdullah proudly moderated the discussion. The lecture stimulated his hopes for more cooperation, more funding for digs, and more income from tourists.

His hotel room TV was not the best, but still he had always enjoyed watching the cultural shows on the national educational channel. As he drank his glass of wine, and flipped through channels he stopped suddenly. There before his eyes flashed Abdullah Koroturk, Marissa Okur, Art West, and some Jewish woman whose name he quickly forgot. As he listened to the learned lecture and saw the reaction, he also saw his own career flash before his eyes. Mehmet thought of a famous phrase he had learned in school:

> For of all sad words of tongue or pen,
> The saddest are these: "It might have been!"[1]

---

1. John Greenleaf Whittier, "Maud Muller," 1856.

63

Winging West

ART WAS A FRUGAL kind of guy, but love can make you do extravagant things. In his satchel he now had two business class tickets on a Turkish Airlines flight from Istanbul to Atlanta, with a connecting flight to Charlotte. After the lecture, the reception and the dinner that followed, Art went to bed and slept soundly. However, a lengthy woman-to-woman chat ensued on the roof garden between Grace and Marissa. Over glasses of merlot, Grace regaled Marissa with stories of past digs in Israel. Marissa filled in details about Art's role during the summer work at Hierapolis.

Grace summed up, "Bear in mind that Art has been singularly focused on his work for most of his life. He can be quite oblivious to things he ought to see and do. He is also naïve about people and situations. But there is hardly a more good-hearted man on the planet. He even respects women—imagine that! He's a rare find, a bit of an 'artifact' in his own right, so to speak!"

"That is all well and good," began Marissa her face clouding over, "but there are many differences between us, not the least of which is the fact that my family is Muslim, albeit mostly secular Muslims. We will soon be traveling all the way to the United States to visit his mother. But for now, I am not comfortable taking Art to see my parents in Izmir. They know nothing about our personal relationship—only the professional side. I am very much afraid."

Grace leaned closer, "We all agree there is one God, the God of the Bible. And Art told me you already consider yourself a budding Christian. Just relax and let God take over for now."

That was all Marissa needed to hear.

The sun rose full bore early on departure day. Art and Marissa enjoyed one more view of Istanbul before catching a taxi to the airport. Given that Grace had her own plane, she could make up her own schedule. Meltem, having a few days off, was hired to escort Grace around the city for two days and then on a leisurely cruise down to the island of Patmos!

Art and Marissa rested in the Turkish Air lounge with a glass of cherry juice before their flight. "You need to give me another short course on your mother," said Marissa.

"Well there's a lot more to tell. She's very old school in terms of her values and habits, and by old school I mean old Southern etiquette school. She's set in her ways, as the old Southern saying goes. Whatever she wants to do, we will do. She keeps busy zipping around in her new Camry. I'm looking forward to seeing Jake again. Mom says he's good company and that he's converted her to Middle Eastern food. That should work in your favor!"

The call to board had just been announced and Art and Marissa were some of the first to get on the plane. They chatted on for a while, and then fell silent as the food service began. They checked the movie listings and decided on *Indiana Jones and the Crystal Skull*. "What do you think? Am I anything like Indiana Jones?" said Art hopefully.

"Sure, except you don't wear a fedora, you're not that cantankerous, you're a Christian and you do real archaeology," listed Marissa. "Otherwise you two could be twins!" she said with a wink. The movie began with Indy already in trouble with a group of Soviets at a military base in Nevada. "What was a battalion of Russians doing there?" wondered Art. "That was hardly likely in 1957."

Marissa looked over and saw Art engrossed in the movie. She smiled. It was nice to have a stable relationship with someone who was trustworthy and honest. What a relief after playing the dating game earlier in life. No more. Marrisa at thirty-six was ready to get married, settle down, and possibly have a child. Was she too old? Would it even be possible? Would Art want a child? This much Marissa knew. She wanted to marry this man, and the assurances of Abdullah after the lecture had made her believe that she and Art could work in Turkey on digs as long as they wanted to. They would have almost a blank check to do so. And there was Art's anonymous independent funding as well. Who could have set that up? Grace and Manny? That was Marissa's guess.

The stewardess came around with a hot towel for her face. Marissa gladly laid it on her face and reclined even further. Her thoughts wandered and before she knew it Art was poking her gently and saying, "Wake up sleepyhead. It's almost time for another meal and another movie. This time it's *Iron Man*. You need to watch especially since you resemble Pepper Potts (aka Gwyneth Paltrow), except with a much better tan and no red hair."

Marissa smiled and agreed, "Okay, movie man, I will watch this one. Is there much violence?"

"Yes. What do expect with super heroes? But it's funny also—after all, it's a comic book series." Art and Marissa felt comfortable enough to express their own opinions and not just go along with each other for the sake of getting along. It was a good sign that the relationship involved a lot of trust and very few cat and mouse games. Trust and freedom to pursue their own interests and be apart from time to time would be crucial. After all, where would they live if they married? The United States? Turkey? Both? As the second movie started, Marissa inserted her earphones and murmured, "Who could have imagined me doing this? It must be a God thing."

Art overheard this as he was wolfing down some potato chips, and he leaned over and gave Marissa a somewhat salty kiss on the cheek saying, "It must indeed be."

"You know, I haven't even been brave enough just yet to tell my parents about you." said Marissa.

"All in good time, all in good time. If they saw the lecture on TV, they have now seen me at least."

"Yes, they did see the broadcast. They understand that we are colleagues—no more," replied Marissa. "My brother married a Scandinavian girl—there is still much tension in our family over this."

"You have a brother?" replied Art with some surprise. "There's still a lot I don't know about you."

"True, but I think you are avoiding the point. Remember, that works both ways. I believe you have a sister, according to Grace!"

"Yes, Laura is now working on environmental issues in Papua New Guinea. She was working with children as a Christian missionary; now she is trying to save their land from deforestation."

As they continued their conversation, all thoughts of *Iron Man* disappeared and the hours winged by as they flew ever westward.

64

Home Cookin'

THERE IS ALWAYS A sense of anticipation when one comes home to a place that one loves. Art was mighty glad to be back in North Carolina. He felt quite light-headed as he waited for all the suitcases. When they turned around with their suitcases, there stood a tall tan guy wearing Nike basketball shoes and a Bobcats jacket.

"Jake!" cried Art. "It's great to see you again. The last time I saw you, you were getting dunked in the Jordan River."

"That seems like forever ago," said Jake, giving Art a hug. "Now I am doing the dunking —on a basketball court with Michael Jordan looking on. And this must be Miss Marissa?"

Marissa smiled up at Jake as he took the two big suitcases. She had never seen anyone so tall! Several bystanders were already pointing and whispering as they recognized the new basketball star. This did not escape Marissa's notice.

"We promise to let you rest tonight! But tomorrow—no way!! You will be shocked to hear that we are heading for Spoon's Barbecue for lunch, after which you will be my guests in a box suite to see the exhibition game between the Bobcats and the Magic. Your Mom seems to have become quite the fan and now she goes to every game, though I keep telling her these are just practice games and she doesn't have to yell herself hoarse at a practice game."

As they headed to the car idling at the curb, Joyce jumped out. Art raced around the car and gave his Momma a big hug. Marissa was right behind him and politely extended her hand, but Joyce called, "Come on over and let me give you a proper Southern greeting. I have a thousand questions to ask. You must tell me all about your family."

"By the way Jake," said Art trying to divert his mother, "I've got a quick question for you."

"Shoot," said Jake, who was sitting up front with Aunt Joyce.

"You haven't recently contributed to an Art West Trust Fund have you?"

"No, sir," said Jake. "But if you are in need of funds, I'm sure I could spare some. *My banker* is sitting next to me, however, and she pinches the pennies."

"Somebody set up a fund to the tune of one million dollars at the Wells Fargo Bank for my archaeological work. My anonymous donor is still anonymous, and *my banker*, Richard Character, will not reveal the information!"

"Did you just say a million dollars?" asked Joyce in amazement. "Am I hearing you right?"

"Yes Momma," replied Art.

"Let's solve that one later," suggested Marissa, "Now it's time for us to enjoy each other's company and get better acquainted."

"I couldn't have said it better," said Joyce. "This lovely lady understands something about manners. And, I might add, your English is just wonderful. How is that true?"

"I spent a number of years in Boston," began Marissa. She continued the story but Art was lost in his thoughts. It was so good to be home, out of harm's way and safe in the company of family and good friends. The ride ended, suitcases were unpacked, a light supper was enjoyed around the dining table complete with grace, and everyone turned in early. As Art shut off the lights in his room, he was reminded of his favorite Gerard Manley Hopkins poem:

> I have desired to go
> Where springs not fail,
> To fields where flies no sharp and sided hail
> And a few lilies blow.
> And I have asked to be
> Where no storms come,
> Where the green swell is in the havens dumb,
> And out of the swing of the sea.

He awoke to a Carolina blue sky. Marissa was already up and drinking coffee in the kitchen with his mother and Jake. Art entered in his running clothes and promised to be back shortly. The early morning air was a bit heavy this late in August but he enjoyed his run through the town and country neighborhoods.

As Jake promised, by lunchtime they were off to Spoon's Barbecue, one of Art's favorite hangouts. To Marissa he said, "Now I need to explain to you about barbecue. I am not talking about the verb 'barbecuing' as in cooking outdoors on a grill. I am also not talking about some sauce you put on meat, as in barbecue sauce. If you only spent time in New England you would not likely have encountered real barbecue by which I mean hickory smoked pork with a certain Eastern North Carolina vinegar and spice combination. Each restaurant cooks the pork its own secret way, but there's a general similarity to what you would find between here and the coast of North Carolina. It also comes with cole slaw, Brunswick stew, and hush puppies."

"You are eating dog meat?!" said Marissa with a very worried look.

"No! Hush puppies are little deep-fried corn meal balls!"

"Well, I've never had any of those food items, so this should be a nice cultural adventure."

"I have survived," Jake piped in. "And your mother has learned a lot about Middle Eastern food. Just ask her about kebabs and baba ghanoush!"

Yes, times have changed, thought Art. And the best is yet to come.

THE END

Authors' Note

ONCE AGAIN THE BASIC characters in this novel are fictitious as is the plot. The historical context and discussions are mostly based in fact, including the Papias stele with its tantalizing inscription, which resides in the courtyard of the Hierapolis museum waiting to be properly noticed and interpreted. Ben spent time studying it in May of 2009.

The exceptions to the fact claim made above would be that Papias's actual house and papyrus have not yet been found, though we live in hope, and the area we are referring to in Hierapolis does in fact contain remains of ancient houses and is a short walk up the hill from the temple of Apollos and down the hill from the Marturium of St. Phillip.

Likewise, the menorah described does not exist, though someday we hope to find some actual remains from the Herodian temple. The demon papyrus is genuine and resides in the museum at Macquarrie University in Sydney where we have visited. The historical importance of Papias for our understanding of the earliest Gospels and their authors has recently been underscored by the important work of Richard Bauckham and this novel is dedicated to him and his ongoing work.